THE *'WHEELSPIN'* ASS

THE 'WHEELSPIN' ASSIGNMENT

The Fifth Château Sarony Mystery

By R C S Hutching

Copyright @ Timewarp Ltd 2016

All rights reserved under International and Pan-American Copyright Conventions. By payment of required fees, you have been granted the non-exclusive, non-transferable right to access and read the text of this book. No part of this text may be reproduced, transmitted, downloaded, decompiled, reverse engineered, or stored in or introduced into any form or by any means, whether electronic or mechanical, now known or hereinafter invented, without express permission of the publisher.

Published by Timewarp Ltd

ISBN-13: 978-1537076065

ACKNOWLEDGEMENTS

The front cover image is an item in the public domain and was obtained via the Pixabay website.

Books in the Château Sarony Series

The Treasure of Chretien De Sarony

The Grace Dieu Project

The Considine Affair

The Centurion's Choice

The *'Wheelspin'* Assignment

For Joanne

who remembers the music I played in the 1970s

Contents

Prologue 8
Chapter 1 - Celeste 11
Chapter 2 - Nikki 25
Chapter 3 - Anne 36
Chapter 4 - Mikey 46
Chapter 5 - Hal 55
Chapter 6 - Griss 66
Chapter 7 - Tatti 77
Chapter 8 - Dave 86
Chapter 9 - Paolo 96
Chapter 10 - Iosif 108
Chapter 11 - Alan 119
Chapter 12 - Vladimir 133
Chapter 13 - Joyce 144
Chapter 14 - Suzie 157
Chapter 15 - Ivydene 166
Chapter 16 - Boy Racer 176
Chapter 17 - Pinky & Perky 188
Chapter 18 - Angelina 198
Chapter 19 - Monique 211
Chapter 20 - Kev 224
Chapter 21 - Jase 238
Chapter 22 - Woman in Black 251
Epilogue 257

Prologue

It was a cold night with no moon visible in the night sky although the couple didn't seem to notice as they meandered along Hornsey Lane. Very few vehicles passed them and the icy breeze combined with the lateness of the hour had reduced pedestrian traffic to zero. An observer of their progress along the road in the direction of where St Joseph's Church sat at the junction of Highgate Hill and Dartmouth Park Hill could not have avoided the impression that the man and woman were suffering from an attack of dual schizophrenia. One moment they were shuffling along the dark pavement with arms around one another, the next they would spring apart and with angry gestures loudly berate each other. The pantomime had been played out repeatedly since a walk in the cold air had seemed like a reasonable idea. The fact that a dusting of frost had already started to coat the wrought iron surfaces of the ornamental ironwork that rose alongside them gave the lie to the wisdom of the excursion.

There was nothing particularly noteworthy about the B504 that was Hornsey Lane, with one significant exception. At the point where it needed to cross the more low-lying A1, it had been necessary to build a bridge following the demolition of the original brick built 'Archway Bridge'. The new, impressive, wrought iron construction, was completed at the very end of the nineteenth century and enabled traffic to proceed directly between Highgate Hill and Crouch End. The official title of the structure is 'The Hornsey Lane Road Bridge' but it is also known by two other unofficial names. One is 'Archway Bridge' due to the fact that the design of the original bridge gave its name to the general area now known as 'Archway' which then returned the compliment to the later structure. The second is far more emotive and, over the course of many decades has more than earned the name most familiar to residents of that area of north

London. The distance to the A1 below is approximately 80 feet onto unforgiving tarmac and paved surfaces. The parapets running along either side are some four feet high, ornamental, and, as a local MP once said, were not even high enough to dissuade a determined child from scaling them, let alone an adult.

That night in January 1978 the cold breeze blowing across the structure added an even harsher wind-chill factor to the night air. The couple were halfway across when the passionate kiss they were indulging in came to a sudden end and the female sprang sideways to the edge of the pavement. She swayed slightly as she stood and hurled what, from the tone and volume of her voice, was unmistakably a stream of abuse. Turning away she began to walk unsteadily onwards and only stopped when, after several paces, she realised that the man had not followed her. She shrugged and muttered to herself but, on finally looking back, saw that he had climbed up onto the parapet and was standing upright with one arm wrapped around one of the half dozen cast iron ornamental posts that support the spherical bridge lamps placed at either end and at the centre point of the bridge. Behind him was nothing but the open air above north London, below lay the unyielding surface of Archway Road.

He began to laugh and shout at her as he balanced there and it made her angry. She turned away and for a moment wondered how it was that she was out in the cold winter night. Then she remembered the party, Jase had unexpectedly put in an appearance, and that bass player had also turned up. She knew she was high, and giggled as she walked slowly onwards. She was only faintly aware of the car engine and what sounded like running footsteps. There was a shout, the voice was different. More running feet. She turned around, almost overbalanced, heard a car door slam and, as she slowly focused her sight on the ornamental lamp, realised that he wasn't there.

Her thoughts were badly confused due to various substances both legal and illegal consumed earlier. She vaguely took in the car that had pulled away from the kerb and was soon past, heading in the direction of Highgate Hill. 'Bastard' she thought 'He's pissed off in that car'. *'Bastard!',* she shouted the word as she walked unsteadily with the intention of retracing her steps back to the party. *Her* party if you please, and what was she doing out here in the cold anyway? Oh yes, as she reached the centre of the bridge she remembered. The bastard had left her here alone. One minute he was up there by the lamp; next minute he'd buggered off with his mates in that car. Bastard. Serve him right if he'd fucking well fallen off. She suddenly walked to the parapet and was aware of the frost beneath her hands as she looked over. She could just make out something in the road a great many feet below. It was picked out by the headlights of a car and, as a second vehicle also came to a halt she saw people begin to surround the thing in the road.

It was almost twenty minutes later when the police car drew to a halt and two officers alighted with the intention of seeing if there were any clues concerning the casualty down below on Archway Road. They were surprised to find an attractive, lightly clad young woman, crouched down against the parapet just below the ornamental lamp. She couldn't or wouldn't speak but offered no resistance as they gently shepherded her into the back of their car. There was no other evidence they could find regarding whatever had occurred and they accelerated away from Suicide Bridge, as it was popularly known, and headed towards their station.

Chapter 1 - Celeste

On 3rd January 2015 two figures lounged on two settees in the library of Château Sarony in a village not far from the French city of Dijon. The pale, blue-painted room would have been in darkness due to the heavy gold curtains covering the windows, but for the diffused light radiating from the two large chandeliers illuminating the elegant interior. One of the figures was a tall blond woman in her late twenties with legs that somehow seemed too long for her dressing gown clad figure. The other was a man in his middle thirties, undistinguished in looks, reasonably well built, and possessing grey eyes which frequently flickered across his wife's form as she vainly attempted to stay fully covered whilst reaching for her wine glass.

"I am shattered." Mission accomplished she sprawled back untidily on the settee before adding "Oh bugger," as some wine slopped onto her hand.

Her parents had left for home earlier that afternoon, and due to the workload imposed initially by the publication of The Considine Affair, and the subsequent discovery of the Boudica remains, life had taken on the nature of a permanent Formula 1 race in order for them to meet numerous deadlines and appearance dates.

The name Timewarp together with the names and images of Anna and Martin Price had been catapulted into public view following their sensational disclosures arising from the Considine investigation. This, in turn, stirred interest in their two earlier, less widely publicised successes with the recovery of the Argenta Treasury and then the resolution of the mysterious deaths of four WW2 US Rangers. Anna's stature and attractive looks combined with Martin's somewhat obscure period of service in the British army served to provide the media in general, and the tabloid press in particular, with the heaven-sent opportunity to depict them as real life equivalents of Lara Croft and Indiana Jones, all of which was extremely tiresome to two very well qualified archaeologists. Anna's comments, fortunately, uttered in private, regarding oft repeated suggestions that her natural assets should be displayed more generously for public consumption, were not for delicate ears.

In an effort to take on work involving genuine archaeology they had accepted an invitation from Grantfield University to examine the remains of three Roman legionaries discovered at an army camp in Lincolnshire. The result of that apparently mundane assignment was the discovery of the remains of Boudica of the Iceni and a veritable snowstorm of publicity.

When, due to the intervention of something called Christmas, the whole of Europe had ground to a halt, the opportunity to relax at their beloved home was welcomed with open arms. Unfortunately, it occurred to Anna's mother that this also presented an opening for she and her husband to spend the holiday with their only child. The fact that she was also able to tell her friends in Grantfield that she would be spending Christmas and the New Year at her daughter's home, 'a delightful French château you know' was an avenue generously explored. Motherly blackmail was swiftly translated into daughterly duty and enabled Anna's parents to spend ten days of idleness at Château Sarony whilst Anna found herself grudgingly embracing the role of hostess. "I don't know why you put up with my mother and still stay married to me. Is it really worth it?" The question was asked as she once more tried unsuccessfully to arrange her dressing gown into an unprovocative cocoon around her long legged physique.

Martin helped himself to another glass of wine and said: "I think it's probably worth the fiver your parents bunged me to take you off their hands."

"Bastard."

"Now, now. It's still just about the season of goodwill to all men."

"But not wine-swilling bastards."

"So you don't want your surprise present then? I've been waiting until your parents left."

She looked at him suspiciously, but he simply pointed towards the fireplace at the far end of the room. Beneath the picture of them both, in the guise of a medieval knight and his lady, Anna saw something propped up against one of the two golden chess king ornaments. Having consumed several glasses of alcohol since her parents' departure she rose unsteadily to her feet, struggled to maintain her modesty thanks to a loose dressing gown cord, glared at an appreciative husband, and retrieved the A5 sized envelope. She was conscious of his eyes upon her as she walked back to the settee and, opening the manilla rectangle. withdrew the folded sheets of paper. "It's in French," she pouted. "Martin. You know I'm still struggling with the bloody language. Come on, read it to me as it's still the Christmas season." She waved the sheets of paper at him and refilled her glass.

"I don't need to read it. What you have is a certified copy of the deeds to Château Sarony. As you persist in referring to the old place as *home* I thought I had better do the honourable thing and make you co-owner. Happy Christmas or, more accurately, happy belated New Year." It was said in his usual casual manner and it took a moment before the words sank in.

"Are you mad? How much is this place worth?"

He shrugged "Search me."

"I already receive a pile of money each month from the trust fund. Supposing I ran off with the chimney sweep or something?"

"If that's your intention can you leave his number. I've been looking for a new sweep for months."

"Seriously Martin, why? I've got everything I could ever want, thanks to you."

"It's not about money, Anna. It's because you and Sarony were made for each other. I've known it since that day in 2013 when you first entered the place. Château Sarony has waited hundreds of years for someone to love it the way you do. I sometimes feel quite envious."

She looked down at the piece of paper and then back at the unremarkable figure with the grey eyes sitting opposite. Her dressing gown gaped unnoticed as she bit her lower lip in an unsuccessful attempt to stop the tears filling her eyes and rolling down both cheeks as she sniffed loudly.

He gave her time to take hold of her ever fragile emotions by quipping, "Now, snivelling is not what I intended you to do. It's all in my own self-interest. By tying you to the Château there is far less chance of you running off with that chimney sweep. Not that he would find you very attractive covered in snot of course."

When she recovered her power of coherent speech it was to ask, "Have we got much in the way of champagne still available following the Christmas onslaught?"

"Plenty, but I think I will stick with ordinary wine, and make this my last one."

She ignored his comment and instead asked: "Have you any plans for tomorrow?"

"Nothing particular."

"And the champagne supplies will last an entire day?"

"I'm sure they will, why the sudden interest in fizzy drinks?"

"Because it's 2015 and the floozy formerly known as Spindles Freemont is due her, hopefully, traditional New Year seeing-to now that her parents have gone. I'm going to turn in soon, as I want to make certain that my energy levels are as high as possible. In fact, I'd advise you to do the same Price old chap. I've got plans for you, buster, you're going to be popping a lot of corks tomorrow!"

The following evening, as they wolfed down yet more cold remains from the seasonal festivities, Anna suddenly said "Thank you, Martin"

"Don't mention it. Nowadays the lady of the house doesn't have to thank her Lord and Master for destroying her chastity, although if you really are still in a grateful mood I'm sure I could……..." She grinned and cut across him.

"I didn't mean for *that* you dirty old man. I meant thank you for the past twenty months or so. I still find it hard to believe we have been together less than two years. It's just been an incredible period. I know how Captain Kirk must have felt each time he was beamed down to an entirely new planet. I would never in my wildest dreams have expected such a breath-taking change in my life."

"Well don't get too excited. I know that Nikki is busy sifting through the incoming mail but, at the moment, the fallout from the last two projects looks more than enough to keep Timewarp going for months. The paperwork and general admin are endless, and the interviews and appointments still piling up look pretty daunting."

She pulled a face and answered. "The phrase 'be careful what you wish for' has never been more appropriate. We wanted publicity for Timewarp and, now our last two projects have turned out to be so high profile, we are struggling to cope. Now the New Year holidays are over I'm bracing myself for a renewed round of calls on our time. Thank God we've got Nikki to organise things."

Those words proved prophetic to the extent that two days later Nikki Prendergast, Timewarp's sole employee, arrived for their first meeting of the New Year. They spent six hours ploughing through various contracts and agreements that included a lucrative offer from *Medieval France* for the rights to print extracts from their forthcoming book on Boudica. This was part of the additional feature run by the magazine to enlighten French readers on noteworthy archaeological and historical subjects in the UK. In the late afternoon, as they began to put business matters to one side so that Nikki could drive back to Duclos at a sensible time, the English girl pulled a small notebook from her bag and said "I almost forgot. I received a call early this morning via the Timewarp answering service we set up. A message was left by a Celeste Palin asking if you would accept a visit from her on either Thursday or Friday and if so at what time? She said it was important but not urgent and asked for a reply via text to a mobile number."

"Celeste Palin, that rings a bell, but why?" Anna frowned and looked across at her husband.

"Isn't that the woman we met at the bank in Basel when we located the Three Sisters? She wore a very smart business suit if I recall, something about that sort of outfit does something for a woman."

"Sounds more like it does something for a man," remarked Anna. She pulled a face and looking at Nikki said: "It's a man thing Nik."

"I thought that was uniforms, or was it armour?" Nikki laughed.

"If the two of you would refrain from making slanderous allusions to my innocent views on female fashion," interrupted Martin, "I suggest, Prendergast, that you tell the delightful Celeste Palin that eleven a.m. Thursday will work for us, and then you can push off back to Duclos."

When Nikki had departed he turned to his wife and asked: "Do you think she wears stockings?"

"Nikki?"

"No, you fool. Celeste Palin, when she's wearing her business suit at CKC Bank."

"Behave Price. Now, why do you think she wants to meet us again? It can't be anything to do with those diamonds, surely that's all the province of the McLaughlin family, isn't it?"

"Yes, it won't be that. Perhaps she's fallen prey to the Considine and Boudica publicity and wants to take us on as clients. We only have to wait two days to find out."

To Martin's intense delight Celeste Palin did arrive in a beautifully tailored black suit and as she elegantly alighted from her car Anna hissed "Happy now?"

They watched as the woman ascended the half dozen steps with a slim document folder in one hand and pre-empted their greeting with "Mr and Mrs Price, how good of you to see me."

"Welcome to Château Sarony Celeste. Please call us by our first names." Anna was determined to match the Swiss woman's courtesy. "Please, come through to the library, it's where we spend most of our time."

Once the usual pleasantries had been exchanged and coffee dispensed Martin asked: "Is your visit connected with the diamonds Celeste?"

She looked momentarily perplexed and then answered in her faultless English "Ah, the Three Sisters, Martin. No, not at all. Having met you both last year, I made it my business to follow your more recent activities. Timewarp has certainly made a name for itself since our meeting, and it is your well-publicised abilities when investigating historical anomalies that have prompted me to contact you."

Having replaced her coffee cup on the small table she carefully crossed her legs and continued. "You may be aware that in recent years our, that is to say, the Swiss, banking system has come under some scrutiny from the major European countries. They were, of course, happy to take advantage of our strict rules on confidentiality when it suited them, but now that ethical matters are popular with modern electorates they have decided that those rules are no longer appropriate. We have been obliged to accommodate this more relaxed approach to confidentiality and as a result, our traditional stance has been amended in certain areas. I will not bore you with too many details as only one of these changes has given rise to my visit." She paused and accepted a second cup of coffee before resuming.

"One of the lesser known amendments, coincidentally, would have had a small bearing on the investigation which occasioned our meeting last year. CKC has asked all of its clients to provide a signed indemnity to the effect that the contents of their security boxes are not the proceeds of theft, terrorism and a great many other areas of illicit activity. Should any statement prove untrue and result in CKC being held accountable, as the new regulations now provide, then the owner fully indemnifies the bank against any financial consequences. Our letters stated that unless a response was received before January 1st, the bank would be obliged to open the security box, photograph the contents, and register the appropriate details with our independent company lawyers. There has always been a scheme in place that enables a box owner to make a single monetary deposit into an account which is linked to the safekeeping facility so that the box was paid for each year out of the interest earned. Whoever was able to provide the account number and password and match the specimen signature held in our records when the facility was initially accessed was accepted as the rightful owner."

"What happens if an owner dies unexpectedly?"

"Provided we are given proof of death, then the heirs can obtain access or even continue the arrangement if they wish, although it was only the original owner of the account who had to provide a signature when it was first accessed. From then on, it is only the account number and the password that are necessary, as when you wanted access to the old Mulder account last year."

"I imagine a deposit can remain untouched for many years if the novels I have read are based on genuine facts," Anna commented.

"Oh yes, that is less usual in the modern age, but when there were valuable items taken during the Second World war, many were placed into our banking system and left untouched for decades. That, fortunately, has all but become a thing of the past."

"So when an owner dies, his heirs have to pay for the facility if they want it to continue, I presume?" Martin asked

"Exactly."

"But supposing an owner dies without anybody knowing a box was held. Doesn't that cause a major problem?"

"Well yes, and that brings us to the point of my visit. If, despite all reasonable attempts, it proves impossible to establish contact with an owner or his heirs then the box is opened and, ultimately, legal title to the contents passes to the Swiss Treasury, the bank submits an invoice for any costs incurred in trying to trace the owner, and the matter is closed. However, the new regulations have rather pre-empted that scenario, although the number of boxes affected is extremely small. This is why I wished to meet with you. Amongst the small number of boxes affected is box 582167745667. Having observed all of the correct procedures during 2014, the box was opened by the bank in front of independent witnesses on January 2nd and here is a picture of its contents." She unzipped her document folder as she spoke and handed them a colour photograph depicting a small gold bust of a uniformed and heavily bearded figure surmounting a blue pedestal, the base of which was also gold.

"The figure is somewhat familiar," said Anna as she studied the subject. "He looks like one of the old Russian royal family members - the Romanovs."

"Very good Anna" replied Celeste Palin. "You have got it exactly right. That is a bust of Tsar Alexander III."

Martin looked closely at the picture. "It's difficult to judge its size, but I imagine it is solid gold and not simply a coating, the stones are diamonds I would think, which makes me think that the blue pedestal is lapis lazuli. Intrinsically quite valuable I suspect, but presumably it is the provenance that makes it worthwhile to lock this up in a bank security box for..........how long Celeste?"

"The box was acquired in 1977 and remained unopened until this month."

"Almost forty years," said Anna. "Why have you come to see us, Celeste?"

"You have no idea what this is?" The Swiss asked and when they shook their heads, said. "Let me show you another photograph." She withdrew her hand from the folder and laid a further glossy picture on the coffee table. It was Anna who answered first.

"I've seen this picture before. It's one of the Fabergé Imperial Eggs isn't it?"

"Yes, Anna. It is the Alexander III Commemorative Egg to be precise. Manufactured for Tsar Nicholas II in 1909. This is or, should I say, was, the only known photograph and the whereabouts of the egg has been a mystery since sometime during the First World War."

"What is the connection between the egg and your security box object apart from the obvious Russian one?"

"Each egg contained a surprise present. From descriptions at the time, the little bust is thought to be the surprise present from the 1909 Egg."

Martin looked again at the two photographs. "So if the bust were to be sold, how much would it fetch?"

"Nobody knows because such an object has never been sold on the open market but, because of what it is, the value will be considerable. Now, let me show you another photograph. This was also found with several identical copies in the security box." She handed them each a photograph and it was Martin who said "Hang on Celeste. I thought you said the Egg went missing during the First World War?"

"Yes, Martin. Until the security box was opened the first photograph was the only known picture of the missing Egg, and that is still the case so far as the world at large is concerned. However, as you will see from the second photograph, the Egg appears to have somehow come to light in 1977."

"I still don't understand why you have contacted us," he said.

"We, that is CKC Bank, want you to see if the owner can be traced. You clearly have an expertise in this type of work."

"An Egg complete with its surprise present would be extremely valuable presumably."

"Somewhere between five and ten million Euros is a *very* conservative estimate. I suspect it would fetch a great deal more, if only because the Russian state would be keen to obtain it."

"What other information can you give us Celeste?"

"The date the security box was opened, the account holder's name and details that were provided at that time. Also, copies of the letters sent by CKC to the account holder last year. Beyond that, nothing that is not already in the public domain. Fifty Imperial eggs were made, seven are missing. CKC wishes you to undertake two tasks. One is to see if you are able to ascertain whether the owner of the box is still alive and, two, whether it is possible to establish the whereabouts of the missing egg. If the egg and its surprise present can be reunited, then together they will be worth considerably more than the individual parts if auctioned separately. You have not asked me the most obvious question, though."

"You are referring to our fee of course."

Celeste smiled and inclined her head in acknowledgement.

"We need to discuss between us whether this is something we wish to take on. Why is the bank going to so much trouble?"

"As I said, we are obliged to try and trace the owner, but because we are able to recover our costs we run no risk whether you find the owner or not. We will be paid either by the Swiss Treasury, or the owner if he wishes his property to be returned. CKC is a very traditional bank. If we advertised for the owner to come forward we would not only be inundated with cranks and con men, but the story would be seized upon by the media and we have no wish to attract that sort of publicity. We are confident that you will handle the search in a more discreet manner."

"We will let you have a decision within forty-eight hours, Celeste. Is there someone working for you at CKC whom our Miss Prendergast can contact?"

Celeste Palin rose to her feet and said "My assistant Angelina Flavio in Basel. If you do take this on she will let you have the further information I mentioned. Please keep the photographs."

"What do you think?" Martin asked when their visitor had gone.

"I think it sounds fun, there are no dead bodies involved and, although it isn't remotely connected to archaeology, it isn't very likely to be quite so sensational as our last two ventures. We may well be able to deal with it entirely from Sarony. Let's talk with Nikki and see what she thinks we should ask for by way of a fee."

Chapter 2 - Nikki

"I think you should take it on," said Nikki Prendergast. "There is no great pressure to produce a positive result. Succeed or fail, you still get paid. If you fail, it's not going to be of great public interest so won't harm Timewarp's reputation. I will agree on a fee with CKC, and you can have a rest from all the TV work and interviews."

"That settles it for me," said Martin, and Anna nodded her agreement. "OK, Nik. Let us know what deal you negotiate with Angelina Flavio and if it's quick we will start next week."

As Nikki drove out through the gates of Château Sarony Anna said: "Come and walk with me husband, we could both do with some fresh air." As they strolled down the gravelled drive she linked an arm with his and Martin knew she would steer them down to the old vault that lay just inside the perimeter wall. He was correct but, on this occasion, she was content to stand tightly against him as she contemplated the place that had figured so prominently in their early relationship. "Do you realise Martin that if this CKC work goes ahead, it will be the first time we have actually undertaken a commercial assignment."

"What about the Boudica project?"

"That was more a favour for the Professor that evolved into something else. Our other three were all embarked on without the expectation of profit."

They had reached the vault and stood in silence for a while looking down into the open area that lay to the front of the oaken doors. "Don't think it's creepy or anything, but I've always felt a peculiarly strong bond to Lady Sarony who died all those centuries ago. I know it's odd, and I don't believe in all of that spiritual stuff. Well, not usually, but I am absolutely convinced that the story we put together about what happened when Chretien de Sarony returned from Italy is correct. Ever since then I become very emotional whenever I think about her. She wasn't well served by circumstances she had no control over, and by contrast, I have been extremely blessed by random fate in the form of meeting you. Oh, bollocks." Once more her voice became choked and Martin slipped an arm around her shoulders but said nothing. She regained control and continued. "You know that I fell in love with our home at the time of my first visit, and I know that she loved it here as well. That's why I come down here so often, I feel that in some way I am confirming how much I understand the pleasure she derived from this place. I'm not being very clear, I know, but just in case you thought I had some sort of morbid fascination with death, it isn't like that at all."

He relaxed his grip on her and gently tugged the golden ponytail, "You both belong here, Anna. You bring the old place something it hasn't had for a great many years, and I think you will be surprised at how much the local people appreciate that fact. Seeing the château occupied as a proper home means a great deal to Sarony. I hadn't understood the depth of feeling until a couple years before we met and since then I've tried to play my part. Nothing can change the fact that we are not in any way related to the original Sarony family, but there is now a kind of continuity by virtue of how we both feel about the place. I'm sure Lady Sarony would fully approve of you. But was there another reason you wanted to take this stroll?"

"You know me so well Mr Price. It's about Nikki. I'm pleased we have her working for us, it's unbelievable how wasted she was on the reception desk at Grantfield, but I think we ought to think of offering her more."

"A pay rise you mean?"

"Well, that also. But what I did wonder was if we should give her some shares in Timewarp Ltd? Perhaps twenty percent to make her feel that she's more than just an employee. It looks as if her partnering up with JP is a permanent arrangement, and she works really hard and always uses her initiative when we ask her to meet up with the various media people. I would hate to lose her if somebody else spots just how good she is."

"Fair enough. Let's see how she handles things on this CKC project and then make a final decision."

Nikki phoned the following day to say she was coming over to Sarony, and her little sports car arrived outside at 11 am. They sat in the Library and listened as she outlined the terms agreed with CKC. "It's all fairly straightforward, they have agreed to allow a three-month period for your research. After that, if it is judged that the task is doomed to failure then your involvement will cease and their duties deemed to have been carried out in a reasonable manner. The item will then pass into the ownership of the Swiss Treasury. For that three-month period, Timewarp will be paid a retaining fee of 20,000 Euros per month, on top of which, reasonable expenses such as travel etc will be reimbursed. If you succeed in locating a verifiable owner, then he will be charged 5% of an estimated market value based on independent expert opinion and you will be entitled to 1% in addition to your retainer. I was surprised they didn't try to drive a harder bargain. How does that sound?"

"Reasonable I think," answered Martin. "I agree," added Anna.

"Good. Sign this contract, please. I will email it across to Angelina at CKC and ask her to forward whatever information she has to the main Timewarp address. You can pick it up wherever you may be."

When they were alone again Anna remarked "Well, it looks as if we have got a little project to keep us thinking during the winter months. I will be interested to see what the further details are that come over from CKC."

They did not have to wait very long. Within two hours an email and attachment arrive from aflavio@ckc.com with an attached pdf. Superior PC skills allowed Anna to assume pole position as Martin gracefully withdrew to the settee for an auditory role. It also meant that through half closed eyes he could ogle his wife's alluring form whilst adopting a pose of deep concentration. Anna, however, had tumbled to this particular ploy many months before. "You don't fool me Price. Stop the mental assault on my virtue and listen to this. She read aloud from the monitor screen, *'Jason Sumner Wooldridge, 56 Vosper Place, London SW5. Born 8th September 1957. UK Passport No 213804806.'* Also, some copies of the initial documentation when the account was opened."

There followed a silence that Martin ended by saying "Well get on with it. The suspense is killing me."

"That's it."

"What do you mean, that's it?"

She glared at him as if he was a naughty child. "Now which of the two words don't you get? Or is their order confusing? There is nothing else. That explains why they didn't negotiate harder over our fees. They know they are asking for the impossible."

"It certainly looks as if they expect us to work hard for our money, doesn't it? A bit of a turn up him being British though. I wonder if that was a factor in Celeste's decision to approach us?"

"Probably, but now we have to work out a plan for finding out a bit more about this chap."

The first breakthrough came almost immediately and from a totally unexpected quarter. The Auberge Fleurie in Sarony village was still catering for diners despite the patio being unsuitable in the cooler weather. With fewer patrons outside the tourist season, the small dining room, accessed via the doorway between the bar counter and the stairs, provided adequate facilities for those Sarony residents wishing to dine out. Martin and Anna had arranged to meet Nikki and her partner Jean-Paul Ricard for dinner and the two couples arrived only minutes apart. As they settled down to eat Nikki asked: " Did CKC come back to you then?"

"Yes, just a few hours ago, but the information consists of only the name, address, date of birth, and passport number of the person who opened the account plus some copy bank forms," Anna replied.

Jean-Paul paused in his dissection of the guinea-fowl and said: "If it will help, I can run a check on the details through our database Mes Amis."

"Thanks, JP, but it turns out that the owner of the box was British and lived in London. The box was opened in 1977 - Silver Jubilee year. The chances of our man appearing on your database are pretty remote," answered Martin. "It won't hurt to try, though. The name is Jason Wooldridge."

"Ooh. Wheelspin, Burnin' Rubber, Tread Care.......What?" Nikki broke off and looked at her friends. Her spontaneous outburst had a similar impact to that of Medusa on the companions of Perseus. Knives and forks had halted, frozen midway between plates and mouths. Eyes were riveted on the slim woman enthusiastically waving her arms to a rhythm audible only to herself, as her body twitched in time to the hidden music.

The state of suspended animation stretched agonisingly until the French policeman spoke. "What are you talking about Mon Petit?" JP was as surprised as Anna and Martin.

Nikki was unrepentant. "Hah, I've obviously had a broader musical education than you old fogies," she laughed. "One of my first boyfriends had an older brother who was seriously into seventies music. *'Wheelspin'* were a rock band. Quite big back then. Don't tell me you've never heard of *'Burnin' Rubber'* and *'Tread Carefully'* their first two albums?" She stared at them in mock horror.

"Nikki my darling. Much as I love you, there are times when I think you are more than a little crazy," said JP.

It was Anna who came to the younger woman's rescue by commenting "Actually I think I recall hearing the occasional reference on the radio. What made you suddenly mention them Nik?"

"The name. Jason Wooldridge. 'Jase' was his stage name. He was the lead singer, frontman, wrote most of their stuff. Then there was the lead guitarist - can't recall his real name but he was known as 'The Mad Axeman' because of his antics on stage. Don't remember the other two. They looked as if they were heading for the top and suddenly it all fell apart. The band split. Jase dropped out of sight and *'Wheelspin'* became just another casualty of the seventies drink and drugs culture. It's almost the only thing I can remember about that particular boyfriend and his family. It's funny how when you look back over life, it's the music that often stands out, isn't it? I mean to say, I never think back to my younger days and think 'oh yeah, that's the year I learnt all about simultaneous equations' but then I can't say I ever enjoyed school. It was just something that got in the way of my social life. There's a lesson to be learnt isn't there - you guys go to University and I end up as an expert on a nineteen-seventies band that nobody has ever heard of."

"Well your knowledge may well be what pays off in this instance Nikki, but it's a bit unlikely that your hero Jase is the very man who opened a safety deposit box with CKC. On the other hand, if it is him, this could turn out to be the shortest and most remunerative assignment ever."

Nikki grinned happily. "You never know Anna; did you get a date of birth?"

"September 1957 I think. It's in the right area by the sound of it. OK, Nik we'll check him out if only because it is our first and only lead."

Back at Château Sarony the next day Martin and Anna started their research. "Hmm, not a great deal to go on is there," remarked Anna as they read the blurb on the website dedicated to *'Wheelspin'*. "According to this the band had released two highly successful albums and there was a third scheduled for release three months after a proposed US tour. The idea was to reinforce sales of the first two albums in the States so that the American public were fully exposed to the latest British music sensation. Then they would tour again three months later, starting in the UK and then go straight back to America to promote the third album. It seems as if all was not well between the members of the band though because they were literally at Heathrow and about to set off for the US when a massive row erupted and Jase stormed off. The tour was cancelled, the band never played together again and a third album was never released. Jase refused to undertake any further work as part of *'Wheelspin'* and having subsequently been sued by his record company was declared bankrupt. The remaining three band members drifted into obscurity and from then on worked mainly as session musicians."

"It all sounds depressingly familiar," commented Martin "When was it that the row at the airport happened?"

"Let's see, ah, September 1977. That's the same year the box at CKC was opened isn't it?"

"Yes, but what would a young musician be doing with an exceptionally valuable Russian artefact? More to the point, why would he go charging off to Switzerland and plonk it into a safety deposit box?"

"Do you think there is more to this than meets the eye?"

He looked at her and cocked one eyebrow aloft as he said "Well, it's rather unusual behaviour don't you think? For instance, the fact that he put it somewhere for safekeeping indicates he knew it was valuable, but it doesn't necessarily mean he knew exactly what it was. On the other hand, if he did know what it was, then did he also know where the Egg was? I doubt that in 1977 many people had generally heard about the Faberge eggs. I don't suppose there is a picture of this *'Wheelspin'* outfit is there?"

"Not here but let's see if anyone else apart from Nikki knows they ever existed shall we? Aha, there is still at least one other dedicated fan. I've found the *'Wheelspin'* appreciation site, and there are even some pictures. Oh yuk, what a hairy unkempt bunch."

Martin leant forward for a closer look. "Fairly typical rock band from those days. With all that long hair and beards it's difficult to tell them apart. Look, it says here that both the albums they released went gold. Can you pull up the details of this Jase character and see if there is a date of birth."

"Hang on, yes here it is 8th September 1957. That's the same as the date CKC gave us. Looks like Jase is our man, ah now I knew there would be a catch. This website was last updated in 2006, let's see what the contact details are." She manoeuvred the mouse and said. "Would you believe it. There's only a name and a postal address in London. Anne Silverdale, 47A Grove Road, Holloway, London N7."

"I realise that it's a novel idea, but instead of writing and waiting forever for a reply, why don't we see if we can trace her via Directory Enquiries?" To the surprise of them both this idea proved successful and it was agreed that Anna should make the call, as being female, it could prove less off-putting than an unknown male caller. She sat waiting as the ringing tone sounded and was about to cut the connection when a woman's voice answered.

"Hello."

"Is that Anne Silverdale?"

"Who's asking?"

"My name is Anna Price. I got your number from the website."

"Website?"

"The *Wheelspin* appreciation website."

"Oh, that's all over and done dear. I thought it might have generated some interest back in 2006, but nothing came of it. Their stuff isn't even available on cd. Sorry."

"Oh, don't go, I'm not a fan of theirs. I'm hoping to trace Jase - Jason Wooldridge."

"Well, good luck dear. Nobody's heard from him for almost forty years. I knew him very well. Helped to set up the Wheelspin fan club and everything, and I've never heard from him in all that time."

"Look, Mrs Silverdale...."

"Miss. It's Miss Silverdale."

"Sorry, Miss Silverdale. Could my husband and I come and visit you? Perhaps get some information from you that isn't generally available?"

"Why? Are you writing a book, or doing a newspaper article?"

"No, nothing of that sort. Look, if we could meet up it could be of help to us, and I can explain further."

"Alright dear. When do you want to pop round? Are you in London."

"Well, no. We live in France actually."

"France?" The surprise in her voice couldn't have been greater if Anna had said they lived on Mars.

"Yes, so what about one day next week?"

"Alright dear. Will next Wednesday afternoon be OK, about two o'clock?"

"That's fine Miss Silverdale."

"Anne, call me Anne. See you next week."

Martin was looking at Anna in surprise as she replaced the phone. "I thought you wanted to spend time here in Sarony?"

"I do, but as we've taken on this job I want to get it moving, and this is our only line of enquiry. Let's take enough stuff for several days and hope we can wrap it up in that time."

"OK Mrs P. There's no sense in taking a car. If we are going to be based in London, I'll book us in somewhere decent and we'll rely on taxis to get around. London in January! You're so good to me."

"Huh. We're only doing this because of your infatuation with Celeste's underwear."

"It will have to be a bit special to match what you bought in Belancourt when you went shopping with Nikki and Aggie. Talking of which, as we appear to be treading water until next Thursday why don't you try on that dress you bought for the Summer Fair, you know, the one that laces up at the front?"

She gave him what is generally referred to as an 'old fashioned' look and said "And unlaces the same way! Well, I suppose I could indulge your animal instincts. The enforced celibacy whenever my parents come to stay drives me crazy. OK Price, you get the champagne while I transform myself into a medieval damsel. Now take your hands off my bum and clear off to the kitchen."

Chapter 3 - Anne

The Highbury Skyline Hotel was one of the splendid new buildings that had sprung up in the wake of the Arsenal football ground development and was very handily placed for access to Grove Road, one of several mainly residential streets running between Holloway Road and Hornsey Road north of Seven Sisters Road. The houses had been built in Victorian times and formed long terraces three stories high surmounted by large attics, ideal for modern-day conversion into more affordable units. The January weather had descended into grey chilly dampness and as they travelled along Holloway Road and passed the Nag's Head junction with Seven Sisters Road Anna felt relieved that she did not have to experience the big city scenery every day of her life. The taxi ride lasted less than fifteen minutes before they were deposited outside ground floor flat number 47A.

Anna had phoned Anne Silverdale when they arrived in London the previous day, and then again from the taxi to ensure that there was no misunderstanding about their arrival time. The door was opened immediately in response to the chimes of an electronic bell and the founder and former president of the *'Wheelspin'* fan club greeted them with a smile and asked them in. Anna thought she detected a north of England accent when the woman spoke but only in the pronunciation of some words. What they saw was a nice looking woman in her fifties neatly dressed in clothes perhaps a little too young for her years, but with a surprisingly trim figure. She ushered them through to a clean and tidy living room, tastefully furnished with items bought from John Lewis rather than Ikea, and generally displaying an air of quiet prosperity. Having performed the usual introductions, and declined the offer of coffee, Anna explained in general terms the reason they were interested in locating Jason Wooldridge, saying that a friend of theirs living in Europe was keen to trace him. She was about to ask her first question when she was pre-empted by their hostess interrupting with "Now I know why I thought you were familiar. You're the couple who found Boudica. I've seen you on TV and in the papers. This is a bit off your usual line of work, it's not historical or anything is it."

"Our friend helped us out last year with a problem we were having, and, knowing that we quite often visit family and friends in the UK, asked if we could return the favour. We're not expecting our search for Jase to be at all high profile Anne" said Martin. "Can you tell us what happened with *'Wheelspin'* back in the seventies?"

It was as if his words had ignited an internal fire. Anne Silverdale suddenly smiled and leant forward in the easy chair as she spoke. "They were one of the earliest bands to produce what we now call 'Rock', but at the time was just referred to as Rock 'n' Roll. The sound those four lads could produce made your whole body vibrate - like a jet fighter taking off at an air show. I was a precocious and I must confess, promiscuous, seventeen-year-old, and very happy to be part of what was then a flourishing groupie scene. Great days they were. Something new and different happening every day, or so it seemed. I'd left school as soon as I was able and come down to London. I'd always loved music and I started to visit the various record company premises in London."

"So you were on personal terms with the members of *'Wheelspin'* then," said Anna.

"That's a delicate way of putting it dear. At one time or another, I slept with all of them. I even thought at one point that me and Jase had something special going, but he eventually dumped me for some posh tart who started hanging around."

"So what caused the band to disintegrate so dramatically?" Martin asked in order to move the conversation onto more relevant ground.

"I don't know exactly, not first-hand so to speak. That was after Jase dumped me, and I'd tried to get him out of my system by latching onto that good looking singer from *'Krakatoa'*. I don't suppose you've ever heard of that band have you - they never did make it." She sighed and added "Rock music and leather jackets always loosened my knicker elastic. Oh and the pills and booze of course." She looked at the expression on Anna's face and burst out laughing. "Don't look so shocked, it was all different in those days. Now where were we? Oh yes, the band breaking up. Well, it happened when I was up north with *'Krakatoa'* and all I know is that Jase turned up late at the airport when they were due to fly to the States. There was a massive row and a few punches were thrown before he shouted that he was resigning and they could all fuck off to America permanently for all he cared because he had never wanted to be a rock star and he'd had enough. He stormed off and although he collected some things from the flat, he has never been heard from since as far as I know.

Now he was the creative heart of the band and wrote all of their stuff so without him they were scuppered. I heard that Hal and Mikey tried their hands at some writing but they weren't any good. Without Jase writing and singing there wasn't really anywhere they could go. I still used to see the *'Wheelspin'* boys around for a while during the following months and they filled in those details."

"Hadn't they done alright for themselves from the two albums?" Anna asked.

"Oh no dear. You see Jase wasn't stupid, although he did have a bit of a quick temper. It's the music publishing royalties that bring in the big money. In those early days when the young musicians were still being ripped off big time by managers and record companies, Jase was canny enough to set up his own music publishing company from day one. All the big money went to that company. The record company and the band shared the performance royalties, but with that arrangement - I'm guessing a seventy-thirty split in favour of Tornado Records - there wasn't a lot left for the band to split four ways. Also, of course, the record company will have spent a lot on early promotion, touring costs and the like, to say nothing of paying a basic living allowance to the boys so they could actually eat and have somewhere to sleep. All of those costs would be charged to the band members and deducted from the royalties when they began to roll in, before anything was paid over. The royalties were accounted for half-yearly as well so there was always a delay which made the money supply even more difficult, and almost impossible for the lads to figure out exactly what they had available for themselves.

What I've heard called a 'cash-flow' problem by my accountant on occasions, was a permanent state of affairs for many of those lads. That's why so many of those old sixties and seventies bands, that everyone assumed were making a fortune, ended up broke. They may have sold millions of records and generated large sales receipts, but by the time everybody had taken a cut there was often very little available to pay for the millionaire lifestyles that many of them indulged in." She paused and looked at them.

"You know quite a lot about how it all worked Anne," ventured Anna.

"I told you dear, I was a groupie which I know has rather shocked you, but it was actually quite a decent life. Being a groupie didn't mean I was some little slag who just slept around. Us proper groupies knew a lot about the music, the bands, the music business in general and we got a lot of respect within the industry itself." She suddenly giggled and added "The shagging, boozing, and other stuff was just the icing on the cake."

"You said that Jase had a bit of a quick temper Anne."

"That's right he did. Don't get me wrong, though, he never laid a finger on me. He wasn't the sort of bloke who hit women. Not like Hal. He was hot tempered as well and the drugs made him worse. That's why I left him."

"Weren't you Jase's girl then?"

"Not at first. I told you, I had all of them, but at first, I did have a real thing for The Mad Axeman and I was with him for a good long time. The trouble was he used to thump me occasionally when he was off his face, and one day I turned up at a party with two black eyes. Jase knew who was responsible and he went after Hal. For all that Hal was a lot bigger it was Jase who came out on top because he was genuinely angry. Hal was just a bully who threw his weight about and scared people because of his size and aggressive attitude. He couldn't handle Jase who just sailed into him like a man possessed. That's how I ended up with Jase, he just told me that I wasn't to have anything more to do with Hal and that I could move in with him until I found somewhere to live. Well, one thing led to another of course and we became a couple."

"But why did you set up the website all those years later?" Martin asked.

"I was going through one of those patches where I suddenly realised how old I was and thought it would be good to get back in touch with faces from the old days. When I was twenty-two I decided that I was getting a bit long in the tooth for the groupie game, and things were changing by the start of the eighties. I found a chap who was a nice ordinary lad from where I grew up in Halifax. I learnt to type and became a secretary and, for a few years, it all went quite well. He was manager of a store in Halifax, and by the time I was thirty-five I was bored out of my mind. We split up and I headed back south to London.

I was lucky to have enough for a deposit on this place, before the smart set from Canonbury began to creep up the Holloway Road. I got myself a job at a branch of Jezebel Records and worked my way up to branch manager. Then, when they were bought out in the nineties, the buyers didn't want my site. I took over the lease from Jezebel at a bit of a knock-down price and started my own music store. Without exaggerating I've always had a good knowledge of the music scene and so I've earned a decent living. I try and get my hands on some of the more obscure albums, and spot trends in the market like the renewed interest in vinyl. I've made a lot of money in that sector. I like it here in north London and my store is along Junction Road, so it's all very convenient.

One day back in 2006 a kid came in and asked if I'd ever heard of a band called *'Wheelspin'*. It brought back a lot of memories so, in a fit of nostalgic enthusiasm, I set up the website. It didn't attract much interest which was disappointing, but it was really just a bit of an ego trip, so I'm not too bothered, although it would have been nice to see the old faces again."

"So you haven't had any contact with either Jase or any of the other band members for years?" Martin observed.

"I've seen Mikey and Griss now and again but nobody else, although I did bump into another ex-groupie about six years ago in central London, and we had a drink and a chat about old times. She said that Hal Blenkinsop was last heard of working as a session man for one of the small record companies. Over near New Cross in South London, I think she said, but she'd heard nothing of Jase.

Mikey the drummer, is out of the music game entirely and works for King & Northcote, the big estate agents. Haven't met up with him for quite some time so whether he is still with them I couldn't tell you. Griss works somewhere in The City but I'm not sure where. That's pretty much it, I could ramble on to you for hours with tales from yesteryear, but my contact with Jase finally ended that day he walked out on the band at Heathrow. Up to then, although he was still banging that posh tart, and I was with the guy from *'Krakatoa'* I honestly thought he would get tired of her and come back to me." She sighed and for a moment there was silence until she added, "But I never heard from him again."

Anna looked at the older woman and wondered whether she had felt about Jase in the same way as she, Anna, felt about Martin. If so, then she could understand the sadness that had seemed to envelop her when she uttered that last sentence.

"From the little we have been able to find on the internet; it seems that nobody has seen anything of Jase since the kerfuffle at the airport. We were hoping you may have been in touch with him at some point over the years."

"I'm sorry dear. the best I can do is suggest you try and locate either Hal Blenkinsop or Michael Harvey - that's Mikey. They may have heard something. I can't imagine a talent like Jase will have given up the music scene entirely."

"What do you think?" Martin asked as they travelled back in the taxi.

"She seemed quite nice, although I wish she wouldn't keep calling me 'dear'. It always sounds so condescending and reminds me of my mother. Apart from that, she was a mine of information about the music scene in the seventies, although her cheerful admission that everybody seemed to be bonking everybody else took me by surprise."

"It was all before the big Aids scare of the eighties don't forget."

"I guess so. I just think I'm by nature a bit of a prude, and it made me feel a bit uncomfortable."

Back in the hotel later that day a decision was made. "It's either The Mad Axeman or Mikey," said Martin.

"Let's try Mikey. I don't much like the sound of the other chap. King & Northcote are quite a large outfit. I think we should try them. I'll phone their main office and lay it on a bit thick. I can be quite honest and maybe the recent publicity we've had will actually be useful."

It took half an hour before Anna finally ascertained that Michael Harvey was manager of the King & Northcote office at Guildford. She had been correct in assuming that there would at first be a reluctance by the company head office to confirm that it had an employee of that name. "Everybody's gone so bloody security conscious nowadays that it's a wonder the entire country hasn't ground to a halt," she muttered as she finished her call.

"Well, you could be a malicious ex-girlfriend, perhaps a former groupie desperate to re-ignite an old flame." Martin's comment earned him a withering look and he subsided into silence as Anna launched into her routine.

"I'd like to speak to Mr Harvey please."

"May I tell him who is calling?"

"Anna Price."

"Hold on please," there followed a short pause before, "Hello, Ms Price. I'm sorry but he's rather busy at present. Can one of our other negotiators help you?"

"No thank you. Would you tell Mr Harvey that he was recommended to me by Anne Silverdale? If he could call me back, I'd be very grateful."

"Hold on a moment, please. Ah, Ms Price he's just become free. I'm transferring you to him now."

Anna smirked and thought 'Bloody liar, he was free all along.'

"Hello, Ms Price. I'm so sorry to have kept you waiting." The smooth and pleasant voice trickled into Anna's ear. "Am I correct in thinking you are a friend of Anne Silverdale?"

Anna was determined not allow an opportunity to be given the brush off a second time and shamelessly decided to capitalise on recent publicity. "Not a close friend Mr Harvey but she did suggest I should speak with you. My husband Martin and I are in London and, as a result of our success with the Boudica remains and before that the Considine matter, a friend has asked us to look at something on her behalf, and it appears to have a tenuous connection to *'Wheelspin'*. We are hoping that you may allow us to stand you lunch so that we may trespass on your time." There was a moment of silence before the reply came.

"Oh, so you are *that* Anna Price. I've seen and read a lot about you both during the past few months. Extremely interesting work you have been doing, and now you want to talk about *'Wheelspin'*. That's a name from the past Mrs Price. My goodness, I haven't thought very much about those days for years. I'm not sure how I will be able to help, but if you and your husband are willing to travel down here to Guildford then we could meet in The Onslow Arms in Sydenham Road at, say, 1.00 on Friday. Would that work for you?"

"Friday at 1.00 it is Mr Harvey. I will phone now and book a table."

She broke the connection and looked at her husband. "Why don't we take tomorrow off Martin, and see the sights? Then we can hire a car on Friday and we will have wheels for the weekend."

"You think we will still be here over the weekend?"

"Well let me put it this way. It's an awfully long time since I did some shopping in Oxford Street, and I've never actually walked into any of those wonderful stores knowing that I had a pile of money in my bank account to indulge myself with."

"OK Mrs Price, why not! It's still the January sales so let's combine business with pleasure."

Chapter 4 - Mikey

They hired a Toyota RAV4, which brought back to Martin memories of his time in Lincolnshire some months earlier, and successfully negotiated both the London traffic and the M25 before arriving at their destination.

Anna's passage through the restaurant area drew a number of admiring glances from male diners, and the tubby little man seated at their table joined the appreciation society as he rose to greet them. Their first impression of Michael Harvey was a favourable one. He was dressed in a smartly tailored light grey suit. A crisp white shirt was adorned by a pale blue and yellow striped tie indicating the wearer had not bought into the modern open collar look. A good head of fair hair and gold-rimmed glasses gave his blue-eyed clean shaven face an open fresh appearance.

"I wasn't sure how we would recognise each other so I took the liberty of waiting at the table you had booked." They shook hands as he added, "But seeing you being shown across I suddenly realised that you do both look exactly as shown on television and in the magazines. I've sold houses to a number of quite famous people and it's surprising how some of them look absolutely nothing like their portrayals in the media. Before we talk about *'Wheelspin'* would you mind autographing this Sunday Times magazine for my daughter? She's a history buff and has been absolutely nuts about Boudica since your huge discovery."

Rather self-consciously they obliged their companion and he gratefully tucked the magazine into a slim briefcase before smilingly asking,

"How is it that the people who found Boudica, and revealed the Considine plot, are interested in poor old *'Wheelspin'*? How does an old seventies rock band fit into such exalted company?"

They ordered drinks and explained that it was actually Jase they wanted to contact. "You were the drummer I believe," said Martin.

The man laughed. "Would you believe it. *Mikey* of *Wheelspin* is now Harvey of King & Northcote. Where did I go wrong?"

"Did you?" Anna asked.

He shook his head. "No, not really. The real me was *always* Harvey of King & Northcote. I was brought up in a nice ordinary family down here on the outskirts of Guildford and to the despair of my parents became infatuated with music in my teens. I wasn't that good, none of us were apart from Jase. Don't get me wrong, we were as good as a lot of bands flogging round the pub and university circuits in those days, but Jase was what made us just that little bit better and got us the recording contract with Tornado Records. Once Jase left none of us had the talent to compensate creatively or attract a decent replacement for him."

"Do you have any idea of where Jase might be?"

"No. I haven't seen him since that day at Heathrow. My God, almost forty years."

"Were you good friends?"

"Not particularly. Just workmates really. You know, you rub along happily enough most of the time, but nothing like true friends. Not hearing from Jase hasn't exactly blighted my life. I can't say I liked him that much but that was because he was a bit intense and very serious about his music. I was only a suburban bit part player and I didn't expect it to go anywhere."

"But Jase did?"

"Well yes and no. He wanted his song writing to be accepted and his music aired, but, on reflection, I think he saw the band just as a vehicle for that. I don't think he ever really liked the whole playing in a band thing, and it was quite easy for him to just walk away. I can't say I hold a grudge against him."

"But you lost out on fame and fortune."

"That's debatable. I had some fun while it lasted but never made any money from it. I never was that good, and there was no guarantee that I wouldn't be booted out if a better drummer came along. We all had individual contracts from Tornado Records, but Jase was the man, despite what that idiot Blenkinsop thought."

He laughed derisively and added "The Mad Axeman, Lord save us" in a contemptuous tone.

"You didn't get on with Hal?" Martin asked as their food was served.

"He's a moron. In those days he was quite good looking, could play a bit, but because of the quality that Jase brought, in terms of singing, writing, everything really, he, like the rest of us, was carried along on Jase's coat tails. Then, because he could jump around and pull fierce faces on stage he began to believe his own publicity. Started griping about the fact that Jase was interviewed more often than him in the music press. The fact that there were umpteen silly little girls happy to drop their knickers - excuse me Mrs Price - and get laid convinced him that he was a great talent who was being unfairly held back by the favouritism shown to Jase. He wasn't a great talent, I wasn't, Griss wasn't, Jase was or, rather, would have been, if he had continued."

"Was Anne Silverdale one of the silly little girls?" Anna asked.

Mikey shook his head "No, she was OK. One of the proper groupies who helped all of us when we were touring and playing a different gig each night. That clown Hal was too stupid to know a good thing when he saw it and he treated her badly. She ended up with Jase as a result. A good move for both of them at the time, but it didn't last."

"But you'd slept with her. Weren't you jealous?"

He raised his eyebrows at that comment and for a moment Anna thought she had overstepped the mark. Then he smiled and said, "You can only have got that from Anne so fair enough. We had a one-night stand, or maybe it was two or three nights. I was feeling depressed and she gave me the bit of affection and confidence I needed at that time to get me over it. I wouldn't have agreed to see you today if you hadn't mentioned Anne. I always felt she was a bit hard done by, and she was never anything other than a good friend to me. She deserved better from Jase and, although she was with him because he had stood up for her against Hal, I thought that she became genuinely fond of him. Not just the way she was fond of the rest of us, something a bit deeper."

"Do you think she was in love with him?"

He shrugged and pursed his lips before replying "Maybe, or maybe it would have developed. He dumped her and that was that."

By now they had eaten and moved onto coffee as Mikey had patted his stomach in deprecating fashion and refused a dessert.

"What actually happened at Heathrow that day?"

He laughed and took a mouthful of coffee. "Despite what you may have heard it was not a Beatles style event. There were no hordes of screaming girls lining balconies or throwing themselves in front of police horses. Three of us, myself, Griss, and Hal had arrived reasonably on time, an achievement in itself. I have to admit to a certain cynicism on my part even then, but it was quite exciting, and we were just about to fly off for what was to be our ground-breaking tour of America. We hung around waiting, and Ronnie our manager paced up and down a bit as the time ticked by, and still no Jase appeared. There were also a couple of roadies, and a guy from Tornado Records."

"No groupies?" Anna couldn't resist asking.

"No, plenty of free sex to be had in the States. Sorry if that sounds unpleasant, but that's how it was. Nobody thought anything of it. We knew what it would be like. It helped combat the boredom of touring. Anyway, Hal was still resentful about having been shown up by Jase and losing Anne to him months before, even though by then Jase had gone off with some upper-class slapper and Anne was out of the picture. Jase was nowhere to be seen and our flight was due to be called. We were all a bit on edge and Hal was effing and blinding about 'who did Jase think he was' and he treated us 'like bloody session men'.

Well, Jase finally surfaces and confesses that he won't be coming on the flight with us because he's lost his passport, and hadn't been able to find it. He didn't seem to think it was a big deal even when Ronnie said a press conference had been organised for when we landed. He just shrugged and said we should go ahead without him as he couldn't do anything about it and needed to organise himself a new one. He said he would follow as soon as Tornado Records sorted things out.

Ronnie our manager should have been on top of all this but he was worse than useless and just stood there without making any comment. Hal had been drinking and taking God knows what else the night before and was more strung out than me and Griss. I think it was Jase's casual attitude that sent him right off the deep end. He freaked out big time, accused Jase of deliberately pulling a stroke so that he could make a later grand entrance to the States and focus all the attention on himself, with us being treated like a backing band. It struck me when he said it that, well, that's what we were really, but as I said, Hal had a different view and so went absolutely ballistic.

It didn't help that Jase wasn't in the least bit conciliatory. His attitude was simply that he couldn't do anything more and so we all had to make the best of it, no big deal. He just stood there looking bored as Hal was ranting and raving. The more he shrugged and looked around while Hal was raising hell, the angrier Hal became. He was a big bloke, but Jase had already bested him once in a fight and so, when inevitably, Hal lost it completely and threw a punch Jase just stepped back and laughed. That was like pouring petrol on the flames because Hal began shouting at the top of his voice and other people in the vicinity were looking alarmed. Whatever Hal had been taking or drinking slowed him up so when he went towards Jase and threw another punch, Jase just ducked and it sailed over his head. Then, as another punch was thrown, airport security turned up and grabbed Hal who stood there bright red in the face and still swearing and calling Jase everything he could think of. He finally ran out of breath and all of a sudden everything went quiet. There was a whole group of us, as I've said, with Hal in the centre being held by the security guys Jase was standing by himself facing us, and I saw this thoughtful look come over his face as if he'd suddenly got the point of some obscure secret. It was weird, and then he said. 'You know what? I don't need this. I don't need to put up with a prick like you Hal and I'm not going to do this anymore. You can all fuck off to America or Timbuctoo for all I care. It's over I've never needed anyone, and I don't need you lot.' And he turned around and walked off. We all stood there for some few seconds watching as he walked across the lounge area and was then hidden from sight by a mass of foreign tourists and their luggage.

Ronnie, ineffectual as usual, said something along the lines of 'take no notice, he doesn't mean it, lads'. The bloke from Tornado Records had a bit more about him and said, "I think you should go after him Ronnie, we need to sort this out, and we can always try for a later flight." By the time Ronnie got moving Jase had disappeared and there never was a later flight. I remember feeling slightly relieved and thinking to myself that I could stop pretending and go and find myself a quieter sort of life, and I never saw Jase again. In fact, as far as I know none of us ever saw him again. That was the end of *'Wheelspin'."*

He looked at them both and grinned "It's no big deal. Sex, drugs and rock 'n' roll' as they say. Fun while it lasted, but I've no regrets. I don't own a drum kit. Telling my wife and kids that I've had lunch with the people who discovered the resting place of Boudica will be a far more interesting topic of conversation in the Harvey household this weekend. The only one of us who would have made it big time was Jase."

"But you can't just walk away when you are under contract," said Anna.

"Jase did. He just walked away. Tornado Records ended up suing him, but he had got good independent advice, and when the bankruptcy proceedings took place he had no assets of any great significance. So that was it, we all went back to living normal lives, well, most of us did."

"Most of you?"

"Pretty much. I'm an estate agent, Griss went to work for a firm of publishers - in Holborn, and I see him once in a while for a pint. Out of nosiness more than anything else I've looked up the old names from time to time to see how they are doing. Ronnie Keenan continued in the management business but unfortunately contracted cancer and died. Anne Silverdale went back up north to one of those Yorkshire towns she grew up in and then suddenly popped up in London again years later. I met up with her by accident and by that time she was running her own record store. There were another couple of girls who, for a time, were regular features of our lives, and I presume are probably happily married and settled down with children. I heard that one of our ex-roadies has ended up as a record producer in Texas, another one died in some bizarre accident. They came and went so I never could keep up with them.

Hal 'The Mad Axeman' Blenkinsop is the big exception. He was convinced he was God's gift to rock but when his contract at Tornado ran out they wouldn't offer him another one, nor would any of the other companies. He did session work at various studios for a while then set up his own band, but as far as I know he has never landed a recording contract and he is still knocking around the pub and club circuit even now. He played a venue here in Guildford a few years ago and true to form managed to get in a fight over a woman. The bloke's in his late fifties for heaven's sake, still, acting like he is eighteen. I actually saw it mentioned the other day on a poster that he's playing a gig near here tomorrow over at Dorking if you want to speak to him."

He leant back in his chair and added. "Unless there is anything else I can help you with I'll say thank you for lunch and I hope my ramblings are of use."

"What do you think happened to Jase?" Anna asked.

"For quite some time I imagined Jase living in happy anonymity somewhere, but I don't recall ever hearing of him since those old days in the seventies following his bankruptcy. It caused a bit of a storm at the time because he wouldn't answer any letters, nor attend the hearing. He was adjudged bankrupt in his absence, following which, when his personal possessions were seized, it was realised that he owned very little and Tornado were left empty handed. What he is doing now I wouldn't know."

He stood up and placed a business card on the table. "If you decide you want to buy a property in this neck of the woods I'll be happy to help." They shook hands and watched him depart as Martin signalled to a passing waiter for the bill.

"Seems like a nice bloke," said Martin as they drove back to north London. "At least we now have a first-hand account of how *'Wheelspin'* fell apart."

"But no further clue as to where Jase might be" replied Anna. "It looks as if we are off to Dorking tomorrow doesn't it, that is if we can trace 'The Mad Axeman' and his pals."

"But that still leaves Sunday for shopping," he laughed.

Chapter 5 - Hal

Fortunately, Dorking is not overburdened with theatres and it took only a few phone calls to establish that a band named *'Dreadhead'* were appearing at The Prospect Theatre on Saturday evening and featured *'The Mad Axeman'*.

"Sounds delightful. Are we going to have to sit through an entire performance?" Anna groaned.

"I hope not. They may well be staying somewhere locally so I suggest we get to Dorking tomorrow morning and see if we can track them down well before they perform."

Having arrived at 10.00 am they were fortunate to find that The Prospect Theatre opened its box office at 11.00. At Martin's suggestion, it was Anna who approached the young man behind the reception desk to ask about *'Dreadhead'*, although the further suggestion that she should pretend to be an anxious groupie earned him a deserved punch in the ribs. Nevertheless, Anna was aware that there could be a reluctance to divulge the whereabouts of the band's quarters.

The man at the desk was no more than in his very early twenties and so she beamed brightly at him as she asked him to confirm that *'Dreadhead'* were appearing that evening. "We are thinking of booking them for a university gig" she stated, then as he was answering, she brushed at the front of her blouse and asked if he could see a mark on it. There were few young men who, if invited to look at Anna's generous chest, would decline the offer and the receptionist was no exception. Seated as he was his eyes were conveniently placed for the task. Thus distracted, he sat mesmerised as she asked what time *'Dreadhead'* were expected as she wanted to sort out a possible booking before their performance. They were expected to arrive at 1.00 pm and unload their equipment came the answer. Brushing her hand over her chest to expunge the imaginary black mark enabled her to find out that they usually booked rooms at 'The Foxglove' public house on the outskirts of the town just off the A25.

Very little eye contact had been made and when Anna returned she said "I don't like indulging in this *femme fatale* stuff Martin. It was just like when we hired that equipment in Dijon and the man conducted the entire transaction with you via my boobs."

The note of outrage in her voice made him laugh and he replied "Yes, but on that occasion, he undercharged us as I recall. You must be losing your touch because this chap in the theatre didn't even offer you free tickets."

"I consider that a plus rather than a minus thanks very much. Now, what do we do next?"

"Let's give them time to drop their gear and get out to the pub. We can grab an early lunch here in town and then drive out and see if we can catch them at this 'Foxglove' place early afternoon."

Located a short drive from the 'Silver Cockerel' roundabout The Foxglove was not what could be described as either a family pub or character inn. In truth it was a somewhat grubby looking Mock-Tudor fronted building, on two floors, standing in its own grounds with no other buildings nearby. There was an unappealing poorly tended 'garden' at the sides and rear, and an asphalt parking area between the pub and the road. "Interesting," remarked Martin as they turned off the road and he noted at least a dozen motorbikes adorning the front area. He nudged Anna and indicated a large van with the words *'Dreadhead' - Making Britain Rock'* emblazoned on the side.

She looked with dismay at the two wheeled machines and said "Do you think it's OK? I've been a bit twitchy ever since that time in Sarony with the Coubert gang."

Martin just patted her arm and said "It'll be OK. Come on."

'It might be OK for you Mr bloody ex-army man but this girl isn't a member of the US Marine Corps like our friend Aggie,' she thought as she extended her stride to catch up with him.

There was a small entrance lobby and a second set of doors inside through which Martin breezily led her. As they entered the bar Anna's stomach did a double flip when she saw that most of the clientele were men dressed in motorcycle leathers. Her own choice of a denim jacket, jeans, and an unmarked white blouse, all surmounted by a golden ponytail drew interested looks from the drinking fraternity. None more so than a noisy group of four sitting at a table in the far corner of the room. This group were not leather-jacketed but dressed in a variety of scruffy casual clothes. The largest of the four wore a black T-shirt displaying the word '*Axeman*' in bright red with red flecks scattered below in a suggestion of dripping blood. They made their way to the bar and, as they collected their drinks, Martin nodded towards the corner table and murmured to Anna "I think those are our lads, come on. Let's go and say hello."

The big man with the paunch and the ponytail, that helped emphasise the fact that he was losing his hair, must have been six feet two inches tall judging by the size of him even from a sitting position. As they traversed between the tables en route from the bar he stared intently in open appraisal of Anna as she approached. It was a challenging, almost insolent studying, often used by some men to signify their interest in a woman.

With her high heeled boots, she was almost six feet tall herself, and the steady clip-clop sound they made on the wooden floor gave an impression of self-confidence that their owner did not feel. Most of the clientele gave the blonde a second look before resuming their own business and it was easy to ignore the man accompanying her, despite the fact that he was of similar height, and seemingly in good physical condition. The 'Axeman' however continued to fix an unwavering gaze on her as they drew near.

The other three occupants of the table were clearly several years younger than their large companion and although they also passed cursory glances over the newcomers, it was in the more normal detached fashion of pub customers. "Are you the band playing The Prospect this evening?" Martin opened the conversation with a smile. One of the younger men began to answer with "Yeah, that's right…," but was cut short by the big man's voice

"Who's asking?" The tone was belligerent but his eyes continued to sweep up and down the woman's body, inviting eye contact that was not forthcoming as Anna stared at an invisible point just above his head.

"Martin Price. We are……."

Again there was an interruption "Never heard of you, but she can stay if she wants to." Hal Blenkinsop laughed at his own comment and looked around at his cronies with a smirk, that duly elicited a couple of low chuckles.

Anna half turned towards Martin and was about to suggest they retrace their steps when her husband chose to ignore the rudeness and said: "Your old friend Mikey from *'Wheelspin'* said it could be worth asking you about Jase Wooldridge."

"Did he? That was good of him."

There was no invitation to join the group and the couple remained standing, although that was not the only reason Anna had begun to feel uncomfortable. Bikers, bikers' pubs - for that was what The Foxglove clearly was - and people like Hal Blenkinsop had never been part of the general scenery for Anna other than something to be studiously avoided when spotted on the distant horizon. She had never been a 'Saturday Night Girl' who went out with friends hoping to meet boys in pubs and clubs. Fully equipped by nature on a physical level, she lacked the self-confidence her looks should have provided, and had always found the whole 'boy meets girl' routine a painful and uncomfortable experience. On a social level, she liked environments that she was familiar with and, even in adulthood, was still on occasion unnerved by the unfamiliar.

Martin was naturally less inclined to let such things bother him and ignoring Hal's clumsy attempts at verbal jousting persevered with "If you don't want to discuss it just say so and we will be on our way."

Hal was nothing if not a showman. Being the centre of attention was something he always relished and he was beginning to enjoy playing the tough guy in front of the other band members. He responded with "If I didn't want to discuss it I'd have said so wouldn't I? What do you think blondie?"

Despite being caught off guard by his direct question Anna found her temperature rising and for some reason couldn't restrain herself. She didn't like the place, nor the clientele, and in particular, she didn't like the loud-mouthed oaf who for some reason thought he was someone important. Before she could stop herself she suddenly snapped "What I think is that I'd have to be a corpse before I found you worth listening to. Come on Martin, I've had enough of this idiot."

One of the younger band members laughed and the grins on the faces of the other two showed their enjoyment at Hal being so scathingly put down. Even Martin was surprised by the way in which his usually timid wife had lashed out. One or two of the drinkers at the nearest tables had begun to take a keen interest particularly as the voice of the blonde had carried above the rumble of an otherwise all male population. They tuned in to the atmosphere in the corner and heard an angry Hal retort, "Your mouth's bigger than your tits blondie so shut it before you get a slap."

Later, Martin observed that although Anna had rather unwisely offered her condemnation of the big man's attitude, threatening her was not something he was going to let pass without comment. "Still like hitting women do you Mr Axeman?"

Hal's face flushed an even deeper hue at the jibe and he got slowly to his feet "If you and motor mouth aren't out of here by the time I've counted to five you'll be very sorry."

Martin said nothing and stared at the man who was slowly counting aloud against what was now a backdrop of total silence. Turning to his wife he quietly said, "Go and stand at the bar."

As the ultimatum expired she hastily complied and then watched nervously. She knew from experience that Martin would not back off, and she had no doubts about his ability to look after himself, but as she glanced at the sea of leather-jacketed men now intently watching the free entertainment she knew the odds were impossibly high. Hal walked around the man sitting to his right and advanced on her husband "I warned you" he shouted, but Martin took a step back and deposited his glass on the nearest table before standing his ground and replying.

"We simply want to know if you've seen Jase Wooldridge."

"Too late mate, you should have left while you had the chance," came the reply as Hal lunged forward and made a grab for Martin's shirt front. His outstretched arm was knocked sharply aside and the fact that the seemingly casual blow with the edge of the man's hand set up an unpleasant tingling sensation briefly surprised him. His opponent again took a backwards pace beyond his reach.

"No need for any of this."

It was said in a calm, almost friendly voice, but an aggressive Hal, once set on a course of action, was not easily put off. He moved quickly forward arms outstretched in a semi-circular stance with the clear intention of enveloping Martin in a bear hug and wondered for a long time afterwards how the man had managed to hit him so hard. The punch, when it came, sank deep into his over-generous stomach and, as every last cubic centimetre of breath left his body, he found his right wrist caught in a steely grip that twisted his arm up behind his back as his assailant stepped behind him. Finding the ponytail handily placed Martin grabbed it with his free hand, wound it around his fist, and yanked hard, jerking the taller man's head sharply backwards so that he could only stare helplessly at the bar ceiling with its nicotine-stained patina. He gave the trapped arm an extra upward shove that elicited a yelp of pain from his captive before propelling the gasping musician ahead of him on rubbery legs. Using Hal as a battering ram Martin strode through the inner and then the heavier outer pub doors with the musician's chin taking the initial impact on both occasions.

As they exited it was as if an electric current had suddenly been switched on and animated the Saturday afternoon drinkers of The Foxglove. The band members got to their feet but were blocked from pursuing their colleague by a sudden surge ahead of them by some of the biker clientele. The barman tapped Anna on the shoulder causing her to jump and then nod in relieved understanding as he motioned her to join him in relative safety behind the bar, having checked that the cricket bat he kept for such emergencies was in its usual place. The crowd headed for viewing positions at the windows, and several of them congregated in the small lobby area between the inner and outer doors through which the two combatants had lately passed.

What they saw as they surveyed the front parking area was Martin suddenly spin his man around, grab his T-shirt in both fists and slam him backwards over the bonnet of the RAV4. With the wind knocked out of him for the second time Hal opened his mouth to gulp but immediately found the smaller man's forearm jammed across his throat. What the onlookers were not close enough to hear was the exchange of words that then took place. "If you don't want a fractured larynx please tell me whether you know the whereabouts of Jase Wooldridge."

The grey eyes had taken on an unpleasantly cold, almost venomous look which, combined with the staggering strength pinning him to the vehicle, made Hal's blood turn to water. The pressure was mercifully eased sufficiently for him to whisper a reply.

"Griss," he gasped. "Griss said he saw him. A few months after he took off. I haven't seen him since he walked out at the airport in 1977." Martin stepped back and with the sudden removal of his assailant's arm Hal's legs buckled and he slumped downwards into a sitting position on the ground with his eyes watering, a throbbing stomach ache and a nasty raw feeling in his throat. He wondered just how things could turn from suddenly teaching a man and a mouthy bimbo a lesson to putting himself in danger of losing his life. Dramatic though the thought seemed, Hal was in no doubt that he had come very close to an early and permanent end to his afternoon. He shuddered as he sat with dulled senses watching as the man walked back towards the building.

The lobby was clear as Martin re-entered and he noticed that most of the drinkers had resumed their seats, including the trio from *Dreadhead*. He saw Anna making her way back into the public area and as he looked towards her she pointed urgently saying, "To your right Martin." Turning he saw that one of the bikers, a man in his forties with a broken nose, and dressed like Marlon Brando in 'The Wild One', was almost upon him. He instinctively shifted both his centre of balance and the angle of his body as he saw the hand movement but at the last second checked his reaction on realising that the outthrust hand was open and reaching for his.

The handshake was firm and the voice that accompanied it said "Fuckin' brilliant! What a delivery! That tosser has been mouthing off ever since he arrived and I was going to have a word with him myself if it had carried on."

Martin smiled "Sorry to have spoilt your fun."

"He and some others blocked off the doorway" added Anna."

The biker smiled and gestured towards the three band members at the corner table. "Just making sure it stayed a fair fight, although I don't reckon they were up for it. Probably just as irritated by that loud-mouthed git as the rest of us. My name's Kev by the way, this is our pub on a Saturday and we like it quiet and peaceful."

"I'm Martin, and this is Anna, my wife. I think we have probably done enough to disturb your Saturday, but it's been a pleasure to meet you Kev. I'll take my wife home now and let her relax on the drive back to London."

The man nodded and said, "If she was my wife, Martin, I'd wrap her in cotton wool."

By the time they re-entered the parking area there was no sign of Hal. "I'm so, so, sorry Martin" gulped a distrait Anna as they walked to their car. "I've accused you in the past of provoking a fight and then I go and do exactly that. I just saw red when he kept trying to act as if he was being clever."

"Nothing to be sorry about. That tub of lard is only tough when he's hitting a woman. That's why I thumped him so hard; he actually thought he could threaten you and get away with it, and we know he once knocked Anne Silverdale around. Anyway, I hope you're impressed. Not a broken bone nor a speck of blood to be seen."

"But how did you know the bikers wouldn't come in on his side?"

"I didn't know for sure, but they were all older men, forties plus. They're genuine bikers, not scruffs. They only want a drink and a chance to break the speed limit. They don't go looking for trouble. I gave the barman twenty for taking care of you, that was good thinking on his part."

"Yes, the only person not thinking was me wasn't it?" She replied disconsolately. "I looked around that pub when we arrived and wrote the whole lot off based only on how they dressed and the bikes we had seen outside."

She subsided into a morose silence and he knew that hiding behind her sunglasses her eyes would be full of tears. The icy detachment was used by her to disguise the self-doubt that would bubble to the surface in situations where she doubted her own actions. Allowing the silence to prevail was the kindest way he could manage to let her undertake what he knew would be a period of severe self-recrimination. They drove without speaking for almost the entire journey back to the hotel until Anna finally re-established lines of communication by saying. "I suppose we had better phone Michael Harvey and see if he knows the name and phone number of the company this chap Griss is working for. I wish we hadn't taken this assignment on now Martin. It doesn't have the remotest connection to archaeology and only a very tenuous link to history."

Later that evening when Martin finished his phone conversation with Mikey he announced "Griss is working at Clutterbuck & Co, in Chancery Lane, apparently they publish technical books mainly for the legal profession. Let's give them a call on Monday morning."

Chapter 6 - Griss

"That would be our Mr Bruce Grissom you are referring to Sir," responded the switchboard to Martin's enquiry. "He's our sales director. I'll put you through to his secretary, hold on please." A surprised Martin did as he was told and was quickly rewarded with the words "Good morning. Marion Tutt speaking how may I help?"

"My name is Martin Price and this is in the nature of a personal call. I am a friend of Michael Harvey and I would like a word with Mr Grissom if he is free please."

He held on for a minute or two before a male voice came on the line. "Mr Price? Bruce Grissom here. How is Mikey? I haven't seen him for quite a while."

"He is well but I admit I have only met him once, a few days ago. I'm actually trying to track down Jason Wooldridge."

"Are you now, why is that?" The friendly tone had been replaced by a more formal one.

"A friend of ours has recently found something - a quite valuable artefact - that belongs to him. She lives abroad, as do we, but as we were visiting the UK we said we would try and trace him."

"I see, when you say 'we', who else is it you refer to?"

"My wife, Anna."

"Price you said. You're the couple who found Boudica aren't you?"

"That's us. We met up with Anne Silverdale and she put us in touch with Mikey. He mentioned the name of your employers and so here we are. Would you mind going over things for us regarding *'Wheelspin'*, we haven't made a great deal of progress so far."

"Can you make Monday evening in High Holborn, say 6 o'clock? Next week's a bit hectic for me but I can finish around 5.30 and meet up with you in a Wine Bar called The Bung Hole, it's almost opposite where Chancery Lane emerges."

When the call finished Martin said, "It looks as if you will have most of Monday to go shopping as well Anna."

They arrived ahead of time and took one of the circular polished wooden tables on the ground floor. A bottle of French red familiar to them both was opened, and three glasses provided. They had only just poured their drinks when a tall dark haired man entered, immediately looked towards them, nodded, and with hand extended walked over.

"Excuse me saying so, but I know you are Anna and Martin Price because I have seen your pictures in all of the glossy magazines. I'm Bruce Grissom, more usually known as Griss, and former member of a seventies rock band, embarrassing though that is. I do hope that third glass is for me?"

As an opening, it served to break the ice and having commented approvingly on their choice of wine he asked how he could be of help to them.

"Out of those with *'Wheelspin'* connections you seem to be the only one who actually saw Jase after he walked out at Heathrow, according to Hal Blenkinsop, that is."

"Mad Hal eh? Good luck with that. He hated Jase, you did well to get anything from that lunatic. For once in his life, he is right, though. I did run into Jase some months after he split. There was a party at Tatti's and I went along, and out of the blue Jase turned up. That was a big surprise because I knew they had broken up due to her inability to keep her underwear in place for more than five minutes.

"You didn't think much of Tatti I take it?" Anna asked.

Griss shrugged his pinstriped shoulders and she remarked later to Martin how difficult she had found it to reconcile the city gent who had shared a bottle of wine with them, with the long-haired moustachioed bass guitarist of the nineteen-seventies. In contrast to the tense encounter with Hal, Bruce Grissom proved a charming and candid companion.

"When Jase walked out at Heathrow he only beat me to it by a matter of weeks. I'd had enough of that scene and decided I would quit after the American tour. I was a competent enough bass guitarist but nothing great, and although the girls and the booze were fun for a while, I couldn't imagine it as a permanent way of life. Music was just a teenage hobby to me, like growing my hair long and wearing those daft high heeled shoes that were popular in the seventies. There were too many people in that world, like Hal Blenkinsop and the usual hangers-on, who took themselves far too seriously. We were an average band of the era and we were taken out of the pub circuit level by the talent of Jase Wooldridge. Mikey and I had talked about it for some time and although I had already made my decision to jump ship, I don't think he would have been far behind. As it happens Jase throwing in the towel pre-empted us. I had a brain and immersing it forever in a solution of booze and drugs wasn't my intention. I'm the senior sales director of Clutterbucks with a seat on the main board and that's what I always wanted, together with the comfortable, stable, life that goes with it. Sorry, that must sound terribly smug, but the fact is I like my life."

"But you were an up and coming band with two gold albums and a big tour in the offing" protested Anna.

Griss pulled a face before taking another sip of wine. "Frankly, I think that if the US tour had gone ahead and proved successful, then Jase would have been hijacked by Tornado Records and the rest of us would have been dumped. There were a lot of far abler musicians in the market and we didn't even own the right to use the *'Wheelspin'* name, Jase had got all of that sewn up and, to be fair, the name was his brainchild so I never had a problem with that. Even our earnings were being whittled down to a basic level due to Tornado Records recovering the advances it had made to us when we were struggling. The truth is we were always struggling, apart from Jase because he had the income from the song writing royalties."

"You don't make it sound a very attractive existence," said Martin.

"Things are not always what they seem" answered Griss. "That is especially true when applied to the entertainment business. We were taking a basic wage, and yes, enjoying a superficial lifestyle that all youngsters would have envied. Wall to wall women and unlimited booze and drugs were great but one way or another it all had to be paid for, and we were spending it faster than it was coming in. When the music stops, to coin a very appropriate phrase, the bills still have to be paid. Jase walking out didn't cause me a single sleepless night. I had never expected, nor wanted, a long-term career in the music business. As it transpired, Tornado got totally shafted when Jase walked, because they found they couldn't touch any of his money. We, Mikey, Hal and myself, hadn't broken our contracts and so we farted about until they expired and then Tornado was forced to write off the money we owed them." He laughed and added ironically. "Life's tough if you're a record label. We weren't unique and having been provided with individual contracts Tornado couldn't come after us when Jase walked."

"You were going to tell me about your last meeting with Jase," put in Martin as the narrative paused.

"Oh yes, so I was. Now let's see, the old memory is a bit reluctant after all the years that have passed. Jase walked out September 1977 and our contracts with Tornado weren't due to expire until 31st March the following year. The three of us bummed around Tornado Records studios just off Sloane Street doing a bit of session work here and there. We had time on our hands and drank a bit too much and also partook of various illicit substances. Hal in particular used to be wandering around stoned out of his mind a lot of the time, and if I remember correctly that's why he missed out on the party invite, and why he's remembered that I saw Jase after the Heathrow fracas. You see a couple of months after that bust up Tatti started hanging around the Tornado studios again. Just like she had when she first got off with Jase.

"Hang on a minute," interrupted Martin. "Would this Tatti girl be the same person who caused Jase to break up with Anne Silverdale. She has referred to him going off with what she called 'a posh tart'."

"Sounds like Tatti alright," chuckled Griss. "Yes, she was what can only be described as 'a bit of a goer' - without being too crude. Tatti had only one thing going for her and that was the fact that she was bloody gorgeous, and she put her natural attributes to frequent use. You see, she was the product of the public school system, she knew how to look good, spoke in a very well educated fashion, and generally exuded an air of complete confidence. The combination of natural good looks, a wonderful body, and a willingness to hop into bed at the drop of a hat - or, in her case, her knickers, made her a very attractive proposition. Quite why she had decided on a career of self-destruction I don't know, although I suspect that once she hit puberty she found schoolwork very difficult to do from the horizontal position, if you get my drift.

The thing was that Tatti was seriously into drugs, and I do mean serious. She made Hal Blenkinsop look like a member of the clergy, and she had a thing for musicians. The talk was that although her parents were divorced, she received quite a generous allowance from both of them, although it was her mother with whom she had lived during her teenage years. Even so, whatever her income was I should guess that it was barely sufficient to pay for her flat, her clothes, and all the other expensive things she liked and it had to keep her in drugs as well. To be fair, I don't think she hung around the studio so that the artists would subsidise her habit, at least not at first, but she soon learnt that she had something to offer if a trade was necessary. A lot of the artists and some of the technical guys weren't slow to pass up an opportunity for a bit of upper class bonking.

Jase fell for her big time and poor Anne Silverdale was gradually edged out of the picture until she eventually took the hint and found herself another band. So when Tatti began turning up at the studio again it was pretty clear that Jase had dumped her and she was back in circulation. Hal Blenkinsop who considered himself a bit of a ladies' man with the added attraction of being an ace musician - wrong on both counts of course - fancied his chances, but she would never have anything to do with him. I expect she had heard stories of how he could turn nasty so she always gave him a wide berth. One day, as Hal and I were heading out of the studio, we bumped into Tatti who was a bit pissed. She was pretty rude to Hal who stomped off in a real huff, but I thought I would try my luck. She wasn't exactly difficult to get into bed, or anywhere else for that matter, provided she thought you were OK. So I drove her back to her place and nature took its course. At the time I thought she just wanted a lift home because she wasn't capable and was quite happy to let me shag her as a thank you, but when I was leaving she told me she was having a party that coming Saturday evening and I'd be welcome. Bingo, I thought. Maybe it was going to be more than a one-off."

"So that was when you met Jase."

"That's right, and bang went my chance of a return match with Tatti."

"You don't sound too bothered."

He laughed and drank some more. "Time's a great healer, and it wasn't as if I was in love with her. I wasn't really upset, more annoyed that I wasn't going to follow up my initial encounter. Tatti was very decorative but I didn't actually like her that much. I confess to being a bit of a hypocrite though because I admit that I felt a bit peeved when I got to the party and thought Jase was already there. I'd got myself a drink and was wandering through the flat when I saw Tatti in a corner talking in what seemed a fairly intimate way with this guy I took for Jase. It wasn't, but the dim lighting, smoky atmosphere and heaving bodies made it difficult to see clearly across the room. All of a sudden Tatti moved away from him and headed in my direction. 'Result' I thought, but as she got close she suddenly called out 'Hey, look who's decided to pay a visit. What do you want you bastard?' I turned around and blow me, but there was Jase. He nodded to me and edged through the crowd to where Tatti was, and I thought then that I really wasn't in the party mood after all. So I left, and that was the last I saw of Jase Wooldridge. I made a point of telling Hal that I'd had it off with Tatti because I knew it would really wind him up, and it obviously succeeded because he apparently still remembers it to this day."

"But you didn't actually speak to Jase?"

"No, I just stayed long enough to finish my drink and then went home."

"Have you any idea where Jase would have been living, or where he might be now?"

"Well, there wasn't a family home because he was an orphan and was brought up in a children's home. He used to rent a small flat over in Earls Court, and as far as I know he was probably still there. Apart from reading about Tornado bankrupting him, I haven't heard anything of him for about thirty-eight years."

"Do you know of anyone else he may have stayed in contact with?"

Griss fell into silence as he thought back over the years but when he finally spoke it was to say "I honestly don't. It's not as if we were bosom buddies, apart from Tatti of course, and her bosom was everyone's buddy. We had all met by accident at an audition staged by a record label wanting a four-piece band to promote. A sort of publicity stunt. We were all individually rejected but got talking when we were in the pub afterwards. We decided on the spur of the moment to have a serious crack at forming a band and seeing whether we could earn a living from it. So you see, we weren't old mates who had grown up together or anything like that. We never did form deep personal relationships and after we split up we haven't bothered that much to keep up with one another. Mikey and I meet for lunch now and then, but we tend to talk about family and of course property prices. Nothing left to say about the days of our misspent youth. Jase has never had anything to do with anyone, and Hal was always a nutter. I haven't the faintest idea who could give you a clue about Jase and what he's been doing for the past thirty-eight years."

"What was Jase like? Was he what you would call the leader?" Anna asked.

"There was no official leader. Hal tried to promote himself into that position particularly with all that 'Mad Axeman' stuff, but we tended to defer more to Jase. He was the lead vocalist and he wrote all of our stuff. That's one thing that has often puzzled me. He loved writing songs and I've never understood why he dropped all of that. Unless he hasn't and has carried on but uses an alias. Apart from his talent, he was just an ordinary bloke, but quite hard headed. He wrapped up his publishing royalties very tight and we never saw anything from that source. He was quite tough with women as well. I don't mean like Hal; I mean in the ruthless sense. He was quite capable of making a girl feel she was the love of his life and then dropping her when he found someone he thought was more attractive."

"Like Anne and Tatti for instance?"

"Yes, although Anne was a groupie and had been around the block a few times. Tatti was basically an upper-class bike who knew nothing about music but liked the glamour of the music scene. She was stunning and poor Anne never stood a chance based purely on looks. Personally, I would have stuck with Anne, but for Jase, it was a simple decision. He wanted Tatti and so goodbye Anne. Like I said, a fairly typical young bloke. Maybe it came from being brought up in a children's home and having to always think of himself first."

"Do you know where the childrens' home was?"

"Sorry, not with any accuracy. It was definitely in Sussex, and he mentioned Eastbourne quite often. On several occasions, he remarked that he was going off to Eastbourne for a day or two. Not exactly the vibrant venue to attract an up and coming rock star so I'm guessing it was in that area. You really need to speak to Tatti if you can find her, but before you ask - no, I don't know her whereabouts. In any case, she probably either succumbed to the ravages of drink, drugs, and STD or if she found herself a rich old man to keep her in funds she has probably died through excessive abuse even more swiftly."

"One last thing. Do you know what Tatti's surname was?"

"Mmm, let me think, Drake I think, yes, I distinctly remember her introducing herself as Tatiana Drake."

"Tatiana? That was quite exotic for an upper-class English girl."

"Not in her case. Her father was a member of the Russian embassy staff. Of course, in those days it was the USSR. He was some big wheel in their trade delegation and was pretty much permanently based at their embassy in Kensington."

"But you said her name was Drake."

"That's right, I remember her saying she had changed her name when her parents divorced, and she went to live with her mother. Drake was her mother's maiden name I believe."

"I don't suppose you know what her father's surname was?" Martin asked.

The question was met with a shrug and a smile. "I'm afraid you have just about exhausted my fund of information on Jase and Tatti." Griss replied, "But I hope that it's been of some help."

They left shortly afterwards and as Martin and Anna walked down towards Holborn Circus on the lookout for a cab Anna said "At last, something that gives us some sort of link to Jase Wooldridge and Mother Russia. We are making some form of progress." It was a chilly evening and she slipped her hand inside her husband's arm and drew herself close to him.

"I suppose we should do the decent thing and send an update off to CKC," answered her husband. "They are paying for our happy holiday here in dear old 'Blighty' so deserve something if only to have the opportunity to pull the plug on it. Ah, here comes a cab at last."

Chapter 7 - Tatti

"How much use is the knowledge that Tatiana Drake had a Russian father if we don't know what his surname was?" Anna asked as they sat in the bar of the hotel the following day.

"Apart from providing us with a Russian link, not very much. Perhaps we ought to look at other aspects. For instance, why would Jase go haring off to Switzerland to open that account?"

"To make sure his bit of contraband was safe and secure I imagine," answered Anna as she wondered why her husband had asked such a pointless question.

"Yes, I appreciate the basic intention, but first of all, how would he know just how valuable the bust was and does the average twenty-year-old think 'I'd better stash this somewhere, I know, I'll nip off to Switzerland and open a secret account'? Granted, he wasn't perhaps a truly average twenty-year-old, but wouldn't he have been more likely to choose somewhere closer to home?"

Anna considered the point as she slowly rotated her glass on the surface of the bar and finally said: "Supposing he didn't go charging off. What if he was already there? They were a touring band actively engaged in promoting their records. They may have been touring in Europe."

"That's a bit more logical, but I still think it's far-fetched for a Swiss Bank account to be a natural choice. More to the point, why take the wretched thing away on tour?"

"Perhaps he didn't. What if he came by it when he was already abroad?"

"It's all rather flimsy isn't it Anna. Let's check with Mikey whether *'Wheelspin'* were touring at that time before we spend any more time on that theory. What else have we got?"

"Precious little, although I have emailed a progress report to CKC as discussed. But going back to your earlier point, just how would a twenty-year-old rock singer know that the gold bust he had was valuable enough to warrant opening a security box to keep it in?"

"This Tatti girl may be the key to it. Do you feel like another trip up the road to see Anne Silverdale?"

A telephone call enabled them to arrange a visit to *The Rockery Music Store* on Junction Road where they were greeted with the words "Welcome to my musical world" as Anne Silverdale led them through the racks of vinyl records and more modern CD offerings to her small office at the rear of the shop.

"We would like to find out as much as we can about Tatiana Drake, the posh tart called Tatti that you mentioned last week Anne," said Martin.

The woman sighed deeply and then nodded her agreement. "She first turned up in The Troubadour which was the pub just round the corner from the Tornado Records studio. A lot of the recording sessions at that time went right through the night with the facilities in use virtually twenty-four hours per day. It was after one of those sessions that we had all ended up in the pub for early doors at ten-thirty in the morning. We were regulars and the landlord used to cook a full English breakfast for those who wanted it. He also turned a blind eye to some of the other substances being consumed or sold on his premises."

"You mean drugs, I presume," said Martin.

"That's right, various dealers got to know where the Tornado Records people hung out and made a point of paying regular visits. The Troubadour was our hangout of choice and we had just finished our food when this Tatti creature walked in. This was 1977 and it was still a little unusual for a woman to come into a pub by herself. She was smartly dressed, not frumpy or anything you understand, but it was obvious that her clothes were top drawer. It was even more noticeable because the Punk revolution had started that year and styles were changing. A lot of girls had started to dress down, but not her. She did no more than walk over to us and ask if the boys were the band named '*Wheelspin*' and when that was confirmed she offered to buy everyone a drink, even us girls and the roadies. Nobody turns down a free drink and she was invited to join us. The boys were very taken with her of course and I have to admit she was extremely attractive. The next time she turned up was a few days later and having already broken the ice, nobody objected when she came over and joined us. Before long she became a regular member of our little group and eventually the inevitable happened and someone invited her along to a recording session. Gradually she became part of the scenery and of course she wasn't short of admirers. It wasn't just our crowd either, I know for a fact that she got involved with several of the Tornado executives and studio staff before she drifted back to our group." She was one of those clever girls who could mix with smart well-educated people and was equally at home with more ordinary folk. She just didn't let things knock her off balance, like when she got herself in the papers over the scene she had caused at the Russian embassy."

Anna pricked up her ears "What was that all about then Anne?"

The older woman frowned as she searched her memory before saying "I'm not sure for certain. Her father was Russian and the newspaper report said something about her having gone to see him and then a massive domestic row erupting. It led to her being forcibly ejected from the embassy and standing on the pavement ranting and raving. It was bad luck that a newspaper photographer happened to be passing and took a series of pictures that subsequently appeared in the *Daily Mirror*. The day the story was published Tatti was hanging around with us as if nothing had happened and just said that her father was a tight-fisted pig and the next time he told her to see him at the embassy he could whistle."

She shrugged before adding "Anyway, as I've already said, she had a lot of poise and self-confidence. She was a very attractive girl and if she chose to put it about then nobody took much notice, particularly at a record company. It wasn't exactly a morally correct environment. By this time, I had moved in with Jase and we were roosting in his flat in Earl's Court, and I was a bit slow to notice that she had begun to take more and more interest in him. Hal was trying to get off with her at the same time, but although she obliged a few of the boys, she always avoided him. I suppose her readiness to drop her knickers for all and sundry was why I didn't notice that she was particularly homing in on Jase."

"But didn't her promiscuity put Jase off at all?" Anna asked.

"Not really, it was a strange world we were living in back then, and there didn't seem to be anything we couldn't have if we wanted it. I'm not sure Jase realised she had him in her sights initially. There were recording sessions, parties, plentiful booze and drugs. Hal was still resentful over me and Jase, and now he could see that Tatti was happy to not only hop into bed with whoever she liked the look of but was eyeing up Jase in preference to him. Lots of things were happening, lots of tensions and temperamental incidents. I wasn't really aware that he was especially keen on her and the fact that he may have bedded her at some point wasn't much of an issue. Then of course when the boys went off on their European tour it all came together - for them of course."

"European tour, do you remember when that was?" Martin asked.

"I'm not likely to forget in the circumstances. They toured from early August to the end of the month and they were taking just a few days' break before setting off for the USA. I hadn't gone, because I didn't like the hectic schedule. At least if I got fed up with a UK tour I could just come home, but out there I couldn't even talk to anybody very much because I didn't speak a foreign language. It didn't register with me that Tatti had stopped hanging around until after a couple of weeks and then when I managed to phone Jase up he said that she had turned up out of the blue at one of their venues in France. He tried at first to say that she was staying on with them because she could speak several languages and it was very helpful for the band, but finally admitted that he was sleeping with her the whole time. This was all a bit weird because one of the roadies hired for the tour was particularly close to Tatti and they certainly had an ongoing relationship of some sort.

Anyway, I threw a tantrum, and told him that I wasn't prepared to sit around while he was having fun with Tatti, and the singer from 'Krakatoa' had hinted a couple of times that he liked the look of me. Jase just said if that was how I felt perhaps it was a good idea if I moved out. That was it, bang. Just like that." She gulped as she said it and added "So, little northern groupie chick shown the door, and posh, clever scrubber moved in. Mind you, in some ways it probably did me a favour because I did exactly what Jase said, and so I was on tour in Scotland with 'Krakatoa' when there was that big police raid on Tornado Records"

"What was that all about?"

"Drugs, in a word. There had always been plenty of stuff to be had if you wanted it, and I did my share, but only the softer varieties. Some of the bigger bands and artists were into the more exotic and expensive lines and a number of the Tornado executives were also at it. Mainly the older blokes with big salaries who realised that they could not only get high themselves but having a ready supply was also a good way to land some of the younger girls that hung around and were already hooked."

"You mean they used it to trade for sex?" Anna asked.

"Well not quite as overtly as that, but if a girl was invited to a party by one of the execs, then it was very often a party for one, and if a ready supply of coke or whatever was made available then she would naturally show her appreciation in the usual way. It wasn't that unusual, but it's a scene I'm glad I never got into. I only did the business with musicians I fancied, not some fat bloke old enough to be my dad. Yuk, I may not have been a model of virtue but I wasn't a junkie slut. Over the months the drug thing had got progressively more and more part of the daily scenery. It was getting ridiculous, and then one day bang, the police turned up, busted a whole bunch of people at Tornado and at the time it made big headlines. I was a few hundred miles away as I've said and was as clean as a whistle.

"What about *'Wheelspin'*?"

"They were still on their European tour so they were also in the clear. I seem to recall that a couple of executives and a few artists were prosecuted for possession, but I think it was just one of those raids that were undertaken from time to time as a sort of advert to show that the forces of law and order were combating the excesses of the permissive society." She laughed before saying "The irony is that if they had busted the *'Wheelspin'* caravan they would probably have got a far more impressive result."

"I didn't think *'Wheelspin'* were seriously into drugs."

"The boys weren't, but Tatti was, and so was her friend on the road crew. He'd been one of the major suppliers to the Tornado crowd. He had hung around the studio for months and been hired, on and off, as a roadie for *'Wheelspin'* and other Tornado Records bands. He was a dealer and was one of the reasons the drug usage at Tornado had escalated."

"So where did he get his stock from?" It was Martin who asked.

"No idea, but he was Tatti's main source, and I know he used to supply several of the other users at Tornado."

"Do you remember his name?"

She shook her head "Not all of it. Dave something. He wasn't on the full-time payroll. He was actually quite good at his job, and not a bad bloke really. Not some thick ex-school friend being given a sinecure by an old mate. He was definitely quite a switched on character and a cut above a lot of the dimwits who often turned up. As I recall, he was very often hired for the foreign tours, or if one of the full-time roadies was ill. Don't forget, Tornado handled quite a number of bands, and a roadie with a brain who knew what he was doing was always able to find work. He could probably have landed himself a full-time job if he'd wanted it."

"Did you see Tatti again after she and Jase got back from the tour?"

"Only once. Sometime close to the big scene at the airport Jase dumped her and then when I came back from the *'Krakatoa'* tour I hung around Tornado for a while, hoping to meet Jase again but he had dropped completely out of sight. I saw Mikey and Griss and, unfortunately, Hal. We had a few drinks and laughs but nothing more. Then all of a sudden Tatti started to show up again. I gave her the cold shoulder but one day she cornered me in the ladies' toilets and begged me to tell her where she could find Jase. I told her straight that I didn't know and hadn't seen him since they had all gone off to Europe. By that time, I was living with the *'Krakatoa'* guy, so I told Tatti that if Jase wasn't at his Earls Court flat then she could try looking for him down near Eastbourne where he had been brought up. That was the last direct contact I had with her. As far as I knew she was still living in her posh flat in Highgate by the time I went back to live in Halifax."

"He was raised in a children's home wasn't he?" Martin asked.

"Yes, I don't think his parents were ever married and his mother put him into care before he was a year old. He never was adopted and came out of the system aged sixteen and made his own way in the world.

"Did you live it up when you were with him?" Anna re-entered the conversation and added, "I mean, according to you and others he was the only one actually making decent money."

"Oh, I see. No, we just lived in his flat at Earls Court and as far as I know, Jase was no better off than the other guys. I think what I said was that he had got his music publishing income tied up securely and that when Tornado sued him for breaking his contract they found he had nothing in his name that they could get their hands on. How the money was actually stashed I've no idea, but Jase certainly wasn't receiving a huge amount in his own bank account. He sometimes had trouble paying the bills, just like the other lads. I think that was another source of Hal's resentment because he would often have a dig at Jase, saying he was 'the rich one' to which Jase would just smile and say nothing."

"Did you ever try and contact Jase after you split up?"

"A couple of times. I hoped I would see him when I went back to the old haunts at Tornado Records and The Troubadour but he never showed. Before then, though, when I got back from the *'Krakatoa'* tour and I couldn't get an answer when I phoned the Earls Court flat, I went round there and as I still had a key, I let myself in. It was obvious Jase had been there because when I left I had made sure everything was clean and tidy - the product of a good northern upbringing. On that occasion though it looked as if a bomb had hit it. Even for Jase, the place was in a mess with things everywhere, and so I just sat down, had a cry, slung the key onto the table and never went back. That's why I was surprised when Tatti asked me if I knew where Jase was. I had assumed he was living happily with her in Highgate but from the little she said, he had dropped her after the tour ended and just before the Heathrow meltdown. When I look back now I realise how lucky I've been. The seventies were great, don't get me wrong, but for a teenage girl seriously into music and musicians, it was a dangerous place. Drink, drugs and STD have accounted for a lot of us, but I survived. Me, with no great talent for anything. I'm still here and keeping body and soul together."

They made their way back out onto Junction Road and stood for a while as the busy north London street flowed around them. A young black man in an expensive looking leather coat hurried past and into the music shop. A bus pulled in and disgorged a clutch of passengers. An old woman scuttled past, muttered to herself, dropped several bulging plastic bags to the ground, thrust an arm into a waste bin, and with a grunt of displeasure withdrew it before picking up her possessions and moving on. Anna shivered and wished she was back in Sarony. Even Grantfield would be better than London on a winter's day.

Chapter 8 - Dave

When asked for an assessment of Iosif Gusev the usual response from his superiors was 'diligent'. Being of a diligent nature had taken him on an unspectacular course through the diplomatic service of the Soviet Union and earned him a posting to the London embassy. Iosif, although diligent, was not without ambition, but that ambition was not to progress on a career path for the glory of Mother Russia that would eventually provide him with a pension and small apartment in Moscow. Iosif's ambition was to accumulate sufficient personal wealth to enable his comfortable retirement to the United States of America. Once there he could then indulge his fondness for the little luxuries such as women, alcohol, and further wealth. All items that were, regrettably, not part of the Communist ideal, and would never be achievable on his government earnings. In the days of the Soviet Empire long before the advent of Gorbachev, the state edifice was still being run by what are now regarded as 'Cold War Warriors' who, having lived through the creation of the Bolshevist system followed by the purges of the thirties and the Nazi onslaught of the forties, were still secure in the knowledge that what they saw as the ideal way of life was exactly that. Secret would-be capitalists such as Iosif would not find a comfortable future within that philosophy.

Hidden deep below the self-effacing exterior lay an entrepreneurial spirit that his employers had no idea existed and which, when allied to his commendable diligence, had for some years enabled him to slowly build up a small but steadily increasing retirement fund. His liking for western luxuries had mistakenly led him into marriage to an English woman with whom he had fathered a daughter. That union had foundered on the rocks of his wife's refusal to accept the restrictions of his official salary when she accidentally discovered his secondary source of earnings. They had reached an agreement via the time honoured methods of blackmail and extortion, which enabled Sophia Gusev to acquire a house in her home county of Sussex, change her own and her daughter's surnames to her maiden name of Drake, and obtain a generous monthly financial allowance for each of them. All of this was paid for from Iosif's illicit retirement fund, the diminution of which, as Sophia reasonably pointed out, was nothing compared to what he would suffer if she exposed his criminal career to his employers via The News of the World.

Iosif sat back in his chair and cast his eyes down the column of figures painstakingly entered in the small notebook he always carried with him. Since being seconded from Moscow to the Cultural Attaché's section of the London embassy he had put his time to good use. The small network he had built up over the years was beginning to pay handsome dividends, despite the depredations of a rapacious ex-wife and a spoilt daughter. It was, however, the remarkable unexpected discovery of only two weeks earlier that made his carefully managed source of illicit income appear very hard work indeed.

He reflected on the pure blind luck arising from when the all-powerful Senior Cultural Attaché ordered him to extract from the embassy basement a file detailing the coal production statistics for the year 1948. Quite why that information was required was beyond his imagination, although he had a feeling it's sudden importance may have been connected to his having inadvertently parked his car in the space regarded by his superior as his own. Rummaging among the dust-covered papers and assorted junk from the Stalinist era would take several hours and result in his suit needing to be cleaned and, most probably, a throat infection from the dust and grime which his labours were injecting into the enclosed atmosphere of the basement. For more than an hour he had toiled away at the badly indexed racks of mouldering boxes and files until his irritation got the better of him and he swore long and loud as a cardboard box labelled only '1948' proved heavier than expected as he removed it from the metal shelving. One of the hand-holes set in either end slowly tore as he was lifting it off the shelf and, although he attempted to quickly ground the box, the weak cardboard gave way and it pitched sideways dislodging the flimsy lid and causing a shower of paper to cascade onto the floor. He resentfully wrestled the box onto the small table beside him and in exasperation scuttled about the dimly lit area scooping up the pages of reports that had escaped. He was about to dump them back when he saw that, instead of the expected bed of yellowing paper, the unspilled contents comprised a solid object of some sort, wrapped in a grubby cloth, around which further material was wedged in the spaces between the sides of the box. This unexpected item had obviously been carefully hidden by the layers of paper accidentally dislodged by Iosif's clumsiness and the decaying effect of a damp atmosphere on thirty-year-old cardboard.

He had perched on the basement table for a long time looking at the unwrapped object, not quite willing to believe what his eyes told him he held in his hands. Finally, when he opened it and found the small gold bust of the Romanov Tsar inside he knew that he held the means to change his life at a stroke.

Iosif, diligent as ever, worked late that night at the embassy and when he deemed it safe to do so returned to the basement and recovered the item from the broken box. Who had originally interred it he had no idea, nor did he much care. It had clearly been hidden away in the basement of the London embassy during those turbulent post-war years, having somehow been spirited out of Russia. It no doubt represented some other disenchanted diplomat's retirement fund but, with the frequent changes of personnel during the period of Stalinist paranoia, the would-be owner had never returned to collect his treasure. When he drove to his apartment that evening he carried in the boot of his car the means that, with careful management, would provide him with a new identity and the ticket to a life of luxury in the United States - far, far, from the reach of the Soviet Union and its numbingly grey way of life.

Transporting the Imperial Egg - he could hardly bring himself to even *think* those words - from the car park to safety behind his front door was without risk, and he had carried it, still wrapped in its old piece of cloth, tucked nonchalantly under one arm. He chuckled, poured himself another whisky and, having made his decision, picked up the telephone and dialled the number of the one person he knew, who could help him. The call would be welcomed as there was always a need for money and, with another shipment of the usual merchandise now ready to be taken and hawked to one of a number of enthusiastic bidders in the UK and Western Europe, a golden opportunity now presented itself. For once the phone was answered almost immediately, and the slurring voice betrayed its owner's recent indulgence in alcohol or something more exotic.

"Tatiana Drake, who is this?"

"It is Papa, Tatti."

"Oh, what do you want?"

The comment and tone were indicative of her mother's influence, he thought bitterly. They had not spoken since the unfortunate incident on the pavement outside the embassy some weeks before when she had waited for him and asked for money because her month's allowance had run out. She had obviously been under the influence of drink or drugs and became hysterical when he had refused and suggested she ask her mother. The damned photographer who had happened to be passing had sold the pictures to a newspaper and he had been hauled up before his section head. His explanation had been accepted but with the veiled threat that any further such indiscretion would be viewed in a far different light. He was so shaken by the thought of the possible consequences that for the only time since their final parting he had contacted Sophia Drake. It did not take very long for her to realise that an ignominious return to Moscow would cut off his illicit income, and so she, in turn, would be left without money, the bloodsucking bitch. He told her in no uncertain terms to impress on their daughter that there should be no repeat of the public scene, or they would all regret it. For once his ex-wife actually took on board what he was saying and he knew that she had given their daughter hell.

"I want to give you and your boyfriend the chance to earn some extra money."

"You mean by Dave peddling your stuff don't you?"

"Not exactly, but close. Tell him to meet me at our usual rendezvous tomorrow evening at 8.30."

"What's this all about? We run the risks while you rake in the real money."

Just like her mother he thought.

"Shut up and do as you are told, you avaricious little slut. You will be well rewarded for your meagre efforts, as will your boyfriend."

"Well he may not be my boyfriend for much longer if you must know, Papa dear, so what will you do then, when you can't use me as a go-between?"

"I will find an alternative, one that doesn't involve the use of a junkie tramp."

"And when I tell Mummy she will shaft you good and proper Papa."

Suddenly, now he could see a realistic end in sight, he no longer feared his ex-wife's vindictiveness "Where are my manners Tatti dear? I forgot to ask you how that greedy old bitch is didn't I? Not fallen off the end of a bottle and drowned in a sea of puke I hope."

He put the phone down before the fruit of his loins could respond.

Seated at the table at one end of the saloon bar of the small public house just a few minutes' walk from his apartment, he appraised the young man sitting opposite. Long hair, a beard and moustache, fashionably unkempt and wearing a non-descript pair of blue jeans, check shirt and unbuttoned waistcoat. Every inch the 1970's male that morons such as his daughter happily welcomed into their beds. All the money extorted from him to provide a top notch education at an English private school had produced a tart with a foul mouth and an appetite for the very product he had been basing his financial future on. He eyed his companion with distaste as he listened to his summary of the task he had put to him.

"So let me be clear on this. When I go on this next trip to Europe you want me to use what I unload the stuff for to open a security box and account at a Swiss bank, and you will tell me how that is to be done? I must then pass to you the access codes or passwords, or whatever so that you can manage them. You will also give me some photographs to give to my contacts with instructions to pass them up the line to their employers and invite bids to be made for the object in the photographs. I will receive three times my usual, um, commission for this on top of my normal pay for the shipment?"

"Correct. Once the winning bid has been received, you will deliver to the successful bidder a note of the location from which he may collect his purchase. That location will be arranged by me."

"This object must be very valuable."

"Yes, it is. That is why I am willing to pay you a ridiculous additional sum to handle such a simple task."

"So what is there to stop me just taking whatever it is that you want me to put into the box, and disappearing?"

"Quite simply the fact that you would have no means of converting it into cash, and I would let it be known what you had done to the people in Europe who will be the willing buyers. Let me be clear, you will only be in possession of part of the object. It is unique enough that any attempt by you to sell it would be as good as identifying yourself with neon lights. You would not last very long. I am not stupid, young man, and I trust you only to do what is in your own best interests."

He watched as the long haired lad - he couldn't think of him as a man - licked his lips and ran over the plan in his head before saying. "OK, it's a deal. What about Tatti?"

"My daughter is my problem," he snapped, but then it occurred to him that the lad would need to be kept onside for future use, and so he added in a softer tone "Because I value our working relationship I will tell you that it may not always be possible to use Tatti, and you should think about letting me have a more direct way of contacting you."

The younger man frowned and replied, "Why would you want to cut her out?"

"It's not so much *me* wanting to cut *her* out as *her* wanting to cut *you* out." He noted with satisfaction the look of alarm that passed over the other's features. "I'm telling you, as a friend, that you and she as a couple may be coming to an end. I will leave you to assess the situation and act sensibly if you think my words look as if they have substance. If you and Tatti are no longer together that does not need to affect our business relationship. My daughter is her mother's creature."

He got up and left the younger man puzzling over the evening's revelations.

Tatiana wasn't puzzling. She was fuming. Not only was her money stretched to the limit, but only weeks earlier the man who was pleased to call himself her father, had caused her mother to contact her and give her the sort of telling off that only a mother can inflict on a wayward daughter. Now, he treated her like an unpaid lackey running messages between him and her boyfriend. He wasn't going to get away with it, she told herself, somehow he was going to pay for the humiliation.

She thought about Dave and how she was hoping that her efforts to attract the remarkably similar looking Jase of the *'Wheelspin'* rock band would allow her to move on to a more rewarding longer term relationship. It was not that she was in love with Jase or anything like that, and she certainly had no particularly deep feelings for Dave. Jase, however, was going to the top. He and his fellow musicians were on the verge of the genuine big time, whereas Dave would always be a second-rate drug pusher. She looked at herself in the mirror. She needed to look her best because she had been invited to a party by an executive of Tornado Records to whom she had recently been introduced, and she knew exactly what was on his mind when he made the invite. What she had on her mind was an expectation that he would demonstrate his appreciation in the form of the illicit substance that she knew he was heavily reliant on. Short term problems required short term solutions, and if that meant obliging a not terribly prepossessing forty-year-old, then she would do so without regret whilst she pondered the method by which she would even the score with her swine of a father.

Dave meanwhile was wondering why Iosif Gusev should have hinted that all was not well with Tatiana and, although he was aware of her infidelities, he had always relied on the fact that he was a reliable source from which she supplemented her drug taking. The irony that the drugs in question partially emanated from her own father via his Russian suppliers was not lost on him. Tatiana had originally been no more than the convenient link between himself and her father, but her own growing fondness for the illegal substances had now skewed the tripartite relationship. Now, he was forced to admit, his feelings for her had grown beyond the need for regular sex. He was shocked to realise that the possibility of her permanently transferring her affections alarmed him on a more intimate level than he would have imagined.

Although he made good money from placing the drugs he received from the Russian, Dave also had his own separate network of suppliers providing him with merchandise that he sold on to the people in the music business. Tatiana was now an invaluable intro to that market, and it was via her that he had landed the work as a part-time roadie with *'Wheelspin'* and via that connection to the larger consumer market at Tornado Records. His feelings for Tatiana were mainly financially orientated with the added bonus that she just happened to be extremely attractive. Falling out with her need not mean disaster, but, if she just happened to latch onto somebody in the same line of business as him, then a very lucrative source of income could well disappear. He was realistic enough to understand that there was little he could do to stop Tatiana transferring her affections elsewhere, and so a contingency plan was called for.

He began to think about the 'object' that Iosif Gusev had mentioned and whether there was any possibility of making more from the arrangement than had so far been offered. Iosif trusted him well enough when it came to the drugs, but this new item was obviously far more valuable. He was even willing to finance the cost of a security box at a Swiss bank but then, all he was going to trust Dave with was a photograph of the item and only a sample to verify its existence - whatever the thing was. Even so, the Russian was expecting the top men in the European networks to bid serious money which indicated that not only was the object extremely valuable but must be easily identifiable for what it was. Clearly, it was in a different league to what he was usually concerned with. A work of art perhaps? Something told him that the Russian was telling the truth when he said it would be unwise for him to try a crude theft of the intended deposit. The item itself must be so desirable that any attempt to cut a would-be purchaser out of the deal, and then try and sell it 'privately', would be suicidal. The conclusion he drew was that if anyone was to be cut out of the deal it had to be the Russian himself. A risky enough business to be sure, but the man had an Achilles Heel in the desirable shape of his daughter Tatiana. The beginnings of a plan formed in Dave's mind, and the more he thought about it the more convinced he became that Tatti would be the key to unlock the door to something exceptional.

Chapter 9- Paolo

Tatiana returned to her Highgate flat at lunchtime with enough of her beloved white powder to keep her on an even keel until the usual monthly deposit was made in her bank account. She had worked hard for her present, much harder than she had expected an overweight executive to require, but they had both got what they wanted. Now she could relax for the weekend, concentrate on how to further her aspirations so far as Jase was concerned, and look for a way to gain revenge on her father. She lay floating, in more ways than one, in her hot bath when to her irritation the telephone sounded, and she was forced to slither into the living room.

"Hello, baby." Dave's voice caused her to frown, and it was only when he uttered the words "I'd like to talk to you about your father. Can I come over?" That she focused her attention.

"Where are you?"

"South Ken, I can be with you inside an hour."

"Alright. I've got the new 'Stones LP, we may as well make a night of it. Pick up some food on your way." When she had hung up she went back to the bathroom, looked at herself in the full-length mirror, shrugged, and climbed back into the water.

Food, in this instance, consisted of Spag Bol and crusty bread, washed down with Ruffino Chianti poured from its distinctive raffia wrapped bottle. This was followed by a smoke, combined with the double live album from Mick Jagger and the boys. It put Tatiana in a relaxed and receptive mood as she contemplated her boyfriend sprawled on the settee opposite. Certainly better than her partner of last night and earlier that morning, but not as attractive as Jase, despite the similarity in looks. She suddenly realised that the reason for his visit had not been touched upon and asked, "So what does the pig want you to do now?"

He looked blank for a moment before recognising the allusion to the Russian. "Yeah, right. How are you getting on with your old man?"

Her eyes narrowed as she answered "I hate that mean bastard. Why?"

"You don't have a key to his apartment I suppose?"

She laughed and the thought of her father set her off on a scornful tirade "You must be joking. It's rented by the Russian embassy and although he's not involved in any sensitive stuff, they still keep a tight control on who is allowed access to what they regard as 'their' property. You know that the USSR is run by a bunch of geriatric paranoiacs, and that spreads right through the whole system. Whatever possessed Mother to marry a Russian I'll never know; bloody nutcases the lot of them! Convinced that everybody is out to get them when the reality is that most of the world couldn't give a shit and is quite happy for them to cower behind their Iron Curtain and stay there. Even the cleaning company looking after his apartment was vetted and hired by the embassy."

He leant forward, glass in hand. "And you can't get hold of a key I suppose?"

"Keys are registered with the embassy security section so if one goes missing the careless owner finds himself in extremely hot water. They actually require all key holders to present their keys once per month to the security staff to prove all is in order. As if anybody thinks that a junior Cultural Attaché would keep state secrets in his apartment." She sniffed scornfully and then inhaled deeply.

"But someone could nip off and have a key cut during the month and nobody would be any the wiser," he persisted.

She laughed and changed the record on her newly acquired teak music centre before saying "Come on Dave. Do you think Russian security hasn't thought of that? All the locks are Russian and no honest locksmith would risk his livelihood by trying to copy one of their keys - always assuming he could do so."

"So how do the cleaners gain access?"

"He hands his key over to the apartment security desk each Thursday. They give it to the cleaners when they arrive and then receive it when they leave. Daddy picks it up when he returns from work in the evening. All nice and tidy."

There was a silence as Dave digested this information before saying "Do you happen to know the name of the cleaning firm?"

"Britannia Janitorial," at least that was what I saw plastered across one of those little vans they use when they pitch up once per week. What's all this about Dave? Has my father shafted you on one of his drugs deals or something?"

He hesitated before reluctantly concluding that he had to bring her into his thinking and described the conversation with her father. For the first time in her life, she wished Mick Jagger would shut up as she thought through what Dave's news could mean. "And you think this, um, item is stashed in my father's apartment?"

He nodded and swigged some more wine. "Think about it Tatti. He won't be stupid enough to keep it at the embassy will he, so where else could it be? He's not likely to entrust it to either you or your mother so it has to be at his place. A third-floor apartment with unusually secure locks is as safe as anywhere." He paused before adding "I don't suppose he has a safe does he?"

Her eyes lit up as she answered "Of course he has you idiot. But what he doesn't have is the knowledge that I also have the combination. When he first moved into that apartment he and I were on far friendlier terms and I helped him move in. It was very busy, with phones being connected, and his possessions being unpacked and I heard him mutter something about the safe combination just as the doorbell was rung for the umpteenth time. He dropped a piece of paper onto the coffee table as he went to answer and, being nosy, I took a look and memorised the numbers. I'm good at that sort of thing, and later I jotted them down on the off-chance they could be of use."

He had listened carefully to her with mounting excitement and said "So it's a fair bet that he will have this object of his locked up in his safe. All we now have to do is figure out how to get into his apartment."

"You mean to steal this thing of his?"

"Why not? He's giving me the means to sell it on to the highest bidder. If I have what they are buying, then I can direct the money to wherever I like. Do you know what he is asking for as a good faith deposit?"

She shook her head.

"£50,000 to be transferred into the account he wants me to open."

"But that's as good as giving you the freedom to run off with the money, why would he do that?"

"Because he is going to pay me more than that if everything runs smoothly."

"How much?"

"None of your business. Once I've set up the Swiss account and box I have to give him a receipt from the bank confirming the contents of the box, the password, and any other relevant information."

"Just how much do you think this thing is worth?"

"I reckon your loving father is looking to sell for a couple of million at least."

She sat silently as his words sunk in before pouring herself another glass of wine. Then she made her decision. "If I help you what is my share?"

"If we pull it off we share the proceeds fifty-fifty, and if we get the timing right he won't realise that it's us who have cut him out until it is way too late."

"I don't understand why he needs you to open a security box, though."

"If you didn't shove so much stuff up your nose and down your throat you would think more clearly. In case you've forgotten, your father is a Russian diplomat. He's not exactly free to go swanning off around Europe, apart from which, I've got a network of buyers, some of whom are answerable to far bigger fish at the top. Fish who will be willing to pay big money for the right item.

He has told me that this thing he is selling is in two pieces. The idea is, firstly, that not only do I drop some photographs in the box to somehow prove he has possession of the whole thing, but secondly, and more importantly, I actually include part of the object. This means that when the buyer has made a bank transfer in respect of his deposit your father gives him the access details so that he can retrieve the item from the box and take it away for authentication. When the buyer is satisfied that his proposed acquisition is genuine he will be directed to proceed to an appointment at which he will authorise a transfer of the balance into the associated Swiss account and, on receiving telephone confirmation, I will then hand over the key to a left luggage box at Waterloo railway station here in London where the main object can be picked up. One of the buyer's men waits with me until he receives a message that all is in order."

"I see. So at no point does my father become personally involved, and you never get your hands on the whole object. Very shrewd."

"Yes, but if we can somehow get into his apartment when he is at work we can take the main object from the safe and I have worked out an alternative plan so that we are able complete the deal ourselves, always assuming he hasn't decided to change the combination of course."

"But how will we know who the buyer is?"

"Because he uses me all of the time as his go-between. Your father is the usual paranoid Russian. He is convinced that his phones are bugged and that if he steps out of line he gets hauled off to Siberia. That scene you created outside the Russian embassy not only pissed him off big time but it convinced him that it won't need a second slip up for them to send him back to Russia."

"I do not understand why he puts so much trust in you."

"What trust?" The drugs money isn't enough to tempt me, and in any case he's not my only supplier. I'm not likely to try and pinch the object to be authenticated because everybody would know who had done it and my life wouldn't be worth living. Getting my payoff from your father depends on me concluding the various elements of the plan he has set out for me. And to cap it all he holds onto the main part of the object until almost the last minute. It's pretty much fool proof."

"Unless we can get hold of the main object first," she added excitedly. This was beginning to look a serious proposition.

"As I said. Now this will mean that we have to rob your father and I think we need to do that after I have opened the Swiss account and when we get back from the *'Wheelspin'* tour."

"But when he finds it gone the shit is going to hit the fan big time."

"That's why I want us to pinch it then. I will be back in the country and carrying on as normal. With any luck, he will have no idea how the theft occurred, and if it takes him some time to discover the theft so much the better. Logically I wouldn't come back from abroad, pinch the thing and then hang around. I'm bound to come under suspicion so why would I invite it to that degree? Your expensive education should have helped you understand the meaning of reverse psychology."

"But won't the people who have bid for this thing be furious at being mucked about?"

"No, because they won't have been. I'm going to do exactly as your father has asked which means that they will make their bids by phone to me. I simply won't pass the highest one on to your father. So I will wait until a few days before the auction closes, contact the 'successful' bidder myself, and you and I will go to Switzerland. We will take the object from the box, have it authenticated to the buyer's satisfaction and conclude the deal then and there. All safely completed out of the country with your father still waiting in England for the auction to close."

"But supposing he's in the habit of gloating over this thing every evening, or he goes to the safe a lot. He will see it is missing. Suppose that's just hours after we have taken it Won't he just contact the bank and tell them to change the password?"

"No, that can only be done in person by whoever opened the account. He will have lost all control. If he discovers the theft early on, it just means that I have to weather the storm and carry on as the innocent party for longer. I suspect that he won't even tell me the object has been stolen because he will be waiting for me to betray myself"

"So where do we keep the object in the meantime?"

"With you."

"Me? Why me?"

"Because he knows you don't have the brains to put all of this together. I've told you, if he discovers the theft before we have gone to Switzerland I'm going to be the logical suspect, but it will probably take him a long time to figure out how it was done. If I can just bide my time and carry on as usual, it should throw him off the track. Blood is usually thicker than water and it will be very hard for him to believe you would sell him down the river to that extent."

"But I'm going to be sitting here with the incriminating evidence and if he somehow decides I'm involved I'm going to get it big time."

"OK, that's a fair point so you must stash it somewhere safe so it cannot be traced back to you if it's discovered. Use some imagination for once."

She frowned at that final comment but could see that the plan had been carefully thought through. "Is holding onto the object the only thing I have to do?" She asked hopefully.

"Don't be daft, your part is crucial. You and I together are going to actually pinch it. In the meantime, I want you to telephone Britannia Janitorial and then figure out how to safely hide the damned thing. It can't be too large, but I wish I knew what it actually is. I also want you to be the telephone contact with the buyer. There is no reason for the buyer to think I am anything more than a courier, and you can give the impression that you are part of a larger operation. Just make sure that you are not off your face when you are making the calls." He smiled and topped up his wine glass. "So how about it then? Clever or what?"

She thought about what he had said and finally said "Alright, let's go for it. I'm getting excited already. You are planning to stay tonight aren't you?"

Shortly afterwards, when the *'Wheelspin'* tour dates were finalised, Dave contacted Iosif Gusev. The following evening, he was handed the package containing the 'present' from the Imperial Egg together with two sets of photographs. One of those sets showed the famous only known photograph of the Alexander III Egg. The second set pictured the same item but this time, it was standing in front of an English newspaper front page from which the headlines and the date could be clearly read. It was at this stage that he, at last, found out exactly what the subject of his proposed larceny was.

The *'Wheelspin'* members and their entourage took the cross-channel ferry from Dover and were carefully shepherded through French customs by Dave. He then dutifully waited with them by their hired car while Ronnie their manager took responsibility for ensuring that the van containing their equipment was driven over to them by the other roadie. He and Dave then swapped places and Ronnie drove the car with Dave and the junior roadie following in the van.

The first full day in France was a Wednesday and it had been decided that once the road crew had delivered all of the equipment to the first venue they could have the rest of the day to themselves. This suited Dave very well and he was soon busy making half a dozen telephone calls. The tour was due to last for several weeks with the highlight being the final Sunday evening show set for the Elysee in the town of Dijon on 28th August. Tuesday 17th August would be a free day and it was then that Dave would complete the sale of the Russian drugs and use the money to set up the Swiss account and security box. In response to his telephone calls of several days before, various individuals arrived at the hotels used by the band on its travels and collected the brown A4 envelopes that had been left for them. It was only when he was actually in France that it occurred to Dave that a further precaution could be taken to help muddy the waters if things went wrong.

Although he was clever enough, Dave had only received a basic education at a secondary modern school and nurtured a strong inferiority complex when confronted with what he still thought of as the superior upper classes. He had taken care to dress as smartly as possible, but even so, when sitting in the small office at the bank he felt decidedly uncomfortable amongst the well dressed and suited employees. Switzerland was still somewhat conservative in nature and he was aware of being in a small minority of males sporting shoulder length hair and noticed that there were also very few with a full set of beard and moustache. He had never liked the thought that he was being looked down upon and detected a definite air of superiority and condescension emanating from the individuals with whom he was having to deal. It was this feeling of irritation that prompted him to respond somewhat aggressively to the various questions put, in what he thought were oily tones, by the middle-aged nobody sitting opposite.

"And what is to be the term of the security box?" Paolo Mersini of CKC Bank asked.

"Uh, what do you mean?" he replied, confused.

"I mean how long do you want it for, Sir?"

It seemed to Dave that the final word had been added merely as an afterthought. He felt his hackles rising as he answered, "What's the best, I mean, what's the most ...." He struggled for the right phrase, not wishing to use the word 'cheapest' in front of this superior being. Finally, it came to him. "Cost-effective. What's the most cost-effective?"

"Well, Sir. If you are unsure how long you will need the facility you can simply leave a minimum balance in the account, and the interest it earns will cover all charges, but it is, err how shall I say? It is quite expensive."

Conscious of the fact that he was in possession of almost £40,000 in cash from the recent drugs sale Dave felt a sudden surge of confidence and answered, "Well what do you call expensive?"

With a frown and an upraised eyebrow, Paolo Mersini solemnly intoned "About £25,000 pounds sterling Sir."

Well, it wasn't his money, and if the Russian didn't like it then tough. If all went well Dave was going to be away from all of this life in the very near future. "That's fine," he said and had the satisfaction seeing a look of surprise briefly flicker across the hitherto impassive features.

Chapter 10 - Iosif

The day after *'Wheelspin'* returned to England Mrs Josephine Sanderson answered the telephone in a Knightsbridge office.

"Britannia Janitorial, may I help you?"

"Yes please. This is Mr Gusev's secretary, Irena Karpov. I am calling regarding his apartment at 14 Holland Court. He has a weekly cleaning contract with you."

"How may I help, there is nothing amiss I hope?" answered Mrs Sanderson.

"No, nothing of concern. It is just that some remedial work is being undertaken this week at Mr Gusev's flat, and so it will be best if your cleaning visit for, er, this Thursday is cancelled. Just on this one occasion you understand, everything will be back to normal the following week. Mr Gusev didn't want your people to have a wasted journey, and with him being the only resident it will not matter if a week is missed."

"Very well Miss Karpov. I will advise our people and ensure that Mr Gusev is not charged for this week."

Two days later two people dressed in the usual white overalls and peaked caps of Britannia Janitorial walked in through the glass entry doors of Holland Court, and the man walked across to the reception desk as his female colleague waited by the lift. The security guard behind the desk pushed the visitors book across with barely a glance as the usual uniforms registered and passed over the key to the Gusev apartment without a word. One hour later the key was handed back and the cleaners signed out. This time, the security guard did take a little more notice of the couple as they carried their cleaning trugs towards the front doors, but it was only to note with approval the very shapely bottom of the female.

When the usual security man behind the reception desk handed back the key to his apartment with the words "All done as usual Mr Gusev," the Russian gave a nod of thanks and strolled to the lift. He had no reason to expect anything other than the usual empty, but clean, tidy apartment and so it was only when he went into the bathroom that he noticed the toilet itself had not been properly cleaned. He made a mental note to leave a written instruction for the cleaners the following week to ensure they did not repeat the oversight. His private enterprise had now moved onto a whole new level of trading, with his agent having returned from Europe and passed to him the details of the bank account and box he had opened. He had tried to blot the matter from his mind and concentrate instead on his work at the embassy which had entered an unusually hectic period due to the imminent arrival of Comrade Yelenkov on 3rd September. It was only a routine visit by one of the senior figures in state security, but Gusev and Yelenkov had been childhood friends, and the supplies of the drugs marketed by Gusev came via this connection. This made the visit doubly sensitive and Gusev was deeply involved in the arrangements being made to ensure that the visitor received the impression of a well-run UK establishment.

Childhood friends they might have been, but Yelenkov was not privy to the discovery of the Imperial Egg. The dinner held in his honour in the large banquet room of the embassy went well, and to an uninformed onlooker would have suggested a gathering of well-heeled members of western society rather than representatives of the proletariat of the USSR. Gusev and his old friend talked late into the night and during one of the short intervals when there was nobody else in attendance he confirmed that the latest consignment had as usual arrived safely in the diplomatic bag and via his trusted courier had already been transported from the UK and marketed. They finally said their goodnights and the junior cultural attaché chose for once to walk the short distance through the quiet London streets to his apartment.

It had been a good evening, he reflected, as he poured himself one final small Drambuie, a liqueur he had developed a taste for over the years. Things had suddenly taken an upturn, and not before time he thought. His divorce and the subsequent draining of his savings by the avaricious bitch and his no less venal daughter had all but driven him to despair. Now, with his auction of the Egg not due to close for another twelve days he had already received two substantial bids. He loosened his tie and cast an involuntary glance at where his wall safe lay hidden behind a Matisse print. There lay his salvation and when he gave way to impulse and opened the safe the shock caused him to faint. Fortunately, he avoided injuring himself on any furniture although the small amount of Drambuie did leave a stain on the carpet that would prove difficult to remove.

When he regained consciousness he did the obvious, but ridiculous thing, of putting his hand into the safe, as if something the size of the Imperial Egg would somehow be hidden from sight. Ignoring the sticky patch on the carpet he stumbled to the settee and sat for many minutes with his hands over his face as if blotting out his surroundings would change the reality of what he knew to be true. It was missing. But it couldn't be. He thought back to when he had last seen it. Almost a week ago, he recalled. When he deposited some spare cash in it, and the cash was still there. He hadn't opened the safe since. Could Dave have taken it? He was the only other person who knew of its existence, but how was that possible? He was a drug pusher, not a safebreaker. There were the keys, or rather the lack of them. The front doors leading from the street could only be opened by a key kept on his key ring, but nine times out of ten he was simply 'buzzed through' by the man on the reception desk. His security key to the apartment was never out of his possession - there were no duplicates, and he was the only person who knew the combination of the safe. He groaned and ran his hands up and over his hair. He was alone and had somehow been robbed of the means to transform his life.

He groaned again more loudly and rocked backwards and forwards in child-like misery. He stopped in the midst of his self-pity as a thought came to him. Perhaps he wasn't alone. When was it that Vlad was due to leave? On Monday, and although a busy man who had clawed his way far higher up the Party ladder than Iosif, he would make time to listen to his old friend's troubles. Vlad was clever and had always been streets ahead of his friend when it came to constructive thinking. He slept badly but his slightly fusty appearance the following day was put down by the embassy staff as the result of his late night drinking session with Comrade Yelenkov.

"Now Iosif. What is it that makes my old friend suddenly wish to see me as a matter of urgency on a Sunday?" His expansive manner was due to the ambitious typist with the luxurious figure rearranging her own lunch period to accommodate the unplanned delay caused by accommodating his old friend. "I thought we had a pretty good session last night. Surely nothing has caused you concern in the few hours since then?" Yelenkov stood almost six feet in height and his squarely built frame and heavy-jowled features exactly fitted the Western European view of what a high-ranking Soviet official should look like. He earned a nice little commission from the drug running and was hopeful that nothing had occurred to disrupt the arrangement.

Gusev hesitated, still unsure of whether to reveal his secret, but he finally sat down heavily in the comfortable brown leather armchair and in trembling tones laid out in fine detail the full story. Vlad Yelenkov sat impassively as he listened without comment to his friend's tale. He had always been a good listener and sitting back, with his chin resting on his chest and his eyes closed, the pose could be misconstrued as slumber. Nothing was further from the truth as he absorbed, and dissected the information being provided. His friend had never before seen him in this mode, and hesitantly finished with a rather lame "What do you think Vlad?"

The reply startled him when it came "Have you ever read the stories about Sherlock Holmes, the fictional English detective?"

A puzzled shake of the head caused a sigh to emanate from Yelenkov before he launched into his analysis. "You put the Egg into the safe and now it is gone, yes?"

"Yes, but it is impossible."

"Clearly not, otherwise you wouldn't be sitting there."

"I-I meant......" the sentence was cut short

"So somebody other than you removed it, yes?"

"Y-yes, b-but I am the only one who knew it was there."

"Do not be foolish Iosif. Somebody else knew, or at least knew that it was in your possession. It is simple, who did you tell?"

"Only my courier who returned, as expected, from France and has opened the bank account. He is acting as my go-between and is passing the bids over to me as arranged. He wouldn't be doing that if he had taken it."

"Wouldn't he? Who else is likely to know of the Egg?"

"Nobody, nobody at all, u-unless." He lapsed momentarily into thought.

"Unless?" Prompted Yelenkov

"M-my daughter, Tatiana. She is his girlfriend."

At this point, a soft tap sounded as the wooden door opened and the ambitious young typist looked in. She withdrew far more swiftly due to the ferocious scowl her interruption had elicited from her lunch date and Yelenkov turned his attention back to Gusev with the words, "So we move from only you to your courier, to your junkie daughter, Iosif. Who else, the Moscow State Circus perhaps?"

Gusev winced at the sarcasm. He had never encountered Vlad in this mood and had difficulty reconciling the lacerating interrogator with his affable old school friend. Yelenkov's voice took on a slightly gentler tone as he said "Look Iosif. If they are the only other people apart from you, then it must have been one or both of them. There is no other explanation. It would not take a genius to figure out that you are likely to possess a safe in your apartment, and that is where you would keep such an item. So, we know who the thieves are but we don't know how the theft was achieved." Mystifyingly he again alluded to the great fictional detective before adding "You say there is only one key and the lock was supplied by our security people here in the embassy?"

"Y-yes, that is correct."

"So the only way they could gain access was through your front door by using the only key in existence."

"B-but that's impossible Vlad. I have the key in my possession at all times."

"So you admit it was you who robbed your own safe do you?"

"N-no, of course not."

"Then unless you were under the influence of hypnotism it is clear that the key is *not* always in your possession. So where does it go when it magically leaves your pocket?"

The ruthless dismantling of his statement and the penetrating glare which was now fixed on him made him shift uneasily as he desperately visualised the key in his mind's eye and the circumstances of its use. Almost absent-mindedly he fished his key ring from his pocket and looked at the apartment key, ground floor key, and car key as they nestled in the palm of his hand. He turned an imploring gaze to the man sitting opposite and as he did so he knew the answer. "The cleaners" he breathed. Yelenkov's bushy eyebrow rose a fraction and Gusev added "One day each week I leave my key with the security guard on reception and he gives it to the cleaners to let themselves into the apartment. They hand it back when they leave and I collect it when I return home in the evening. It never leaves the building."

Vlad Yelenkov slapped his palms down on his knees as he said "Hah, and there we have it Iosif. It could be the security guard of course, but there is no real doubt in my mind that it was the courier and your junkie daughter. She must have somehow got to know the combination of your safe and the rest is easy."

"Easy?" His mind teetered as he grappled with the concept. "The cleaning company. It is vetted by our embassy security."

This drew a further glare from his friend. "Iosif please think clearly. Telephone the company first thing tomorrow and ask them for the names of the cleaners who have visited since you last saw the Egg. Oh, and whilst you are at it, ask them how many cleaners they usually send and what gender. Now, go on, shoo, it is Sunday and my lunchtime is ruined. I fly out tomorrow afternoon so come and see me in the morning as soon as you have spoken to the cleaning company."

Gusev scuttled off and on his return the following morning he found Yelenkov wreathed in cigar smoke and humming softly to himself. An upraised eyebrow told him to speak and he said. "Last week's visit was cancelled. They usually use a team of two - male and female."

"Elementary my dear Iosif," responded his friend and burst out laughing at his own private joke. "Now all you need to do is wait. Then, of course, they need to be persuaded to hand back the Egg. You may need my help with that, but I am returning in a few days' time so let us see how this plays out."

Gusev returned to his desk feeling far less confidant than his friend. When his telephone trilled in mid-morning he snatched it up and was for a moment completely nonplussed as the switchboard announced, 'A Mr Dave Smith for you Sir." Trying to keep the shakiness from his voice he took the call and immediately asked "What is it? Why have you called? Is something wrong?"

"Hey, man. Cool it. Why should anything be wrong? You asked me to check in, remember? I've sent you details of some bids and things seem to be moving ahead. It's all cool man." Dave's irritatingly laid back drawl poured itself into his brain. Of course. He had asked him to call and confirm that everything was going according to plan. "I'll phone again in a couple of days, that's if I get through of course. You wouldn't believe how long it takes - I get the Iron Curtain treatment from that old bat on the switchboard." Iosif thought his head would explode as the younger man's babble swirled relentlessly on.

"Yes, yes, he interrupted. "B-but everything is OK? No problems of any sort?"

"Hey, what did I just say? All fine and exactly as hoped. I'll call again soon. If you need us to meet up just call the usual number. Ciao man." Dave replaced the receiver and smiled. That breezy approach should portray a picture of innocence.

Iosif replaced his receiver and scowled. 'Ciao' indeed! The fucking hippie couldn't even converse properly.

Dave was eagerly anticipating the continuation of the plan that should provide him with a life of luxury. His optimistic frame of mind was tempered by the fact that Tatti had now latched onto the band's lead singer and, although he had at first regarded her wandering as no more than yet another infidelity in the long history of her bed-hopping antics, this infatuation looked a little more serious. The fact that he was spending virtually all of his spare time on visits to his various contacts, and continually going over his plan regarding the Egg, searching for loopholes, had meant he could not keep tabs on what the woman was up to. Not that it would matter in the long run. His feelings had hardened and if that was how she wanted it, once he had the money from the sale of the Egg he was going to disappear over the horizon. The last thing he needed tagging along was a junkie nymphomaniac like Tatti. She was, however, the present custodian of the Egg and he was well aware that it would be unwise for him to irritate the volatile aspect of her personality when the stakes were so high. He certainly did not need her to petulantly throw an almighty spanner into the works when she was blitzed out of her mind. So he said nothing to upset her and pretended he was not bothered by the fact that she and Jase Wooldridge had obviously become a lot closer than just good friends.

In his efforts to keep his own actions as routine as possible his next priority was to meet with the Russian and continue with the charade that the sale arrangements were all proceeding as planned. Two more bids had come in and he was holding one of them back as something that could be used as the excuse for one of their usual meetings at the pub. He had a suspicion, though, that the theft of the Egg had already been discovered. Just a nagging feeling at the back of his mind following the last call he had made to the Russian. It may, of course, have been that he too was nervous and excited, knowing that the project was under way, but the conversation had seemed unnaturally flat and stilted. If the theft was discovered and the finger pointed in his direction, he needed to continue allaying suspicion until he and Tatti were ready to make their move. Even so, what contingency plan would the Russian be likely to follow knowing that he actually had nothing to sell?

Iosif Gusev was also waiting for the return of Vlad although 'eagerly' would not be the appropriate description. In truth he had no idea how he should feel, but if he was to recover the Egg he had no alternative other than to follow instructions. Vlad was in Paris and in the meantime, he had directed him to set up a meeting with his courier. This was in the hope of detecting any inadvertent clues that would confirm he was responsible for the theft, and if so the possible location of the missing Egg. The hippy had pre-empted this with the suggestion that he could have details of yet another bid.

He didn't like the situation. He was merely a Cultural Attaché, not one of Vlad's security men. He had no training in trying to worm information out of a suspect. True, the designation of Junior Cultural Attaché had for many years been used as a flag of convenience to mask some of the more dubious activities carried out under the banner of diplomatic immunity, but in his case, it wasn't a cover. He really was what his occupation was listed as in the embassy staffing register. It ought to be Vlad doing this, he thought. A few minutes of being subjected to that ferocious glare would soon loosen the lad's tongue. He sighed and cursed his luck. Life was never fair to him. First, he had accumulated a nice little retirement fund only to see it drained away by that English bitch. Then by an incredible stroke of good fortune, he was offered full recompense and a lot more besides in the form of the Imperial Egg. Now, just as that was on the way to paying off, if Vlad's reasoning was sound, it was jeopardised by a greedy daughter and her hippy boyfriend and would be diluted by whatever percentage he would now be obliged to offer Vlad for his assistance. Iosif Gusev was under no illusion that however far back in time their friendship stretched, Vlad would expect an appropriate reward for his help. He kicked out in irritation at an empty cigarette packet, sending it skidding across the rain slicked pavement into the gutter. He quickened his pace as for the last few minutes he had developed the uncomfortable feeling that he was being followed.

Chapter 11 - Alan

Sitting in the dining room of their hotel Martin and Anna reflected on the further details that had emerged from their visit to Anne Silverdale's music store. "I wonder if Tatiana Drake still lives in London," mused Martin. "We could always ask Griss if he remembers her address. She might have kept tabs on Jase."

"Didn't someone say that he grew up in an area close to Eastbourne? Why don't we take a look ourselves and see if we can trace where Jase was brought up?" Anna replied. "Just how close do you think 'close to Eastbourne' would be?"

"Good question. We could start with a ten-mile radius and look for current children's homes. At least with Eastbourne being on the coast we only have to look north, west, and east. The trouble is that even if we do find a home there's no guarantee that it was operating as far back as the nineteen-fifties. Anne implied that he grew up there so that's how old it would have to be. I suppose that will help narrow our search."

There were seven children's homes within their designated search area and surprisingly two claimed to have been established in the early nineteen-fifties. The remainder either came into being too late to have accommodated a very young Jason Wooldridge, or there was no clue to their date of inception. "It's quite possible that this entire line of research is a waste of time," said Martin in disgust. "If the home that Jase grew up in closed down we are unlikely to ever be able to trace it, and if we can it will only give us a clue as to the area he may have scuttled back to for refuge. Where do we go from there?"

It was a question left unanswered until the next morning when, following breakfast, they settled themselves in the modern lounge on the ground floor of the hotel and watched the rain steadily falling on the outside world. Anna wriggled into a more comfortable position on the black leather settee that, with several identical companions, helped provide an attractive resting place. Martin was absorbed in checking his emails when his wife broke into his thoughts. "I've been thinking about this Eastbourne idea Martin and think we should try a different approach. Hoping to turn up a children's home that was in existence more than fifty years ago by looking in an area that we have arbitrarily decided upon is too much of a long shot. I vote we capitalise on our new found fame. We can contact the local radio stations and newspapers and offer them a short interview provided they let us ask for information concerning Jase. Then, let's see if anything turns up. We can keep the hunt for the children's home on the back burner as a last desperate measure"

Martin looked at her intently before saying "That is a truly inspired idea Spindles old girl."

"Watch it Price"

"Still a bit touchy about the nickname?"

"No - it's the 'old girl' part I'm not keen on. Before we do anything we had better run it past Nikki. We don't want to find we have somehow upset any of her agreements and negotiations that she is working on regarding Boudica. We have to let her truly run that side of Timewarp if we want her involved on a more substantial basis."

Martin duly made contact and when he finished his exchange said, "All OK from her, but she asked if we could get this job over and done with because there is a pile of stuff she wants to go over with us."

"Huh, that's a good reason to string this out for as long as possible as far as I'm concerned; if only we weren't in dreary London."

Because of the publicity generated by the Boudica discovery following so closely on the Considine affair Anna had very little difficulty in making contact with the South Downs Radio director and it took almost no time at all to arrange a visit. They were invited to make an appearance on the *'Alan Keene's Country'* programme that aired live in an 11.00 a.m. to 1.00 p.m. slot every Thursday and was repeated later that same day at 9.00 p.m. "Couldn't be better" exclaimed Martin "That idea deserves a reward; so why don't we do the trip in style. "We can book a room at The Grand in Eastbourne and if we drive down today, we should be in good shape for our visit to the radio station tomorrow morning. It's all down to CKC don't forget."

"I forgot to ask; did you get an acknowledgement to the update you sent them?"

"Yes, it came back fairly quickly from that Angelina woman who assists Celeste. Dead relaxed, just said to carry on as we think fit. She appreciated being kept in the loop, and good luck. I'll try and remember to send her something each time we get a bit further forward."

A phone call secured a Master Suite at the famous hotel and a guaranteed parking space within the front parking area. Once they had dropped down through The City, across the Thames and then through to Bromley, Martin then avoided the M25. "I know a nicer route," he explained to Anna as the Satnav squawked in protest and insisted that he 'turn around when possible'. "Look, Spitfire" he directed her gaze to the RAF Memorial Chapel and the Spitfire and Hurricane fighters positioned outside as they sped past Biggin Hill airport. Down through Westerham and on through Edenbridge they trundled as what would have been a pleasant drive suffered from the continuing rainfall. Enjoying his role as unofficial tour guide Martin took them slowly through the village of Hartfield and appraised Anna of the connection with Winnie the Pooh before taking a left hand turn up a long hill. He turned right at the top and announced "Ashdown Forest, we come out near a village called Maresfield and that's pretty much where we join up with the A22 Eastbourne Road. It should take about thirty minutes from there."

"How come you know your way so well?" Anna asked.

"Part of my training involved learning how to get around the Southeast either on foot or using less popular drivable routes. It's surprising how much has stuck with me, and I couldn't resist trying to impress you. I hate the M25 so even on a lousy day like this I prefer a more leisurely drive. As we are staying at The Grand I hope that some of your Oxford Street acquisitions are going to come into use. You can't wear any old lingerie in The Grand you know."

"You are a lecherous swine Price. If you are hoping for five-star hanky-panky you had best make sure you treat a girl properly. I'm playing hard to get you know."

"How about a delicious Cream Tea?"

"Oh all right."

The rain had eased by the next day and they were able to arrive at the studios a full hour before the show went live. Alan Keene was a pleasant man in his early forties and spent some time discussing with them the outline of the interview that was to take place. Their own previous experiences with the media in general made this an easy process for all concerned. At 11.00 precisely the programme commenced with a brief preamble by Alan explaining that it specialised in news and topics of interest from around the country before launching into their introduction with the words:

"And now I am delighted to introduce two very welcome guests in the shape of the husband and wife team of Martin and Anna Price. For those of you who have been living on a desert island this past couple of years I will explain that Anna and Martin are archaeologists by profession and, via their own company named Timewarp, have achieved spectacular successes in locating a lost Italian treasure, restoring the Three Sisters diamonds to their owners, exposing the Considine plot and, most recently, discovering the remains of Boudica, Queen of the Iceni. It is this final amazing adventure that they are going to discuss with us this morning. This is Alan Keene's Country and it has been enriched by the discovery of the Warrior Queen herself."

And so it went, with Alan keeping to the general line of questions already discussed as the thirty-minute interview took forty-five minutes to air due to the various advertisements that peppered the slot. With five minutes left he wrapped up by saying:

"Now Anna, I believe you have a request to put before our listeners, in the few minutes left will you please enlighten us?"

She explained that an overseas friend had discovered something belonging to Jase Wooldridge and how they had promised to see if they could locate his whereabouts when they visited the UK but had so far been unsuccessful. She mentioned that he had been brought up in a children's home but they only knew that it was said to have been close to Eastbourne. If anyone had any information on the whereabouts of Jase at any time since he dropped out of sight in 1977 would they please phone? Alan then finished the segment with the words

"Anna and Martin will be back in the studio with me at 12.45 to review and comment on any questions or information phoned in by our listeners."

As they sat in the hospitality suite with an hour to kill Martin said "I quite like Alan Keene. Never listened to him before but I thought he stuck to our prearranged agenda very faithfully. Let's see if we get a result."

They returned to the studio on cue and were duly welcomed back by their host as he announced,

"Here are our special guests Anna and Martin Price to answer the listener's questions that have come in following their exclusive live interview with me here on South Downs Radio. I hope that my guests won't mind me saying, that if I had a choice in the matter I would like Warrior Queen Boudica to look just like Anna Price. Now I will read out the first question.

There were half a dozen questions that they were able to cover in their allotted time, and as the programme drew to a close he announced, *"Although we must say goodbye to our guests, who have brightened a winter's day in Eastbourne, I would like to thank not only them both, for an interesting and charming addition to the show, but also you listeners who took the trouble to pose the questions about the wonderful Boudica discovery. Also, I will say that two callers have responded to the question raised about the long lost rock star Jase Wooldridge and I will pass their information on to Anna and Martin immediately the programme ends. Thank you all again for being part of 'Alan Keene's Country."*

They had to wait a further fifteen minutes before Alan Keene was able to join them and drawing a cup of coffee from the machine he grinned and sat down. "I hope you didn't mind my Boudica comment," he cocked an eyebrow at Anna as he spoke.

"No, it's not the first time that has been said. Us strapping Nordic types have to get used to it," she laughed. "I hope we didn't disappoint your listeners."

"Not in the least. We have a very, um, traditional audience. People in their fifties and a lot of older retired folk. Just the sort who enjoy hearing about your discovery. Also, I do have a couple of messages about your old rock star. I deliberately didn't give them air time because I figured it was more personal than anything, but if you would care to let me know at some point whether the information has helped, then I can mention it on air. It all helps to keep listeners interested." He handed over some sheets of paper together with a small cardboard envelope and then added. "Let me know if I can be of further help. We are only a small station so getting you two was a bit of a coup for us. Something of ongoing interest will only be good for our ratings."

They shook hands and Martin slipped the paper sheets into his pocket saying, "Come on Mrs Price, let's get back to the hotel and see what we have got."

They sat in the public lounge on the ground floor amidst the old style paintings and genteel atmosphere that The Grand had successfully nurtured into the modern day. The cardboard envelope contained a CD of the entire show, but with the advertising breaks excluded. Martin handed one of the sheets to his wife and as they read, he realised that they were holding verbatim transcripts of the calls concerning Jase Wooldridge. He became immediately absorbed by the words before him.

"My name's Mark and I shared a flat with Jase Wooldridge back in the seventies before he was part of 'Wheelspin'. He'd been brought up in a children's home over at Normans Bay. We met when I was working on the bar at the old 'Meads Country Club' and he was doing some garden maintenance. We were earning enough to rent a tiny flat between us and for a few months had some good times, the way young lads do. Jase was always keen on his music and used to play as a solo singer-guitarist at some of the local pubs. Then he saw this advert in one of the music papers and went up to London for an audition. He was gone for a few days and when he came back he announced he was joining up with some blokes he'd met and forming a band called 'Wheelspin'. He moved out soon afterwards and I never heard from him again. I moved up to Sheffield later that same year. That's where I still live and I only caught your programme by chance while visiting my Mum."

"This chap thinks Jase grew up in Norman's Bay," he announced to Anna who flapped a hand at him as she carried on reading. When she looked up she said "This person is named Rick and he says he saw Jase Wooldridge in the nineteen eighties. That's well after he disappeared from general view. Listen to this:

"I was a fan of 'Wheelspin' back in the seventies when they were beginning to become well known. I remembered Jase Wooldridge playing as a solo artist at my local pub, 'The Yew Tree' on Alderson Road. I picked up on his name again when 'Wheelspin' played down here in Eastbourne after their first album 'Burnin' Rubber' and got Jase to sign the sleeve of my copy. Then, about 1989 time, well after 'Wheelspin' had broken up and were all but forgotten I saw Jase. I swear it was him. He was sitting in a car at some traffic lights here in Eastbourne. I was in my car and had just turned left but the car ahead stopped because a delivery truck was obstructing our lane. I stopped next to the car waiting to turn right into the road I'd come out of so there was only about a foot between us. I looked at the

other driver and he looked at me. It was Jase Wooldridge, I recognised him! I even told the missus when I got home because we had both been 'Wheelspin' fans."

She looked up and said "If he's right that puts our man in this area twelve years after he was last heard of. Combine that with the comment about Normans Bay and we are a lot further forward than yesterday."

"True, but that sighting was still twenty-six years ago. It looks as if we spend another night here while we check out Normans Bay. I suppose it would also be sensible to take a look at the Electoral Roll for Jason Wooldridge, wouldn't it? We will look pretty silly if it turns out that he is living round the corner in Eastbourne in complete normality, running a music shop like Anne Silverdale for instance."

Not only were they unable to identify a Jason Wooldridge living in Eastbourne but nobody of that surname was listed in East Sussex. "So much for what was a reasonable line of enquiry." Martin reflected. "Were any of those children's homes we turned up anywhere near Normans Bay?"

She flicked her finger across the tablet screen, looked up at him then looked back at the screen before saying "Bingo! Unbelievable! Trafalgar Court Children's Home is situated at Normans Bay. We may have actually found something concrete."

"Definitely another night at The Grand then," answered Martin. "Normans Bay lays east, between Eastbourne and Bexhill. It's a bit late to go haring off there now, and it would be as well to call ahead. I'll do that now."

"What shall we do after that? It's only mid-afternoon."

"I thought we could have another of their cream teas", he replied with a grin.

"And to avoid putting on weight I suppose we then indulge in some vigorous exercise before dinner?"

"Good idea Anna" he replied innocently.

William Goodall was a Chartered Accountant. He was also the chair of the Trafalgar Court Trustees and drew a nominal fee of only £200 for each day he sacrificed from his retirement to manage the affairs of the Charity which owned the Trafalgar Court Children's Home. Under his stewardship, the affairs of the charity had been competently managed for many years. The other four trustees had been carefully chosen and the establishment now stood as a shining example of how a carefully managed home could provide a pleasant substitute for the family upbringing not available to its young inhabitants. There were forty-five boys aged from five to eighteen who enjoyed life in the extended Victorian building that had been kept fully modernised and was set amidst a two-acre landscape of beautifully maintained grounds. The boys who left this environment at the age of eighteen went straight to university. There were no exceptions and being known as a 'Trafalgar Court Boy' was regarded with pride by the bearer and a recommendation to any prospective employer. In its own unique way, it was the equal of many of the well regarded private schools whose names were immediately and favourably recognised when a young man's CV was being scrutinised.

Having taken the trouble to telephone, Martin was put through to the Senior House Parent who in turn confirmed that the Chair of the Trustees would be able to meet with them the following day. At the appropriate time, they halted before the two wrought iron gates that were each surmounted by the representation of a Nelson-era warship.

A small porter's lodge set just inside and to the right of the gates, disgorged a man in overalls who asked for ID and nodded when Martin produced his driving licence. "Won't keep you a moment Mr Price?" he said as he bustled back into his lodge and activated the gate controls. As they edged forward he reappeared and said "Mr Goodall said to expect you. Go straight on up and follow the right-hand curve. That will take you to the main visitors' car park and you'll see the main entrance is only a minute's walk away." They followed his instructions and made their way to a small reception desk in a wood panelled hallway where they waited as the receptionist handed a maroon sweater to an anxious looking fair-haired boy with the words "That's the third time this week James. Having a cold shouldn't affect your memory. I'm going to charge you a finder's fee if it happens again. Now buzz off and do your revision." She chuckled to herself as she turned to her visitors and stood up saying "Mr and Mrs Price? Mr Goodall is expecting you if you would care to follow me please."

"Thank you for sparing the time to see us, Mr Goodall," opened Martin as they shook hands.

"A pleasure to welcome such famous guests Mr Price although I am at a loss as to how I can help you."

Martin explained very briefly the reasons for their interest in Jason Wooldridge and how the radio appeal had led them to hope that Trafalgar Court was the home in which Jase had grown up during the nineteen-fifties and sixties.

"I would like to help Mr Price, but I can state categorically that Jason Wooldridge was never a Trafalgar Court boy."

"But surely no other children's home was sited in such a small area as Normans Bay," observed Anna.

"You are quite correct in that assertion, Mrs Price, but Trafalgar Court only came into existence in 1979. He may well have been in the care of The Bayside Orphanage, though. That establishment occupied this premises until its owners sold up and Trafalgar Court purchased the original Victorian House and grounds. All occupancy was suspended for a time whilst the building was completely renovated and the original small extension added. Youngsters were taken in again later that year."

"So are there no records dating back before 1979?" Anna asked.

"I'm afraid not. The Bayside Orphanage was perfectly adequate when it came into existence during the nineteen-twenties and it provided a very good home for its children in accordance with the expectations of those times. By the nineteen-seventies, however, it was rather outdated and teetering on the brink of insolvency with extensive and expensive renovation costs required. Trafalgar Court was able to acquire the entire business and the property for quite a modest sum and then as I have said, finance the modernisation that was desperately needed."

"What happened to the staff and children?"

"Those staff who fitted into the future plans for the home were given a paid holiday until the work was completed, and the children were temporarily placed with other homes in Sussex until they could be welcomed back. Most of those original staff, and of course all of the children have by now either retired or moved on, only two of our educational staff, and our groundsman-gatekeeper can trace their tenure back to those first days."

"Judging by what we have seen of the grounds and the buildings, Trafalgar Court has turned the enterprise into a profitable concern.

Its owners must be pleased with their investment," commented Martin with a hint of an edge to his voice that drew a sharp glance from Anna.

William Goodall either didn't notice or chose not to comment but instead smiled and sat back in his chair before saying. "It's true that Trafalgar Court as an environment for the children is probably second to none among children's homes in Britain. We educate the children to a public school standard and they also live in good modern accommodation in our houses in the grounds. We are extremely proud of the standards we achieve and the fact that children have here a true home. On leaving they are more than ably equipped to tackle life in the outside world. But Trafalgar Court is not a profit-making enterprise in the accepted sense of the word. It is a registered charity, and although nowadays a great deal of its income arises from donations by former residents, wealthy individuals, and of course its own investments, a substantial amount still comes from the overseas source that originally set up the charity and financed the acquisition of the old Bayside property."

"What is the overseas source, Mr Goodall?"

"I am sorry Mrs Price, but that information has never been made available to me. The apparent settlor is a foreign corporation registered in the British Virgin Islands. Being a notable tax haven there is no way of obtaining deeper information. What I don't understand, though, is how tracing the home in which your Mr Wooldridge was brought up would help you to trace him all these years later?"

"Clutching at straws really," answered Martin "We were hoping that identifying the home would somehow enable us to locate him if he was living locally. It now seems almost certain that he was a Bayside lad but the absence of any records brings us to another dead end."

"It looks as if it's back to Tatiana Drake" murmured Martin as they drove out through the Trafalgar Court gates.

"Oh no! Not bloody London again!" The disgruntled response was accompanied by a heartfelt sigh as his wife slumped sullenly in her seat.

Chapter 12 - Vladimir

Anna not only bitterly resented leaving the Grand, but also taking on the entire assignment. Once again she was stuck back in Britain away from the home she adored, and also now bored by what had all the appearances of a doomed investigation that wasn't even a truly historical project. They were, of course, welcomed back by the Highbury Skyline as it did seem probable that north London would be where they were most likely to pick up the trail of Tatiana Drake. She sat staring morosely out of the window of their suite towards the fine Arsenal football stadium and having spent the trip up from Eastbourne in sullen silence suddenly said, "Martin. If you want to go and watch your favourite football team tomorrow, why don't you give the French chap who manages them a call? You said you met him socially some years ago and you may as well get some fun out of this rotten trip. Sort of payback for being so restrained with the Mad Axeman."

"What about you, shall I see if I can get two tickets?"

"Oh God no. I've been off football ever since you had the run in with that bunch of idiots when we first met. Buzz off and do some man stuff and I will languish here forlorn and forgotten and do a bit of digging via the internet. I want to see if I can find out anything more regarding Tatiana Drake."

Of course, the words came a lot easier than the actions and she soon found out that a super-hot bath followed by some smoked salmon and a small quantity of champagne revived her mood but did nothing for her productivity. Martin had departed at 1.00 pm and the match apparently started at 3.00 so heaven only knew what he would be doing in the meantime. Standing in the cold wind wearing a funny hat and shouting incomprehensible abuse at the opposing supporters, she imagined. She giggled at the mental picture as she sprawled on the settee, stretching out a long leg as she carefully ferried some salmon and bread into her mouth. An occasional muffled roar drifted through the double glazing and she thought of Martin jumping up and down if his team had scored. None of which was any help regarding the elusive Tatiana Drake.

She afterwards convinced herself that the second glass of champagne was what had stimulated her imagination. Well, why not? The Beatles had taken LSD as a mind expanding agent so why shouldn't champagne work for Spindles Price? Why not see if the Russian father was worth looking at? OK, he hadn't risen so far up the Communist Party hierarchy that he had ended up on the podium at the famous May Day extravaganzas in Red Square, but he could have left some sort of trail. She trawled back through the old copies of the Daily Mail, and sure enough, in an edition dated in April 1977 came across a report headlined *Red Diplomat in Domestic Street Bust-up* and there was his name -Iosif Gusev, Junior Cultural Attaché. It was now almost forty years ago which meant that if he was still alive he was probably in his eighties. Then, of course, there were the tumultuous events leading to the end of Communist Party dominance so maybe it was wise to start looking in 1990 and work back to 1977.

The research was not what could be called stimulating but through sheer doggedness fortified by more smoked salmon, she stumbled across a Russian information site purporting to list the diplomatic personnel seconded to London since 1945. Quite why this information was thought to be of interest was beyond her but when she looked at the year 1977 she found I. Gusev amongst the names. From the little they had been told about Tatiana she may have been born sometime close to the mid-fifties – 1957 seemed a good bet - but side-slipping into the Ancestry site revealed no such birth between the dates of 1952 and 1962. She pondered on this mystery before looking into the marriage section and again drew a blank.

Exasperated, she returned to the diplomatic list and followed the name Gusev back until 1958 when he unaccountably disappeared. Undaunted, she ploughed backwards until in 1954 there he was again and for several years before; a picture began to form in her head. Gusev had met his future wife on his first assignment to the UK and they had married in Russia or wherever he was based. Tatiana had resulted before he was posted back to London.

Thinking back to their earlier conversations with the former band members and Anne Silverdale she recalled comments made about a divorce and Tatiana going to school in the UK and living with her mother. This was incredibly frustrating as there seemed no easy way to track her movements other than the sketchy details already known. She rechecked the data and was about to give it up as a false trail when she caught sight of the diplomatic list for 1978 and realised there was no entry for Gusev. Very strange, she thought, and saw that the heading of the final 1977 page stated, 'Staff Retained for Forthcoming Year', so Gusev wasn't expected to be on the strength. In which case, he must have been reassigned before the end of 1977. That was certainly proving to be a busy year, she thought and wondered if there was perhaps another domestic incident that had caused the Soviets embarrassment and resulted in him being transferred. From what she had read they did not have a particularly forgiving view of their citizens being featured in awkward circumstances in the western press.

Returning to the newspaper files she started from the reported row with Tatiana and flicked on through the subsequent editions until in the 7th September edition a report caught her eye that she instinctively knew was about her man. *Soviet Diplomat Killed in Hit and Run*. Her stomach turned over as she read that the body of Iosif Gusev had been found in the gutter on Satchell Street in Kensington having apparently been hit by a vehicle as he attempted to cross the road. There were no witnesses to the incident and the Soviet embassy had asked for his body to be passed to them when all necessary formalities and enquiries had been completed. She worked her way through later editions and found a report dated three weeks later saying that his body had been handed over to the Soviets and would be transported back to his homeland. Some additional information was also added to the effect that the landlord of a pub in Satchell Street had said that it was only when he saw a photograph of the man in the Daily Express that he recognised him as an occasional visitor who would have a couple of quiet drinks with a friend, a younger man if he remembered correctly, and usually, after no more than an hour would leave. He particularly recalled that the young chap sometimes stayed on and was occasionally joined by an extremely good looking young woman who appeared to be his girlfriend. Tatiana for sure, thought Anna, and maybe the young man was Jase? But it was the final couple of lines in the report that made her gasp and nearly spill her drink. *'In a bizarre coincidence, the security guard at Holland Court, the private apartments where the late Mr Gusev had lived was found dead at his reception desk two days earlier. A heart attack was stated as the likely cause.'*

She was about to help herself to another drink when she heard the door open and Martin's voice say, "Is the champagne out to celebrate a famous win for The Gunners?"

"No, it's a football widow's comfort. You don't look particularly damp or windswept, although the little red and white woolly hat is very fetching."

Her husband grinned and whipped the offending article off his head, saying "It doesn't rain in a hospitality box and the food is five star. You're not the only one who has been swigging champagne, although I've been in the company of about sixty-thousand others, not drinking alone like you, you old lush. Mind you, I've noticed before that champagne does wonders for your ability to wear a dressing gown."

"What? Stop leering you dirty devil or I won't tell you what one of us has discovered while the other one has been singing unrepeatable songs with a bunch of strangers. There's a spare glass over there by the way."

He sat in the space at the end of the settee as she drew up her legs and wrapped the dressing gown more modestly around herself with a smirk of triumph at his grimace of disappointment. For the next half hour, she went over with him what she had gleaned from her research until he finally said: "So you believe that Gusev was *deliberately* killed because of the fact that the security guard at his apartment block also died not so long after?"

She pulled a face "When you put it like that, it does sound a bit far-fetched I suppose, but this was the nineteen-seventies and didn't the Soviets kill someone in London with a poisoned umbrella?"

"Giorgi Markov was a Bulgarian dissident. It was a political assassination."

"Alright clever-clogs, but the two incidents I've discovered occurred in September 1977 just around the time *'Wheelspin'* returned from Europe and then imploded at Heathrow. And what about the publican's comment about the young man Gusev used to meet occasionally and the attractive girl?"

"So we have Gusev, Jase, and Tatiana all hanging around a pub only half a mile from Gusev's apartment. I think we can take it that Jase and Tatiana, um, no, wait, it can't be Jase."

"Why not?"

"Because those comments refer to a period leading up to Gusev being killed. Jase had only just got back from Europe and prior to that Anne Silverdale was not only bonking him but said it was only on the tour that Tatti really homed in on Jase. This other bloke must be someone else entirely. More to the point, it looks as if Gusev was only meeting the man, and so Tatti pitching up afterwards would fit in with the fact that she did not get on with her old man and may have been deliberately avoiding him."

"OK. Then why would Gusev be meeting this other chap?"

"Well if it wasn't purely social then I can think of two reasons, neither of which I have the slightest evidence to support. First, there is the cause of us spending this time back in the UK, namely the Egg. Secondly, a slightly more probable reason could be drugs."

"Drugs?"

"Why not? They have been mentioned often enough, and Tatti was a heavy user according to Griss. Also, someone said they thought it was this roadie who turned up around the same time as Tatti who was the dealer. Supposing it was the roadie Gusev was meeting, and Gusev was supplying the drugs?"

"Yes, that makes sense, but I recall you once saying to me that coincidences made you uneasy. We have a whole bunch of them here don't we? Rock-star opens Swiss account and has knowledge of a valuable Russian artefact. Rock-star sleeps with a girl who is half Russian. Her Russian father is meeting someone, a roadie perhaps, who is also sleeping with Tatti and there is a hypothetical drug connection. Father gets killed by a hit-and-run in the centre of London when he is possibly on his way to meet the roadie. A security guard at the Russian's apartment block dies within days from a possible heart attack. Rock-star chucks up his career and drops almost completely out of sight."

"Sounds very melodramatic when put like that, but Jase *must* have come across the present from the Imperial Egg through his association with Tatti. We do know that she didn't get on with her father and he seems the most likely source by which the Egg surfaced after an absence of sixty years. But I don't see Gusev entrusting a druggy daughter, with whom he's had a public row, with anything so valuable."

She thought over what he had said and answered "What about the roadie? If he trusted him to sell drugs would he have also given him the Egg to safeguard?"

"I don't see it. Leaving aside just how Gusev may have got his hands on such an extraordinarily rare and valuable item in the first place, if he did possess it I would have thought it would be the last thing he would let out of his sight. It would have been worth far more than any drugs being peddled at the time."

"But the fact that his body was found on Satchell Street late in the evening does make it probable that he was on his way to meet his usual contact. Could he have been intercepted and had the Egg taken off him, then been bumped off?"

Martin frowned "It's possible, but not very likely. The news report gives the impression that all parties thought it was simply a hit-and-run. No big fuss from the Soviets, they were happy to wait for our police to do their job. They, in turn, don't seem to have found anything suspicious. If we stick with your theory that he was deliberately killed, then I think we have to introduce yet another player into the drama. For the life of me, I can't suggest who!"

"Well going off to watch football hasn't stimulated your thought process very much Mr Price." She retorted. "I do all the hard work and you just pitch up and make it all even more complicated."

"I can tell you what has stimulated my thought process," he replied as he edged closer to her."

"Oh no you don't buster. I've seen that look before, and this half of the Timewarp operation isn't going to come across, what a charming phrase, without some positive contribution. And I bet I can hold out longer than you."

He looked at her grinning face and wondered how on earth he had managed to get through more than thirty years without being in her company. He must have been staring at her for longer than he realised because she suddenly said "Well? Do I get dressed or what?"

"Ah, sorry. Drifted off for a moment. OK, I accept that you have done some sterling work on the Gusev front, but when you were updating me just now you commented that the period of August and September 1977 was a very busy time. Lots happening, at least so far as our little mystery was concerned. So why don't we look through the archives some more and see if anything else was going on that could have a bearing on our thoughts?"

Her eyes narrowed as she said, "Alright then, but I hope this isn't just a cynical ploy to get into my knickers."

"You're not wearing any," he countered with a smile. "Come on Warrior Queen and star of South Downs Radio. Let's see what the papers tell us about that time back in 1977."

Mollified, she joined him and they hunched over their tablets. "Actually, those two months weren't hugely exciting after all, despite it being Silver Jubilee Year," she finally groaned. I see that poor old Marc Bolan was killed in mid-September, but apart from the pop music connection, I don't think that is of any use. Oh, and not long before Gusev was killed the Soviets laid on a bash at their embassy for a chap named Yelenkov."

There followed a perceptible pause before Martin looked up and said "Yelenkov? Does it give the first name?"

"Um let's see. Yes, here we are. Vladimir Yelenkov. Does that ring a bell then?"

"Quite a number, if it's the Vladimir Yelenkov I'm thinking of."

"I'm intrigued, and I presume this comes out of your membership of the Boy Scouts" - she never could resist a jibe at his army days.

"Indirectly, yes. It was before my time of course, but we had all sorts of studies and background gen thrown at us. It is a broad brush approach designed to give everyone a basic veneer of information which they can then build on when they decide which area of the service they want to aim for. This was part of a study pack concerning Intel and so far as I was concerned was never going to be of great interest to me."

She interrupted with "Let me guess. Rather than sit in a nice comfy office, you opted for the line of work that gets people killed?"

"Not quite - Intel can be very dangerous at times. But you did ask and, some years after the period we are concerned with, Yelenkov became fairly well known. You said they laid on a big bash and that indicates he had quite a high status. He was at that time what may be termed 'a rising star' and he continued his upward trajectory. Most of this wasn't widely known at the time of course, and it was only when he kept popping up around Europe that British Intelligence realised he was one of their top firefighters."

"One of their what? I know you can't mean what I would normally infer from that term, so be a good chap, and translate from your handy lexicon of Boys Brigade phrases."

"Wherever the Soviets suspected there could be a security weakness they used someone like Yelenkov to sniff it out and deal with it."

"I might have guessed. You mean he was a killer don't you."

"Well not necessarily directly, although heaven knows what he got up to in his younger days. By the late seventies, he had proved his worth and was moving up the Party ladder. By all accounts, he was an exceptionally clever fellow and it looked as if he was destined for far greater things. However, the nineteen-seventies was a busy decade in more ways than one and in 1979 the Soviets invaded Afghanistan. In 1981 Yelenkov was sent to Kabul to report on security matters. His report commented that the whole thing would turn out to be a total disaster dwarfing even the US experience in Vietnam."

"Wow, I bet that went down well."

"Like a lead balloon. Comrade Yelenkov's star stopped rising and he found himself becalmed. Even worse, his report was leaked to the CIA and then to most of the NATO security services. By the time I first knew of it, it was of course no longer hypersensitive but was considered to be a masterpiece of objective analysis. That's why it was included in our study packs."

"Are you actually saying that this Yelenkov character could somehow be involved with our Gusev?"

"Well, people did have a habit of dying when Yelenkov was around."

"OK. What happened to him?"

Martin laughed and said "That's one of the best bits. It seems that he was less than impressed by the reaction to his Afghanistan Report and so one morning he turned up on the doorstep of the British embassy, in Belgium of all places, and requested asylum. That was around 1983. Since then I believe he has become a British citizen and lives here in the UK, if he is still alive that is. Now are you going to give in gracefully or do I have to shoot you now I've made you privy to stuff that I suspect is still officially on the Secrets List?"

Chapter 13 - Joyce

"I've just thought of something" announced Anna the following morning before swiftly adding "but not that, you perverted individual. Gerroff and pour out the coffee. Hands like a bloody octopus!"

He reluctantly exited the huge double bed with which the Highbury Skyline equipped its suites and attended to the breakfast that had been brought up a few minutes earlier. He grinned and as he turned to her she said, "And any feeble jokes about room-service and you will be wearing that coffee."

Thus admonished he sighed and admitted to himself that the morning was now going to proceed on a more mundane level. "OK Mrs P, I guess this is going to refer to our conversations yesterday about dead Russians."

"Yes, it's this chap Yelenkov. That report about the party they threw for him, it said he was visiting the UK for three days before moving on to their embassy in Paris. That means he will have left London before Gusev's body was found in Satchell Street."

"Did that report say what his function was?"

"My tablet's charging in the living room. Buzz off and get it for me slave, and I'll take a look while you dish out breakfast."

When Martin had done her bidding she again read through the news reports as he filled a plate with scrambled egg, mushrooms, and toast. "Ah, he's referred to as 'a high ranking diplomatic security expert'. Does that help?"

"Not really. I was hoping it might quote a rank, but he was likely to have been ex-GRU or Spetsnaz as they now tend to call themselves."

She glared at him and said "I see we are back to talking fucking Klingon again. Any chance of a translation?"

"Soviet Special Forces, but just from that rather vague job description, I guess he was a formidable operator. Thanks to you, all of my male testosterone has now been channelled into my imagination. Sort of shift from procreative to just creative. So whilst you are shovelling truckloads of mushrooms into your face why not have a look and see if you can find a mention of poor old Gusev's funeral. It might have rated a mention because of where he died."

She tapped away using the obvious keywords and as he carried his own breakfast back to bed exclaimed "Blow me. How did you work that out?"

"Mmm, what?" The toast muffled voice responded.

"Listen. *'Associated Press report that in a small village a few kilometres from Moscow the funeral took place today of Iosif Gusev the Soviet diplomat recently killed in London by a hit and run driver. Neither Mr Gusev's English former wife nor his daughter attended and the nearest family members were understood to be remote cousins. The Communist Party and Soviet diplomatic service were represented by his childhood friend Vladimir Yelenkov'.* You are a jammy bugger; just how did you know?"

He laughed "I didn't. I was hoping we might have got a line on his ex-wife or daughter. Interesting, though. So a few weeks earlier when Yelenkov visited their London embassy he presumably spent some time with his old friend. He then carries on doing whatever his duties required, and then we next find him attending his poor deceased friend's funeral not long afterwards."

"But does it mean anything?"

"I think it probably does. Even if we view Gusev's death as an accident there is a suspicious lack of fuss from the Soviet side, but if we take your view that it was nothing less than a hit then we can really create a perspective. For instance, in normal circumstances, the Soviets would never have passed up an opportunity to create a bit of a scene, but here they are, appearing to happily step back and let our police carry out normal procedures."

"I'm not too certain how that makes their reactions suspicious Martin."

"Well if we take a very uncharitable view we could infer from it that they were unconcerned about the incident and any possible aftermath because they already knew there was nothing to be found. 'One of our diplomats knocked down and killed? Oh well, never mind, these things happen. He was probably just nipping out for a pint with one of his mates.' That doesn't sound like Cold War Soviet attitude. If they didn't have a clue what he was doing or what he may have had on his person why be so relaxed?"

She frowned and said "Yes of course. They would only be that laid back if they actually did know that he had nothing sensitive on him and, in all probability, the circumstances of his death."

"And if that was the case?"

"They must have seen it happen but more likely they instigated it themselves. Hah, so my theory of skulduggery isn't quite so far-fetched. Thank you Mr P. You do have your uses occasionally."

"It only helps us to a small degree though because we have no idea why the Soviets would suddenly decide to bump off one of their own diplomatic staff and attract unnecessary attention. They could have simply recalled him and packed him off to Siberia or whatever they used to do in the seventies. It doesn't feel right Anna; I think this smells more of a private enterprise than anything official. My money's on Yelenkov having a hand in this. He will have been able to organise something with his security pals based in the embassy and made sure Gusev was knocked off when he had left for Paris which would put him in the clear. By the same token it would be the embassy security people who would have taken charge of the incident and adopted a nice friendly attitude to make sure the fuss and bother was kept to a minimum."

"What would the reason be Martin? Could it be something to do with this wretched Egg?"

"I think it's a strong possibility. Supposing when they met up Gusev told Yelenkov about the Egg who then decided that friend or not, Gusev had to be silenced so that he, Yelenkov, could take over."

"This is all guesswork as usual, but why would Gusev have let even an old school friend such as Yelenkov in on the fact that he had the Egg? Gusev was the one on the ground so to speak. Yelenkov was only passing through so how would he have been able to help Gusev out? Even if there was some sort of drugs connection between them, it was Gusev who was organising the distribution. Yelenkov was spending most of his time either in Moscow or being sent off on specific missions to trouble spots wasn't he? Surely Gusev didn't need Yelenkov to help him sell the Egg?"

"But Yelenkov was also a fairly senior security man. Is it possible that Gusev asked him for help in recovering the Egg?"

"We have assumed that Jase got hold of it via Tatiana, and we know that she didn't get on with her father. In fact, she didn't even go to his funeral! Although it happened back in the Cold War days I'm sure that would have been possible given the circumstances. What if Tatiana pinched the Egg and Gusev went to his old friend Yelenkov for help in getting it back? We've got to assume that the entire project falls under the heading of 'personal and private' haven't we. Gusev can't have been acting in an official capacity so far as the Egg is concerned, so he was unlikely to approach anyone on the embassy staff."

"Yes, exactly, and Yelenkov decides to go for the big money himself and arranges for Gusev to be knocked off."

"It works in theory Mr Price."

Her husband sat back and pursed his lips before saying "So are we saying that the death of the security guard at the apartment was coincidental?"

She shrugged "If he was somehow involved then perhaps Yelenkov decided to tidy up and the security guard was a loose end. It will make sense if we imagine that Gusev kept the Egg in his apartment and Tatiana with the connivance of the security guard somehow managed to steal the Egg."

He nodded and said "So she then passes the Egg to Jase who then deposits the present in a Swiss security box whilst on the European Tour. So why do that and at the same time include those photographs, and what on Earth did he do with the Egg itself?"

His wife eased herself from the bed, much to Martin's chagrin and paced slowly across the room and back before saying "Maybe that's the real reason Jase dropped out of sight. Perhaps he flogged the Egg and is living abroad in the lap of luxury. Don't forget, he will have been getting music royalties from the old *'Wheelspin'* recordings at that time. He probably had enough money to set himself up quite comfortably, especially if he sold the Egg." She looked at the frown on her husband's face and asked, "You don't think so?"

"Well it's all possible, I grant you, but there are a few untidy loose ends to all of this. First of all, why leave the present in the bank account? Second, it's all very good saying he had his music royalties, but Anne was adamant that he had no more money to spend than the other band members, even though he had apparently managed to tie it all up beyond the reach of the bankruptcy claimants. Then, what happened to Tatiana who seems to have disappeared just as comprehensively as Jase? Last of all if you are right about Yelenkov, what did he do having bumped off Gusev, and possibly the security man? It doesn't look as if he got his hands on the Egg because he defected to The West a few years later and blew the whistle on a lot of Soviet secrets in exchange for asylum. If he'd made a fortune from selling the Egg then, given his contacts, he would have been able disappear, assume a false identity, and live quietly somewhere without making himself a target for assassination by the KGB."

"Following your reasoning Martin, neither Jase nor Yelenkov ended up with the Egg. That only leaves Tatiana and her drug pushing boyfriend. So where do we go from there?"

"There is only one way my love. Let's see what we can find out about those two. I think it was Griss who went to the party at Tatiana's flat in north London so perhaps he will recall the address."

"What if he does? She's hardly likely to still be there almost forty years later is she? "

He shrugged, "Stranger things have happened, but I agree it's pretty unlikely. We've got to start somewhere though, so what have we got to lose? I'll give Griss a call and see how good his memory is."

He was fortunately able to make contact with the former bass player right away who spent several minutes of fruitless thinking aloud before making the throw away comment "Oh bugger. It was only a stone's throw from that bloody bridge."

"What bridge?"

"The one that crosses the road up near Highgate."

"Hold on Griss. Anna, pull up a map of the Highgate area on your tablet and look for a bridge."

She quickly followed his request and almost immediately announced "Hornsey Lane appears to cross over Archway Road and ends up near Waterlow Park at the top of Highgate Hill," and held the tablet so that Martin could read the names of the surrounding roads. It was when he came to Whitehall Park that Griss said "Hang on, I think that's it. Whitehall Park you say? yes I'm sure that's it. Large Victorian or Edwardian houses, she lived in one that had been converted into flats."

"It's too much to hope that you remember the number I suppose?" Martin asked.

"Actually I do. Dead easy," replied Griss. It was number ninety-nine, the upper flat. She had the top two floors as I recall. God only knows what the people on the ground floor used to think, having a nutcase like her living above them and throwing parties on a regular basis. Can't help you much more I'm afraid because, as I mentioned when we met, I only visited on two occasions and the second time it was dark and I stayed for no more than half an hour."

Martin thanked him and turned to his wife. "Well, there's our starting point, number ninety-nine, Whitehall Park. It's not too far from here and only just up the road from Anne's music shop in Junction Road."

"I feel really stupid, and we haven't even got there yet," muttered Anna as they walked up the front pathway of ninety-nine Whitehall Park. "You can do the talking as I was the one who did the dirty work in Dorking."

The house in question was a large semi-detached which from its style looked to have been built in the early twentieth century. He pressed the bell push labelled 'Flat 2' and after a short wait they were rewarded with the door being opened by a dark haired man in his late twenties. Martin smilingly explained that he was the son of Mr & Mrs Price who had once been great friends with a Mrs Drake who they believed had once lived in Flat 2 back in the nineteen seventies with her daughter Tatiana and finding himself in the area had stopped on the off chance that they may still be in residence. The young man shook his head and said he had only lived there for three years himself and, what with driving out to work in Hemel Hempstead each day, had not really got to talk that much with his neighbours. They were in the process of turning away as he closed the door when he stopped and called, "I've just thought. Old Joyce Enright at number 104 a short way along on the other side may be able to help. She's a helpful old soul, a bit fierce, but friendly enough. I believe she has lived in her house for ages, good luck."

Number 104 did not appear to have been converted and its black front door sported a large old fashioned lion's head door knocker. They waited as the echoes died away and Martin was on the point of repeating his summons when the door opened and a thin, elderly woman with a walking stick stood squarely before them with the black and white tiled floor of the hallway visible behind. "Can I help you?" The question was delivered in a clear authoritative voice. Martin explained that the occupier of the upper flat at number ninety-nine had suggested they should call on her and explained the reason for their visit. She frowned thoughtfully and then abruptly turned to one side and motioned them to come in with a flick of her walking stick and the words "Come on through and I'll try to help."

She closed the front door and, turning to her right, led the way into a bay windowed front reception room. The walking stick was again waved to indicate they should seat themselves on an old style settee. "You are asking about a family by the name of Drake. I can tell you now that no such family ever lived in that house, but a girl named Tatiana Drake lived there for a time during the nineteen-seventies. I can tell you quite a lot about Tatiana. I've lived here since 1967 and seen quite a lot of changes as you can imagine - but let me think for a moment and get everything in order."

Martin and Anna exchanged looks as the old lady leaned back in her chair and closed her eyes. For a moment Anna felt like laughing aloud at the thought that they may have been sitting there watching a complete stranger take an afternoon nap. The eyes suddenly flicked open and Joyce Enright announced.

"Of course, how could I forget? Now what did she call herself? Ah yes, Tatti. My goodness, I haven't thought about her for years. It's not a happy story but, if you are interested, I will tell you what I know."

"Anything may be of help" answered Anna.

"Very well. Now, she made herself quite unpopular with lots of noisy parties and late night comings and goings. There was also talk of drugs, but that is hardly surprising given the people she mixed with. She was very attractive and although I wasn't bad looking myself in those days I would never have got a second look next to her. My husband, bless him, always said that she would come to a sticky end if she didn't sort out her lifestyle. She didn't have much effect on us being on the opposite side of the road, and with our bedroom at the back, but quite a few of the neighbours complained about late night noise."

They had sat quietly listening to the account and although it added a little colour to Tatiana's life in Whitehall Park it took them no further forwards. As Mrs Enright paused in her narrative Martin quickly posed a question. "I don't suppose you know where she moved on to when she left number ninety-nine?"

The old lady gazed at him for several seconds and then her words took him by surprise. "It's funny, but as I said a few minutes ago, I haven't thought about Tatti for a great many years and yet now I've begun it's as if a cupboard door has been opened and everything inside is tumbling out. For a very short time Tatti and I struck up a loose sort of friendship. We used to occasionally get the same bus up from Holloway because we both enjoyed shopping at the big Jones Brothers store. For a while it became a bit of a Saturday afternoon ritual and we used to chat as we enjoyed our cigarettes on the upper deck of a number 4A bus. There was of course a bit of an age gap because even then I was in my forties and happily married, while she was still very much a party girl who never took anything very seriously. Until her last few weeks that is, when her mood underwent a change and she developed what I would now describe as traces of paranoia."

"Paranoia?" It was Anna who interrupted and was rewarded with a steely glare from Mrs Enright who continued her story as if nothing had been said.

"For a while she had become attached to a new boyfriend. She seemed thrilled by the fact that he was a member of an up and coming pop group and was convinced they would become bigger than The Beatles. She actually went off on tour with them, to the Continent I believe, and so I didn't see her for a few weeks. When she reappeared it was with a young man who looked every inch the pop star and seemed to spend more and more time with her. The funny thing was that when I asked her if this was the musician she had been so keen on she said no. But her general mood had changed and she seemed to have lost some of her vivaciousness, although the parties recommenced. When we first used to have our talks on the bus she was always looking forward to the next party, or a new boyfriend, but after she returned from the tour she seemed preoccupied, far less happy-go-lucky.

Then she began to think she was being followed. Stalking they call it nowadays don't they. Well of course it would have been surprising if a beauty such as Tatti hadn't attracted male attention, and no doubt not all of it was welcome. This was something different though. She asked me to tell her if I ever noticed a car repeatedly passing through without ever stopping, or if I spotted anyone hanging around who I didn't recognise. She actually got off our bus on one occasion several stops early and asked me to watch for whoever got off behind her and whether she was followed. It was all nonsense of course, but she had definitely developed a fixation about being watched."

This time when she paused it was in anticipation of a question and Anna duly obliged. "Did she ever clarify why she thought she was being watched?"

The old lady shook her head "No Mrs Price, not in so many words. But when her father was killed in that accident she did say something on the lines of 'I hope the same thing doesn't happen to me'. I thought that was a touch strange but at the time she did appear to be a little the worse for wear if you get my meaning. I knew she liked a drink and she once told me that if I ever wanted something a little more potent than alcohol she would be happy to obtain it for me. Both my husband and I did occasionally smoke a little something, well, it was the seventies, but I think that Tatti was probably referring to a stronger stimulant.

I know that she wasn't terribly fond of her father and had adopted her mother's maiden name. Even so, following his death her drinking and the obsession with being watched seemed to increase, along with the visits from her boyfriend who was virtually living with her. Our Saturday afternoon meetings became less regular and she began to spend more time at her flat. Being a non-working wife I actually saw more of her during weekdays for the short time before she left."

Martin silently offered a prayer of thanks that Joyce Enright had finally got to the point in her tale where they might actually learn where Tatti had moved on to and tentatively asked "Do you know when it was that she left?"

"That's easy enough. It was late January 1978, and things rapidly went downhill for the girl from thereon. She wasn't really a bad lot, just spoilt and misguided I think. It didn't really seem very fair that such calamities befell her."

"What on earth happened?" Anna asked.

Mrs Enright sighed and said "She had thrown what she said was going to be her last party before she moved. She even asked my husband and I, but we would have felt out of place so we didn't go. It was that very night when the second death to affect Tatti occurred and coming so quickly after her father's demise I think it was pretty much the last straw. I only heard what happened sometime after the event. Tatti and this boyfriend of hers had left the party in the early hours and for some reason had decided to walk up to Hornsey Lane bridge.

It was quite a cold night but, according to the police, they had both consumed a mixture of drink and drugs, so probably didn't notice the temperature. As far as I can tell, it was never clearly established what happened, but that bridge has, over the years, earned the unpleasant nickname of Suicide Bridge. Tatti's boyfriend went over the side and was killed instantly when he hit the road below. They found Tatti crouched against the parapet, half frozen and in no fit mental state to give the police a reliable account of what had occurred. She was hospitalised and I think the coroner recorded a verdict of death by misadventure.

Tatti was finally released after several months in an institution for the mentally disturbed. She never returned to Whitehall Park and the next I heard of her was by pure chance sometime in the early nineteen-eighties. My late husband used to buy two Sunday newspapers. The Observer, and The News of the World. Tatti surfaced in a court case concerning the attempted blackmail of a wealthy businessman. She lived in the King's Cross area and had been earning a living as a prostitute. She was sentenced to seven years I think. That was the last I heard of her. It's rather a sad story isn't it?"

They made the short return journey in the RAV4 in almost total silence as they each pondered the story of the beautiful girl who had made such a mess of her life.

Chapter 14 - Suzie

By unspoken agreement, they headed for the hotel bar and it wasn't until they had each taken an appreciative gulp from their glasses that Anna referred to Joyce Enright's story. They remained at the bar perched on the high stools as she said "Well I'm not sure about you, but if we are to believe Mrs Enright we are now well and truly up the proverbial creek. If the chap who fell from the bridge in January 1978 was Jase it would have been quite big news at the time. The fact that it wasn't, points to the probability that it was this mysterious boyfriend."

Her husband nodded, "That's how I see it as well. Poor old Tatti has a bit of a breakdown and ends up on the game, and then inside."

"Do you think she killed him, Martin?"

"It's a possibility I suppose but what would be the point?'

"She could have been out of her mind on drink and drugs."

"Maybe. The trail has almost gone completely cold with Tatti presumably getting out of prison in the middle or late eighties and the boyfriend dead and gone. We are fast running out of options, bearing in mind the objective is to locate Jase and put him in touch with CKC Bank. Who actually ended up with the Egg and who owns it is beside the point. Any bright ideas?"

She rested her elbow on the faux leather apron of the bar and sighed. "We could try for old local newspaper reports relating to the death of the boyfriend in January 1978. Out of all the characters involved, he is the murkiest. We don't even know his surname despite the fact that he is at the centre of the story from beginning to end."

Martin attracted the attention of the barman who confirmed that the Islington Gazette was the major local newspaper but recalled that there used to also be a publication called The Hornsey Journal. He suggested that if they were interested in the area covering Suicide Bridge that could be a better option. "I think it can only be accessed digitally nowadays," he added helpfully.

"In deference to your ancient legs, Martin, I will nip up to our room and bring down our tablets. We can sit here in the lounge area and follow up what our friendly barman has told us" and Martin watched the love of his life stride between the settees and chairs of the lounge and head for the lift. He sat alone at the bar for several minutes replaying the story of Tatiana Drake's downfall, as related by Joyce Enright and found himself feeling sorry for the hapless young woman who, if still alive, would now be almost sixty. He had just taken up residence on one of the settees when Anna returned.

They soon found that the barman was correct and there was a Digital Archive available for those wanting to access back copies. It was an easy matter to locate the incident in the edition covering the week in which it had taken place although it gave only a brief report to the effect that a man had fallen from the bridge and died on impact with the road below. Initially disappointed, Anna then located a far more detailed report in the edition published two weeks later and read it out to Martin.

'The identity of the man who fell from the Hornsey Lane Road Bridge onto the A123 Archway Road has been confirmed as that of David Fairfax, aged 24. Police have confirmed that the incident occurred at 1.30 a.m. on 23rd January and that Mr Fairfax died immediately on impact following a fall from a height of more than eighty feet. The precise circumstances are unclear but it does appear that he had been attending a party nearby and together with a female companion had decided to go for a walk to get some fresh

air. The police would not comment on whether anything other than food and alcohol had been consumed by the deceased. Although initially taken into custody, the young woman who had accompanied the deceased, and was found on the bridge in a distressed state, has now been detained under the provisions of the Mental Health Act pending a psychiatric assessment. During the years since its construction in the late nineteenth century, the bridge has earned itself the unofficial title of 'Suicide Bridge' due to the number of unfortunate persons who have chosen to meet their end by jumping to their deaths. There is no intention to imply that Mr Fairfax deliberately took his own life and police have said that they are not in a position to make any comment. The identity of the man's female companion has not been released.'

"That bears out what we have been told and at last, we have a name. Now, as you were reading I was also looking ahead through some later editions and a few weeks later there is a report regarding the Coroner's Court hearing. It simply says that a verdict of 'accidental death' was returned. An autopsy found significant quantities of cocaine and alcohol in the man's body and it is believed that while under the influence he foolishly climbed onto the parapet of the bridge, slipped on the frosty surface and fell to his death. Tatti may have been good looking but seems to have been pretty unlucky in most other respects and according to old Mrs Enright she was paranoid to boot.

While we are on the subject of Tatti, um, oh heavens, er, there is something else I want to mention."

This was said in such a hesitant manner that Martin looked sharply at his wife before nodding and saying "Well go on then. Why the reticence?"

"It's because I don't want you to think I'm a complete idiot. It concerns what Mrs Enright said about Tatti suffering from paranoia?"

"When she thought she was being watched you mean?"

The blonde head nodded and he could see the look that said she was appealing to him not to belittle her. He waited patiently until after taking a fortifying sip from her glass she said, "Everyone agrees that Tatti was a little too fond of drink, drugs and the good life in particular. That doesn't necessarily mean that she was wrong about everything and supposing she wasn't wrong about being watched? In fact, if somebody thought she and this Dave Fairfax chap had the Egg perhaps she *was* being watched, and when they decided to go for a walk in the early hours whilst under the influence of God-knows-what maybe it provided the watchers with a perfect opportunity to do more than just watch."

"Alright Anna, but why chuck the boyfriend over the side? It's not exactly subtle is it?"

"Not in the least, but I'm wondering if that was somehow accidental. Could an attempted kidnap or some form of threatening behaviour be the reason Tatti was so frightened that it left her deranged for quite some time and unable to talk about what had happened?"

"And this third party intervention could only have come from one source, assuming our hypothesis is correct?" He replied, answering her question with his own.

"Yelenkov. According to our thoughts, he was the only person likely to think that Tatti and her boyfriend could have the Egg."

"So why has this caused you so much angst?"

She looked at him intently for a moment, hesitated, and then replied. "Because I think we are being watched and after what happened to Tatti's boyfriend I'm getting frightened."

He knew better than to treat the comment lightly. "What has given you that impression?"

Relieved to get the matter into the open she suddenly didn't feel so foolish and tried to voice her concerns in a careful and coherent manner. "The day we left for Eastbourne I happened to notice a car parked downstairs in one of the bays with a chap sitting in the front passenger seat. We were walking to our car and as I glanced across he raised his hand and began talking into a mobile. I couldn't see his face because he had turned his head to one side and it was also partly obscured by his raised hand. The only reason I gave him a second thought was because I was surprised he could get a signal below ground; I've never been able to. Later, after we arrived in Eastbourne you parked in the front area of the hotel, and we went for a stroll along the front to stretch our legs. There are public parking spaces available right along that road and I was surprised to see what I thought was the same car from the car park of the Highbury Skyline parked out there at the roadside. I'm certain it was the same car because the last three letters were ORC. You know, like in Lord of the Rings."

As she took another sip from her glass Martin took the opportunity to say "I'm certain I would have known if we had been followed from London, I didn't exactly take a straightforward route and I would have noticed on those quieter roads. Mind you, if your friend knew where we were headed, he could have just beetled around the M25 from Bromley and dropped down to Eastbourne on the A22. Go on Anna there's more isn't there?"

She nodded and said "I still wasn't really associating the car with us but the following day as we came out of Trafalgar Court at Norman's Bay I'm sure I spotted it yet again. We had to wait to turn right onto the road and it pulled away from a layby on our left and you had to wait and let him go. We actually travelled behind him for a short distance but he scooted away and that was that. I did notice there were two men inside and the car is one of those smart BMWs. Not sure of the model though, but it's silver."

Seeing him just silently listening and feeling the grey eyes pinning her to the leather of the settee she ploughed onwards. "Last of all was earlier today when we drove up to Whitehall Park. As Mrs Enright closed the front door when she let us in, I glimpsed what looked like a silver BMW drift past. Then, of course, she told us about Tatti and her so called 'paranoia'. 'My God', I thought. 'History is repeating itself' and I've been chewing it over ever since. What do you think, am I going even dafter than usual?"

He smiled and shook his head as he sat back in his seat. "No, my love. Full marks for observation, I haven't noticed a thing, but from what you have said it does sound as if we are being tracked, although it can't be the same people who were following Tatti unless they are as old as Mrs Enright."

Anna smiled at the thought and said, "I was afraid you would think I was imagining the whole thing."

"I don't think either you or Tatti were imagining it. Somebody, probably Yelenkov, wanted to find the Egg and thought that Tatti may have it. Now, somebody else appears to think we are worth following and the only reasonable connection must be the Egg."

"Surely they can't think we can lead them to it?"

"Not necessarily, but perhaps they are hoping we can lead them to someone who knows where it is. The very same person we are looking for in fact."

"Jase Wooldridge?"

"Exactly."

"Do you think that even though the people cannot be the same as those responsible for the deaths in 1977 and 1978, they are the products of a single source?"

"Are you referring to Yelenkov, Anna?"

"Why not?"

"He would be almost ninety now, assuming he is still alive of course. A bit past it so far as organising some sort of surveillance on us. Also, he would need to be mentally switched on in order to plan, coordinate, evaluate etc. I don't see that as very likely."

"Supposing he made notes, or told somebody about the Egg? Who's to say they haven't decided to do a little treasure hunting for themselves?"

He swirled the liquid in his glass around as he mulled over her comments and after what seemed like an age said, "I'll give an old friend a call and see if I can get hold of some information regarding Yelenkov and whether he is still gracing us with his presence."

"One of your ex- army buddies?"

"Yep. You see, us Boy Scouts have our uses occasionally."

As Anna sat listening to her husband's call she was surprised to hear him say "Hello, Suzie, how goes it?"

'Suzie??'

It was a short call and as he pocketed the phone he said "That paid off. It would seem that Yelenkov is still on this planet although a permanent resident of the Ivydene Nursing Home down near Uckfield in Sussex."

"And Suzie is one of the Boy Scouts?"

"More Girl Guides as I recall" he laughed.

"Do I need to know more?" She couldn't help herself as her usual insecurities peeped above the surface.

"Not really. Brunette, aged around thirty-five, nice figure, not so tall as you, about five-eight I think. One of our best Intel guys."

"Guys?"

"In a colleague sense. Suzie's got a mind like a steel trap."

"Meaning?"

"Once something goes in it never escapes. She's a walking database and has specialised in things of a Russian persuasion. As expected, she came up with the goods."

Somewhat mollified by Martin's off-hand references to his contact Anna let her curiosity subside. "So it's back to Sussex again I guess."

"Yes, today is almost over, I'll get an update off to CKC before dinner and we can get on the move tomorrow morning. I'll phone ahead and see if a brief visit by Vladimir's 'great niece' and her husband is acceptable.

Chapter 15 - Ivydene

The following day they found their way through London, followed through to Bromley and picked up the A21 south. Martin took the turn off for Tunbridge Wells and remarked. "Haven't spotted a tail yet." He made a similar comment as they drove south out of the town and followed the A26 on past Crowborough. The traffic was fairly light and on rounding a bend close to the quaintly named Herons Ghyll they saw a large wooden sign proclaiming the Ivydene Nursing Home to be located along a short driveway behind a dense screen of trees.

"Looks expensive," murmured Anna as they walked into a large reception area, "More like a modern hotel."

"Courtesy of the British taxpayer I imagine," Martin added.

There was a white-uniformed woman in her twenties seated at the reception desk and Anna was momentarily put in mind of Nikki Prendergast when she was at Grantfield University. They identified themselves and waited for a few minutes until another stiffly starched employee approached, asked them to follow her and led them towards the shining aluminium doors of the lift. "Mr Yelenkov is one of the guests housed on the upper floor," she volunteered. "He doesn't very often have visitors, just occasionally old work colleagues. If you believe the rumours, he apparently worked for British Intelligence years ago. Is that correct?" She had addressed the last comment to Anna who, momentarily caught off balance stammered "Wha- oh, um. Yes, I think so."

The lift disgorged them onto the first floor and as they were led along a tastefully decorated corridor Martin asked "Why is the old boy housed up here? He's pretty ancient, wouldn't he be better off on the ground floor?"

"That's a popular misconception" answered the woman. At his age, people can become very confused and naturally, we don't lock them in their rooms. If they were on the ground floor they might just manage to wander off into the grounds which are quite extensive. This way we can keep an eye on them a little more effectively. Here is Mr Yelenkov's room, he has been told to expect you. When you leave, just press the red button by the lift and reception will open the lift doors for you, they will see you via the monitoring system."

They entered the room and found its occupant to be a very old man whose gaunt frame had no doubt once carried a great deal more flesh than it now had to bear. He was sitting upright in bed, although there were two easy chairs and a small settee also in the room. Beside the bed stood a metal cylinder and his left hand rested on the tube of what was clearly an oxygen mask. As they approached, Martin was aware that, despite the aged and shrunken appearance of the body, two eyes were focused on them with an unblinking and penetrating gaze. He was about to offer an introduction when the old man beat him to it.

"If you are British Intelligence then this young woman must be your honey-trap specialist."

He laughed, coughed, and clamped the mask to his face. When he removed it he held up his right hand and looking at Anna said "Forgive me. That was extremely rude. I couldn't believe that after all these years my country of birth was sending someone to kill me, and I wouldn't be too worried if it did. I was intrigued because I am not aware that I have ever had a great niece. So tell me, who are you?"

He took another oxygen break as Martin decided to pretend a confidence that neither felt and answered. "We have no connection with any of the intelligence agencies Mr Yelenkov. My name is Martin Price and this is my wife Anna. We want to speak with you about the Fabergé Alexander III Egg. We are trying to trace a man who we think once possessed it but has not been heard of since early 1978. We know of Iosif Gusev's involvement and death and hope that you may be willing to tell us what you know. We have reasoned that you became involved due to your friendship with Mr Gusev. Our involvement is entirely unofficial and we are concerned solely with putting two parties in touch with each other. The Egg is the common factor but the objective is completely peaceful."

For a moment or two silence descended until the old man lowered the mask and gazed far away at some distant scene that only he could see. His eyes moved slowly from one to the other and he finally said. "Your reasoning regarding Iosif Gusev is sound. Take a seat, please. You have brought back to my mind an episode I thought was buried in the past and has been a permanent source of shame to me. It will be good to share a secret I have carried for so many years although I never thought that anyone else would be remotely interested after all this time. Where should I start?"

"From when you first learnt about the Egg. We have presumed it was in the possession of Iosif Gusev of the Soviet Embassy."

Vladimir Yelenkov nodded. "You are well informed Mr Price. Now let me see, yes, Iosif Gusev and I were old school friends and, during his tenure in London, I was able to supply him with drugs, mainly cocaine, that he marketed with the assistance of a young Englishman. During a visit I made to London in 1977 he came to me in some distress and told me that he had made the incredible discovery of the Egg hidden in the basement of our very own embassy. You will appreciate that our little drug-running enterprise was enabling both of us to slowly accumulate hidden funds as an insurance against whatever the future may have held. Those were dark days and we used to joke about the drugs money being part of our retirement plans.

The discovery of the Egg completely transformed Iosif's plans and would mean that he could escape from his life at the Embassy and the financial demands of his former wife. The reason for his distress was that having wisely kept the Egg locked in the safe in his London flat, he found one evening that it had miraculously vanished. '*Could I help him?*' he asked. Poor Iosif. Blessed with an appreciation of the finer things in life and cursed by a lack of imagination. It took me very little time to determine that the daughter from his disastrous marriage to an English woman was almost certainly the thief, most likely in conjunction with her boyfriend. The boyfriend was Iosif's distribution agent for our drugs and so they had him at their mercy without him realising it." He broke off at this point, taking a drink of water and another oxygen break as they waited for him to continue.

Instead of immediately resuming his narrative he sat silently for almost a minute, staring ahead as if he had forgotten their existence until turning his gaze on Martin as if measuring him up. Finally, he spoke again "I worked for our security service on foreign matters and despite carving a successful career for myself I was uneasy at the way in which the Communist Party was guiding the country. I needed to have a contingency plan in the event of matters taking a downward turn which is why I first inveigled Iosif into the drug running business. When he came to me for help regarding the Egg, I let the scale of his good fortune warp my thinking. For a fool such as him to have such a valuable item drop into his lap was too much for me to bear and, although I initially imposed a high price in return for my assistance, I soon made up my mind to have the Egg for myself. It would afford me the perfect escape plan and the risks of my drug running being discovered could be put to one side.

There was at the time a young man working as a member of the Embassy security staff who was extremely ambitious. Combined with a singularly ruthless streak he was clearly set for a bright future if luck favoured him. I gave him the impression that Iosif had set up the drug business and one of the reasons for my visit to London was to uncover the extent of the operation with a view to closing it down once full details of the network were ascertained. I told him we had received word that the British police were following some leads and it was imperative that the USSR was not implicated. He should pick a couple of reliable fellows from our security staff to assist him, and on no account was any other member of the London embassy to know what was afoot. He was to report only to me when I returned from my short trip to Paris. I strongly intimated that the orders originated in Moscow and success would be beneficial to his career."

He paused and in a more conversational tone addressed his guests. "What I really wanted was to track Iosif's daughter and her boyfriend's movements to determine where they lived - without Iosif being aware of my interest."

"But didn't he ask you what was happening now that he had come to you for help?" Anna asked.

A further application of the oxygen mask delayed the reply for half a minute. "My Paris trip was to last only for a few days before I returned to London and I told Iosif that I would formulate a plan while I was away. I also told him to set up an immediate meeting with his agent so that my men could pick up his trail. You see, I thought it would be possible to either obtain the Egg or discover its location during that short time. Believe me when I say I had no doubt that the man I had chosen would prove far too persuasive for either the daughter or her boyfriend to resist. I would obtain the Egg and there was a strong possibility that Iosif would never know how his old friend had betrayed him."

He sighed and looked from one to the other but as neither of them spoke he recommenced his tale. "Regrettably, things did not go as I had foreseen. I can now only tell you what I was told but I believe it to be an accurate account. Iosif was duly watched in anticipation that he would make contact with at least one of the two persons I was interested in. On the first day, this proved unproductive as he followed an uninspiring routine driving from home to the embassy and back. With my men acting, *ultra vires,* shall we say, it was not possible to initiate the usual lines of enquiry. Then on the second evening Iosif was seen to leave his apartment block on foot. It was a wet showery evening and a decision was made to trail him on foot with a car hanging some distance back. London was less crowded in those days and because of the poor weather the streets were deserted even though it was only nine-thirty. Either due to carelessness or bad luck, it seems he became aware that he was being followed and ran for it but he was not a fit man and was not moving fast. My man simply waited, in the hope that Iosif would think he had been mistaken and watched as he rounded the corner of a street not too far ahead. His own car which had been discreetly following then drew up and my man climbed aboard. As they were about to pull away they were overtaken by another car moving at quite a fast pace. It turned left into the street that Iosif had taken and as they also made the same turn they saw that the car had accelerated and was almost at the end of the street where it was forced to turn right. Having just completed the turn themselves they were unprepared for the figure who raced from one of the doorways and into the road in front of them. They hit him and he bounced up, struck one corner of the windscreen as he descended and hit the road. They stopped briefly, ascertained that he was dead and drove swiftly away."

"You are saying it was an accident?" Anna asked incredulously.

"That is how it was related to me. It looks as if Iosif heard the strange car coming around the corner at speed and, thinking it was his pursuers he hid in the nearest doorway. When it raced past he thought he had gained some breathing space and in panic decided to run back to his apartment. He didn't hear our car following more slowly come round the corner and met his end in a simple traffic accident."

They exchanged looks and Martin asked, "What about the doorman at Gusev's apartment block?"

A look of surprise flitted across the old man's face. "The doorman?"

"He supposedly died of a heart attack."

"Ah yes. Now I remember. You will have to accept my word that a heart attack is exactly what it was. Why would we harm him? It would only have drawn more attention, which of course it did, when that was the last thing I wanted. No, my friends, that is a death which cannot be laid at my door."

"But you didn't give up did you Mr Yelenkov?" Anna reignited the conversation. "You did trace the daughter and continued to have her followed and watched."

"That is not quite correct my dear. Difficult though it may be to believe, I wished Iosif no harm although I freely admit I tried to cheat him. He had no more right to the Egg than me so I do not feel bad about that. His death genuinely upset me and I returned home from London, immersed myself in my work, and resigned myself to having missed a golden opportunity. Trying to continue the operation from back home was too dangerous and difficult to control, particularly as my work involved travelling at short notice to almost any part of the world. Communications in 1977 were not what they are today.

Now I do not expect you to believe me, and I do not much care whether you do or do not. So far as I was concerned, the venture was over. Not least because it had resulted in the death of my oldest friend. However, the young man who I had enlisted as my ally was, as I have told you, very ambitious. He knew that I was unhappy at Iosif's demise, he thought that despite me prevailing on our London embassy to play down the incident, it could be something that came back to haunt him in the future. Remember, I had given him the impression that the matter concerned halting a drug running operation and had been ordered by Moscow. In a misguided attempt to retrieve the position he took it upon himself to continue the search. He managed to pick up the girl's trail from the various comments that were made when the newspapers reported Iosif's death.

He and his men tracked her to where she used to hang out with some pop group in a pub somewhere, and then to where she lived in north London. They seemed confused by whether her boyfriend was actually a member of the pop group or not, but that really did not matter. They kept them both under surveillance as far as possible but it was difficult. Despite them being part of the security service and having a greater freedom of movement than ordinary embassy staff, they could not afford to attract unnecessary attention. Finally, the couple played into their hands by wandering off from some late night party together and they decided to make a positive move. My man told me that they kept them under observation from their car, but when they decided to walk up the steps to the bridge above the road, it was necessary for the car to detour and so contact was briefly lost. By the time they reached the upper road Iosif's daughter and boyfriend were fooling around on the bridge and the boyfriend had actually climbed up onto the ornamental parapet. The girl had wandered further along the walkway and the couple were shouting at each other. They were both obviously very drunk and my man decided this was the opportune moment to pressure them about the supposed drug running operation. Now comes the part of the story that convinced me, when I received his report, that he was telling the truth. As their car pulled into the kerb one of his men opened the door and shouted to the boyfriend to get down. The young man responded by making a rude gesture but his feet slipped and he fell backwards. One hand had been wound around an upright holding one of the lights and was jerked free. He fell to the road below and was killed." He paused and raised the mask to his face.

"So yet another fatal accident with your men in the near vicinity?" Martin asked.

"Yes, Mr Price. Strange as it may seem that is exactly the position. It is what convinced me that it was the truth. It is so unlikely, that a liar would have embellished the tale to make it sound more plausible. My man, despite fearing the consequences stuck to his story. And tell me honestly, what was there to be gained by killing either of that young couple? It would only attract further unwanted media attention, which of course is exactly what happened. Thankfully the girl's name was never released and so no connection was ever made between the two deaths. Until you came along that is."

Anna leant forward and said, "Tell me Mr Yelenkov, who else knows what you have told us?"

"Until your visit, I would have gone to my grave thinking that my guilty secret was mine and mine alone. The ambitious young security man was later killed by Chechen terrorists and the pair he employed would have known none of the details."

"So that leaves you as the only person with a motive to prolong the matter. Two motives in fact. One to continue your search for the Egg, and the second to cover up a badly botched operation that caused two deaths." Martin stated.

The man in the bed nodded. "Superficially that is true, but I have always been a pragmatist. Once back in Moscow, I could no longer effectively and safely exercise control. Times also moved swiftly onwards. The Afghanistan invasion proved a turning point for me and I eventually defected to the UK. I was welcomed and have lived a quietly comfortable life ever since." He laughed and gestured to his surroundings before adding "Even my death will be quietly comfortable."

"And you did not pass on your knowledge of the Fabergé Egg to anyone else?" Anna persisted.

Vladimir Yelenkov smiled and said "Young lady, the Egg was a brief opportunity to save myself years of hard and dangerous work. But the moment passed and I was never likely to be in a position to try a second time. I was certainly never going to broadcast what I have told you both today. I am intrigued by your questions, though. You said at the outset that you were most concerned with tracing a person who disappeared in 1978. Your comments, however, make me suspect that another party may be showing an interest in the Egg and you think I may somehow be involved. Well, nothing could be further from the truth. Sharing my story with you has provided me with a small measure of relief from the guilt that has lain buried for so many years. Betraying and causing the death of a friend is not an easy matter to brush aside, even for someone such as me."

"He wasn't at all what I expected" commented Anna as they drove away from Ivydene. "I think he genuinely regrets having indirectly caused Gusev's death, and that of Dave Fairfax.

Chapter 16 – Boy Racer

"How useful was our meeting with Yelenkov?" Anna asked as Martin piloted the RAV4 back towards London.

"It confirmed quite a lot of our guesswork and provided an interesting insight into Yelenkov himself. It gave us nothing so far as Jase was concerned and, although Yelenkov came to the same conclusion as ourselves, namely that Tatti and either Jase Wooldridge or Dave Fairfax was involved, his money seems to have been on Fairfax. The fact remains though that it was Jase who opened the account at CKC. Yelenkov has never known that."

"Do you think it was Jase who absconded with the Egg?"

"It has never come to light has it. Fairfax is long dead and Jase, apart from one slightly dubious sighting in the nineteen-eighties, has never surfaced. Either of them may have hidden it somewhere and the result will have been the same so far as we are concerned. Oddly enough, the one thing that ties Jase to the Egg also makes it seem unlikely that he took it because if he did then why on earth didn't he also go and retrieve what was deposited with CKC?"

Anna scratched the end of her nose as she thought over the revelations made by Vladimir Yelenkov. "One thing I think we should remember, Martin, is that even though former Comrade Yelenkov was under the impression that he was the only person who knew about the Egg, that's not strictly true. For a start, Jase must have known, but then he was sleeping with Tatti on that '*Wheelspin*' tour, so no surprises there. Then, of course, there is Tatti herself. More recently, we know about it. Hal, Griss, Mikey, and Anne Silverdale all know that we are looking for Jase but none of them know about the Egg, nor does Joyce Enright nor the listeners to *Alan*

Keane's Country. We haven't mentioned the Egg to anybody other than Yelenkov but somebody has started to take an interest in our movements and I don't think it's just because they want to find Jase and get his autograph."

"You're right there Anna. By the way, our friends in the Beamer are sitting about four vehicles back. They latched onto us as we passed that pub called The Crow & Gate. I saw them pop out of the car park."

"What shall we do?"

"Not sure, let me think about it. They're not doing anything wrong and if they are following us because of the Egg, it must mean they know even less than us."

"OK, I'll go with your instinct on that, but it makes me feel uncomfortable. Do you think we ought to have one last try at Anne Silverdale just on the off chance she might recall something helpful from her time with Jase?"

"We can give it a go. Why not phone her and say we would like to bring her up to date with our investigations if she has time to spare. I don't see any harm in telling her about the Egg either. We did spin her a bit of a yarn at the outset and it can't do any harm at this stage."

She reached for her phone and was about to dial the number when he added "No, better still, ask her if she would like to have dinner with us at the hotel, our treat. Also, tell her that we have arranged to meet a former local newspaper man who says he has some information about the chap who was killed at Suicide Bridge in 1978, and we are meeting him in an hour at the Alexander Park Hotel, Turners Hill, not far from East Grinstead."

"What? What the hell are you talking about?"

"Hurry up and do it, my love, we aren't that far from Tunbridge Wells."

Anna knew better than to prolong the conversation and hastily dialled the shop in north London. It was Anne who answered, and the strains of an ancient pop song could be heard playing in the background. Message conveyed, she turned back to her husband and asked "She said she would love to have dinner. So would you mind telling me what you are up to?"

They were gradually reducing speed as they joined a queue of slow moving traffic entering Tunbridge Wells and Martin's eyes kept flicking to his rear-view mirror and back. "The Beamer's only two cars behind now" he answered as they followed the road to their left and stayed in the right-hand lane as they approached a small roundabout of the type merely painted onto the road surface.

"Martin what are………."

She got no further as he raised his voice. "Hold tight."

He jerked the gear stick into second, stamped on the gas pedal and wrenched the wheel to his right. The RAV4 screeched into a tight turn almost hitting a southbound vehicle with the right of way. Careering almost full circle it narrowly missed the rear wing of the BMW which, taken by surprise, was committed to the northbound exit. They flashed past the rear of their erstwhile pursuers and then as he swiftly moved through the gears surged onwards along the road that would have been a simple left-hand turn had he chosen a more conventional form of driving.

"Jesus Christ, that fucking well hurt," Anna shouted as her head banged against the side of the car. They accelerated up the fortuitously clear road and swung left at the roundabout at the top.

"Sorry about that. It was all on the spur of the moment. "Are you OK?" He at last resumed their conversation.

"Yes, no thanks to you, you bloody lunatic. What are you fucking well up to? You've nearly caused a major accident."

"I wanted to shake the Beamer and if we can take the right turn by The Hare just coming up, here we go, I'm going to take us through the country lanes to Turner's Hill."

"Why? We aren't meeting anybody. I've never heard of Turner's bloody Hill."

He didn't immediately answer and instead, she saw his eyes again flicking rapidly from the road ahead to the rear-view mirror and back. Finally, he said "Just after the Beamer picked us up at The Crow & Gate we were talking about the people who knew we were trying to find Jase and you suggested we have a further chat with Anne Silverdale. It was then I thought we should try something out, which is why I asked you to tell her that fairy tale about the newspaper man. Someone is giving the guys in the Beamer the heads up on what we are doing, and they are not even bothering to tail us that closely. They knew we were going to see Yelenkov so they just waited to pick us up on our way back. It was a fair bet that we would come back up the A26."

"But Anne Silverdale didn't know we were going to see Yelenkov."

"I know, but I need to make absolutely sure that she isn't somehow involved in this. At the same time, it was a pretty good way to let the

Beamer Boys know they've been rumbled. Now we will get to the hotel at Turners Hill before them, even if Anne phones them and tells them the latest news. It means we will be able to sit in the warmth and luxury of the hotel and I will go and have a scout round the car park and see if they have shown up. There's nowhere to park along that stretch of road but the hotel parking area is quite large and they will feel reasonably secure. If Anne isn't the one tipping them off then they won't turn up, and I've narrowed the suspect list to just two."

They spent two hours in the comfort of the Alexander Park, during which time Martin made four excursions to the car park. On each occasion, when he returned, he pronounced himself satisfied that their pursuers had not arrived.

"I'm so relieved," said Anna. "I rather like Anne Silverdale and if she had been selling us down the river I would have been very upset. Now, Mr Price, having nearly killed me back in Tunbridge Wells you owe me a full explanation. I've shown commendable restraint so far but now is the time to put me fully in the picture if you value your life."

He laughed and answered "Fair enough, but it was all very much unplanned. As we were saying earlier, not many people knew about the Egg, and we have to assume that Mr Fabergé's creation is what our stalkers are interested in. That pretty much rules out the ex-band members, even Horrible Hal. I'm now happy that Anne Silverdale isn't involved, so that leaves just two. I also took the precaution of checking out our car just in case a tracker had been fitted and I'm sure that we are clean."

"So who has been passing the information on our movements?"

"The simple answer is that we have."

Anna paused with her coffee cup halfway between the table and her mouth "What do you mean, 'we have'?"

"We are the source. That is to say, our updates to CKC have provided the information via either Celeste Palin or Angelina Flavio. I don't see any other possibility."

It took a moment for the meaning of what he had said to sink in.

"Are you serious?"

He nodded and said "Think about it. They are the only other people, apart from Nikki and Jean-Paul of course, who know that a Fabergé Egg is central to our work. More to the point, they are the only two who receive useful progress reports from us."

They finished their coffees and drove away from the hotel in silence until Anna asked, "What would you have done if the stalkers had been in the car park?"

He glanced briefly at her and answered "Nothing probably. Provided they keep their distance I've no reason to quarrel with them. Also, after my boy-racer stunt back in Tunbridge Wells, they know we have spotted them so that's going to be a factor whenever they try to follow us from now on. It will have put a lot of uncertainty into their minds."

"And where do we go from here?"

"Back to the hotel, and then let's go over things with Anne at dinner. We also need to work out how to identify which of our two CKC suspects is the one having us followed."

"A Fabergé Egg?" Anne Silverdale, resplendent in a small red dress, sat looking bemused as she fiddled with the stem of her glass. "That would be worth an absolute fortune, wouldn't it?"

"North of several million pounds I would say," Martin answered.

"And you are trying to find it?"

"Not primarily. We have agreed to try and trace the whereabouts of Jase Wooldridge. Finding the Egg is a secondary matter."

"Well, Jase never mentioned any such thing to me. Don't forget, though, we broke up when he was on that tour. By the time he got back to the UK I had moved out, and then although I did go back to the flat one more time he wasn't there. Although........." The sentence tailed off and remained unfinished as she subsided into thought before finally returning to the present day with the words "Jase was never very tidy, but on that last visit the place was in a real mess. I thought at the time that he was letting things slide rather, but maybe it wasn't that at all. There was stuff everywhere and I wonder now whether the place had been turned over. You know, somebody looking for something."

"Like the Egg," Anna added. "Supposing Tatti gave the Egg to Jase for safe keeping and Jase disappeared, taking the Egg with him."

"No." Anne Silverdale shook her head. "Jase wasn't a thief. He couldn't put up with thievery. It came from his days in the Children's Home when privacy was minimal and things got pinched from time to time."

"In that case who was doing the looking, back then? Probably not Yelenkov's men because they were busy keeping an eye on Tatti."

"What about Dave Fairfax?" Martin asked.

"But we think he and Tatti pinched it in the first place," objected Anna.

"Yes, but let's look at the timescale shall we. Jase opens the Swiss account while they are on tour. Tatti starts sleeping with Jase during the tour. The Egg is stolen from Gusev just after *'Wheelspin'* return from their tour. What's to have stopped her giving him the Egg for safe keeping and the two of them cutting Dave Fairfax out of the deal in just the same way as Gusev was cut out?"

"Anne Silverdale interrupted at that point with "It just doesn't sound like the sort of thing Jase would get up to. Not the Jase I knew."

"But he was totally ruthless when it came to women wasn't he?" Anna responded. "Is it really impossible that he could have seized a golden opportunity, then dumped Tatti? Perhaps that is why he walked away from *'Wheelspin'* and ducked out of sight. He had the security of possessing the Egg."

"It hangs together quite nicely Anna," said Martin gently as he watched the downcast look appear on Anne Silverdale's face "The trouble is it doesn't explain why he didn't go back and clear out the Swiss security box."

They ate in silence for a while, each with different views on the puzzle before them. Finally, it was their guest who spoke. "If somebody did search the Earls Court flat it can only have been Dave Fairfax, can't it?"

"In the absence of any other interested party that is a reasonable conclusion," answered Martin "And that can only mean that he thought Jase had it which runs counter to your assertion, Anne, that he wouldn't have pinched it."

"When was it exactly that you went back to the flat Anne?" It was Anna who asked.

"Exactly? I can't be exact, but it was when I got back from the tour with *'Krakatoa'*. So it was probably October or November 1977."

"And by that time Jase had left *'Wheelspin'* but was presumably still seeing Tatti. Perhaps she was giving Dave Fairfax the run-around so far as the Egg was concerned and that led him to try and get hold of the Egg himself."

"Wouldn't Yelenkov's men have followed him, though?" Anne Silverdale asked.

"Not if they didn't realise he wasn't with Tatti. Look, it's been mentioned a couple of times that Dave Fairfax and Jase Wooldridge were similar in looks. If Jase had supplanted Dave in Tatti's bed, then perhaps he was also living with her in the flat in Whitehall Park. From what Yelenkov said, they weren't able to keep a watch twenty-four seven, so perhaps they didn't realise it was Jase and not Dave Fairfax. That would give Fairfax plenty of opportunity to search Jase's flat undetected." Anna looked at Martin for a reaction.

He nodded slowly and said, "So when Jase reverted to type and decided he didn't want Tatti any longer he simply dumped her and left London."

"Not until early 1978." Anna responded "Don't forget what Griss told us. Tatti let him bonk her as a thank you for the lift home and even invited him to the party. When he got there he thought he saw her at first with Jase, but then realised it was Dave Fairfax. Jase actually did turn up shortly afterwards and I bet it was to tell Tatti that he was pulling out."

"So you think she immediately threw in her lot with Dave again, and that's how come they wandered off together from the party?" Anne asked.

"Well, you said she wasn't exactly averse to a bit of bed-hopping, and if that is how it played out it needn't contradict your view of Jase's character. If he was only holding the Egg in safe keeping for Tatti then he may well have agreed to give it back to her. Events then intervened when Dave fell off the bridge and Tatti had her breakdown."

"Do you mean that he took it to that party and returned it?" Martin cocked an eyebrow at his wife.

"Why not?" She answered. "I don't think Tatti ever went back to Whitehall Park. I think the Egg is lost and gone forever."

"Which brings us no closer to finding Jase." He turned to Anne Silverdale. "I know it's a hell of a long time ago, but is there anything you can think of that Jase might have said about his early life that you haven't told us?"

She shook her head. "Only that he was brought up in a children's home. He didn't talk much about it and at the time I wasn't interested enough to ask. Oh, excuse me." The demanding tones of her mobile phone sounded and she hastily snatched up the small bag she had deposited on the floor beside her chair. Her side of the conversation was short.

"Yes?"

"Yes, it is."

"Oh dear."

"Not with me. I'm not at home."

"No, not far"

"Yes. Alright. I'll pick them up on my way."

"About half an hour."

"Thank you. Goodbye."

They watched as a look of consternation appeared on her face, and she rang off as she rose to her feet with the words "I'm terribly sorry but that was the police. There's been some sort of break-in at the shop, I must get over there right away."

They abandoned their table and as they made for reception Martin said "I'll order a cab. None of us is fit to drive, and you came by cab didn't you?"

"Yes, I wish I'd chanced the car now."

"Don't worry, we are coming with you."

"You don't need to Martin. I've got to stop off at home first, to pick up my shop keys."

"Martin's right Anne, we wouldn't want you to be on your own. There's no telling what needs to be done. We can easily get a cab back if necessary."

Their cab arrived within five minutes and Martin spoke to the cabbie as the women took their seats. They were quickly speeding up the Holloway Road and it was then that he sprang a surprise by saying. "I've asked our driver to pull up just before we turn into your road Anne, and I would like you to give me your flat keys."

A stunned silence followed before Anna said, "What's going on Martin?"

"Nothing, I hope, but I want the two of you to sit well back in the cab, and you Anna, to phone me if you see any sign of our friends. I've told the cabbie to drive on past your flat to the far end of the road. He will wait there until I tell you it is all clear and safe to come back down to the flat."

She knew better than to put up an argument and contented herself with patting Anne's hand reassuringly and saying "What if I don't see their car?"

"In that case get the cab to stop outside Anne's and wait for me to amble up - I'll have the keys don't forget."

Chapter 17 – Pinky & Perky

Anne had dutifully handed over her keys, so bemused was she by Martin's authoritative tone and, she later admitted to herself, by the suddenly penetrating quality his gaze seemed to acquire as he looked at her. Even months after the event she felt an involuntary shiver ripple along her spine at the memory. Anna appeared to be completely calm, however, although as Martin got out of the cab on the corner of Holloway Road she felt sure she heard the younger woman say something under her breath that sounded remarkably like *'fucking boy scout'* but knew she must have misheard. She finally found her voice and, as the cab pulled away and slid past a walking Martin Price, asked. "What's all this about Anna, the police are expecting me at the shop. Why does Martin want my keys, and who are you having to watch out for?"

Her companion waved a hand to silence her and, as they passed a vehicle parked at the kerbside a few yards along from the flat, her fingers tapped at the mobile phone she was clutching. The connection was made immediately and Anna uttered the words "It's there, you can't miss it." She then leant forward and spoke to the cabbie asking him to wait with them at the top of the road before turning to the older woman and saying "I'm sorry about this Anne, to be honest, I don't know what has set Martin off on this particular route. To put you more in the picture I can say that we have been followed recently by a silver BMW, and Martin is sure that this is due to the updates we have been sending back to our contacts at the Swiss bank. We don't know for certain, but it appears likely that they are interested in the whereabouts of the Egg and knowing that we are looking for Jase, have assumed that if we find him the Egg will also be discovered. Something about your conversation with the police put Martin on guard and he clearly guessed there was a good chance that the persons trailing us could be waiting near your flat."

"B-but why? More to the point you just used the word 'persons' which means you think there are at least two. Martin's alone, he will be in some sort of danger if they turn out to be villains won't he?"

Anna sighed. "There is no way I could stop him doing whatever it is he intends, and I know he can look after himself. Two years ago I would have worried myself sick, but by now I've come to understand that I need to have faith in his judgement, even if it runs counter to my own instincts."

The street was reasonably well equipped with lighting as one would expect in a London suburb and Martin spotted the silver BMW well before he arrived at where it was parked. He cast a surreptitious glance to his left as he passed Anne's ground floor flat but there were no lights showing and no sign of any movement. As he drew closer to the car, he became aware of an occupant in the front passenger seat watching his approach despite pretending to gaze in bored fashion through the windscreen. He strolled along, giving the appearance of being in no great hurry despite the chill in the evening air, but instead of passing by the stationary vehicle he stopped, and casually leant back in a half sitting posture on the front wing, as if he was himself the proud owner. After a few seconds there came a loud knocking as the occupant rapped with his knuckles on the inside of the windscreen. Martin turned and, as a hand was waved in irritated fashion to indicate he should move on his way, he smiled benignly at the frowning face and turned back to his contemplation of the hedge that fronted one of the small front gardens. The rapping continued and he continued to ignore it until finally he heard the sound of a car door being opened and then closed followed by footsteps and a belligerent voice demanding "What the fuck are you playing at mate?"

No answer!

A large hand grabbed Martin's shoulder as the man rounded the front of the car. Its owner suddenly accelerated, but the change of pace was entirely involuntary. Martin had gripped the wrist with his right hand and pulled, which, combined with the man's forward momentum, jerked him forward alongside the object of his wrath. At the same time Martin's left arm shot out sideways and his hand clamped around the side of the man's neck. A turn of his body combined with a sharp downward movement of his left arm forced the man to his knees followed by a twist of the right hand which brought his opponents arm painfully up behind his back. A sudden move from the neck hold to the hair was followed by a dull thud as face met car door and a splash of nasal blood trickled down the metallic silver paintwork. A groan of pain escaped from the owner of the face as his assailant seemed intent on forcing his skull through the metal skin of the door. Abruptly the pressure ceased and for the first time, the unlucky lookout heard the voice of his tormentor.

"If you don't answer me truthfully I will break several other bones to match your nose. Now how many are in the flat?"

"One, just one. Honest."

There followed a tense few seconds of silence before the voice asked, "Is he armed?"

"N-no, well, not a gun. A knife."

He flinched as the hand went back to his throat, but it was only to rip his tie from around his neck and use it to bind his hands expertly behind his back before he was thrust unceremoniously into the back of the car. His shoes were pulled off and one of his socks stuffed into his mouth with the other tied tightly behind his head to hold it in place. "Not perfect, but one squeak from you and you will wish you had never been born." In the dim interior of the vehicle, he caught a fleeting view of frightening grey eyes and nodded his understanding as the car door clicked shut.

Martin took a moment to ponder his next move. There was no rear access possible and so he had to use the front door. However lightly he walked along the short pathway from the pavement he had to assume that the intruder could be watching from within the darkened front room and clearly see that it was not Anne Silverdale. He decided that an open approach would be best and so rather than trying to tread soundlessly he scuffed his feet slightly and whistled a favourite tune as he made his way slightly unsteadily to the front door at which point he deliberately dropped Anne's bunch of keys as he fished them from his pocket and muttered "Oh bugger" in a normal speaking voice as he bent to pick them up. Finally, after two apparent misses, he rather clumsily jammed the key into the lock and opened the door with an extravagant sweep of his hand that caused it to bang against the protecting doorstop. "Hey baby, I'm home and hoping for some fun tonight" he called loudly.

He flicked on the light in the small hallway and made his noisy way past the closed living room door to the rear kitchen where he turned on the light before silently thanking Anne for laying such a good quality hall carpet as he noiselessly retraced his steps so that he was positioned with his back against the wall between the living room door and the front door. The seconds ticked past until he heard the slight sound of movement from within the front living room. He watched as the handle slowly turned and the door opened two or three inches. It then remained still as the person inside listened for sounds of movement. The silence must have puzzled him because the door then began to very slowly open, but as with most internal doors, it was hung so that it opened into the room. Martin inched quietly forward and waited until the door opened a further few inches before he took a step forward and slammed his full weight against it. There was an audible crunch as the inside of the door and the head of the other person came together and on barging his way through found a thickset man in his thirties or forties down on one knee shaking his head as a red mark clearly indicated the contact point of his forehead with the door. In his right hand, he held a long bladed knife but as he began to rise a foot connected with his chin and he fell backwards with the knife dropping soundlessly onto the deep pile carpet. Swiftly retrieving the weapon, Martin bent down and held the point against the man's Adam's apple. A brief flash of fear showed in the intruder's eyes before he said, "You're going to regret this mate."

"Now why is it that everyone I meet this evening thinks I'm their mate?" Martin asked in a conversational tone before adding "Now be a good chap and tell me who has hired you."

Feeling less dazed, the man's fortitude was returning and he replied "No chance, just because you got lucky doesn't mean you've got the guts to use that knife. You need to be a pro to use a knife in cold blood, not some amateur lover boy."

Martin nodded and said, "Well, in that case, you had best very carefully stand up and hope that this amateur doesn't slip and aerate your throat."

There was something in the way the words were uttered that suddenly put doubt into the man's mind and he decided to go along with his adversary until his head had cleared and he was back on his feet. As he rose he began to size up the man who motioned him to move past the horizontally pointed knife towards the door. Knowing that an opportunity would arise for him to turn the tables he slowly turned to face the door. He was unprepared when his captor swiftly sprang forward and threw an arm across his throat and held the point of the knife with uncomfortable firmness against the side of his neck.

"Now we are going to take a walk through to the bathroom, and I suggest you think very carefully before you try anything stupid. I am neither drunk nor am I an amateur when it comes to the Gerber LMF II, although it's never been my favourite. So be a survivor and I may even let you keep your ears attached to your head. Am I being perfectly clear?"

'Oh, my Christ.' The thought raced through the mind of Martin's captive "Where did this bastard come from?" The reference to the brand name of his own knife combined with the very calm words that were almost whispered in his ear convinced him that his original assessment of his grey-eyed opponent had been extremely wide of the mark. "W-why the bathroom?" he managed to stammer as they edged in a close twosome along the passage.

"Because that's the place where it will be easiest to clean up any blood. I don't want to mess up the lady's nice carpet. Now here we are. Take off your jacket and trousers and drop them on the floor, then I want you to kneel down facing across the bath and gripping that handle opposite with both hands. If you let go with either hand I will cut off one of your fingers. Tell me you understand."

"I-I understand." The thoroughly frightened man hastily removed his suit, and dropped to his knees as directed. Bent forward as he was, with his waist level with the side of the bath and his arms stretched across the cast iron expanse, he was not only extremely vulnerable but also uncomfortably aware that his arms and back would soon begin to ache.

"Good. Now you just concentrate on staying in one piece while I make a phone call."

The unfortunate man heard the grey-eyed one fiddling with a mobile phone and then say "OK. Better get down here as quickly as possible. Ignore the Beamer and come straight into the flat. I'm in the bathroom. Tell Anne she's got an additional guest, temporarily at least, I'll explain when you get here. Pay off the cab - give him an extra twenty for his trouble. The front door is unlatched."

The few minutes that it took before he heard the sounds of two females entering the flat passed very slowly to the man bent across the bath, and he even winced involuntarily when the bathroom door opened and a female voice loudly exclaimed "Fucking hell Martin. What are you going to do with that knife?"

The reply did nothing to ease his anxiety as the man named Martin said "That rather depends on our friend here. Now please do me a favour ladies and empty everything you can find from the clothing on the floor into the bath. Anne, have you got such a thing as some strong tape or cloth that I can use to tie this chap up - he's not a collar and tie lad like his friend."

Anne Silverdale shook herself out of the daze she been in since entering her bathroom and answered, "No, but I've got some of those plastic ties that are used for electrical work - I bought a box when I wanted to tidy up the TV wiring."

"Perfect" answered Martin and as she scurried off to fetch the ties Anna said "Where's the other one Martin? There were two weren't there?"

"On the floor of their car behind the front seats. Don't worry he is completely unharmed apart from a squashed nose and lips."

When Anne returned he directed her to bind the man's wrists together and said "Now my friend. You can let go the handle and shimmy against the wall between the bath and the toilet in a sitting position, that's right. OK ladies, let's see what was in our guest's pockets shall we? Ah, mobile phone and car keys will be helpful, and a wallet. Oh, about seventy-five pounds, that will more than cover this evening's taxi costs. Credit cards and driver's licence in the name of Raymond Priest. Now Raymond, or may I call you Ray? Never mind, please tell me what your instructions are and who it is paying you for this rather clumsy work you are doing. Bear in mind that you could begin to lose a number of quite useful body parts if you decide to be difficult."

Anne Silverdale had gone a deathly white despite her makeup as Anna flashed a sharp look at her husband. She wisely decided to keep her thoughts to herself and go along with the mind games he was indulging in. At least she hoped they were only mind games she thought as she looked at the ashen face of the man on the floor.

"Well?" The grey eyes swivelled back to their victim. The sooner you speak the faster the embarrassment of being seen in your not terribly prepossessing underwear by these two ladies will pass."

"I don't know the name. At least not the real one," he hastily added as Martin's knife hand twitched threateningly. "There's this bloke we know who sometimes puts some work our way if we want it. Usually tailing or maybe leaning on somebody. Sometimes it's debt collecting, you know the sort of thing."

"Go on." was all the response he received as the two women watched in horrified fascination.

"Yes, well, he contacted us and said that an acquaintance of his needed a couple of people followed. Were we interested? He said I would get a call and that the price was something for us to negotiate ourselves. The call came through a few hours later and we agreed on a figure, paid in advance by bank transfer. We were given your names and where you were staying. We were to report details of your movements using text."

"Was the caller male or female?" Martin asked sharply.

"Male with a bit of a foreign accent."

"So when did the orders change?"

"What?"

"Come on Ray don't mess me about. What were you ordered to do tonight?"

"When we texted that you had sussed us and given us the slip in Tunbridge Wells we were told to grab this woman," he indicated Anne with an inclination of his head. "We were then to rough her up a bit and frighten her so that she would tell us everything she knew about something called 'The Egg' and turn this place over before we left. We were just arriving when we saw her getting into a taxi all togged up for a posh night out. We decided to make sure she didn't go off to spend the night somewhere else by phoning her and telling her it was the police and she needed her shop keys because of a break-in. We were pretty sure that she wouldn't have had them with her and would have to come back here, but if not we would just pick her up at the shop. Harry waited in the car and I waited here in the flat - easy to get into," he added, with a look in Anne's direction.

There followed a period of silence as Martin regarded him thoughtfully and flicking on the man's mobile phone said, "I see you bank with Lloyds."

"So what? There's not much in there for you to nick if that's what you think."

"What are the entry codes?" Martin's voice had again taken on an unpleasant edge. When the man's face took on an obstinate expression he added, "Difficult to use a mobile phone without index fingers."

It had the desired effect and in a shaky voice, the security details were divulged. Much to the man's consternation Martin looked up from the mobile phone and said, "Now Ray, it's time we went for a little drive." Then he laughed and said, "Don't worry, you've been a good boy." Turning to Anna he said "It's late, and I suggest you book Anne a room at the hotel for tonight as I imagine she will want to have new locks fitted here. I'll get rid of Pinky and Perky and join you shortly."

Chapter 18 - Angelina

It was nearly 11.00 pm and Martin immediately spotted the two women as he entered the lounge bar of the hotel. He bought himself a drink and settled at their table as Anna confirmed that Anne had been booked in. She then said, "Now Price, am I going to regret asking what you have been up to *and* how you knew Anne was being set up?"

Anne Silverdale nodded her agreement and Martin surveyed the two inquisitive faces before him.

"Not a lot to report actually. I dumped Ray in the back of the Beamer on top of his pal and decided it was time for a bit of poetic justice, so I parked the car right on Suicide Bridge, having first also removed all of the guy named Harry's ID. I've got his wallet, phone, the whole lot, so now we've got two lots of address books to look through, and two lots of credit cards and driving licences to cut up and throw away. Then I walked over to Highgate Hill and was lucky enough to flag down a cab just as I'd started to walk down towards Holloway."

"What about the men, Martin? Did you do anything else?"

"Not really."

"What does that mean. You've got that look of injured innocence on your face. Come on out with it. You didn't do anything with that knife did you?"

He chuckled and saw the infuriated look begin to spread across his wife's face before raising a placatory hand and hastily adding "I dropped the knife down a drain without using it. Then I opened the electric sliding roof, locked up the car, dropped the car keys down a different drain and, well, here I am." He smiled and took a slow drink from his glass."

"Martin," it was Anne Silverdale who spoke "It's already quite a cold night, and there is even the chance of rain according to the forecast. I mean, if you left that car roof open won't those two men……?" Her question tailed off as Martin laughingly finished the sentence for her.

"Won't they get very cold and maybe even wet, possibly catch something nasty? Yes, I certainly hope so. They were pleased enough to accept instructions to 'rough you up' if you recall. Someone will find them eventually and with luck, I have made life so awkward and uncomfortable for them that they will now keep well away from this little job of work. Oh yes, I had some fun on the cab journey home as well. I was a bit bored so I accessed Ray's bank account. Contrary to what he said there was a little over £5,000 in it so I took it upon myself to make a donation on his behalf to the Great Ormond Street Hospital for Sick Children via BACS."

It was all said in a nonchalant fashion and accompanied by a wink as he took a sip from his drink. Anna burst out laughing. "You are a real bastard Martin," although Anne looked worried.

"Won't they come back after me?" She asked.

"No Anne," reassured Martin. "I made it very clear, in particularly lurid terms, precisely what would happen to them if they ever come within shouting distance of you again. Also, the report I'm about to send off to Switzerland should bring the whole thing to an end."

"What do you mean? How is that possible?" Interrupted his wife.

"When I went into Ray's bank account I took the opportunity to have a look back at his bank statement, handy things these apps, and, sure enough, found a BACS payment into his account for £10,000 dated four days ago. The payer was none other than CKC Bank. So I am going to put together a carefully worded report that should shake up the person who has been directing this attempt to track down the Egg on the back of our efforts."

Anne Silverdale looked a little more relaxed and asked, "How did you work out I was being set up just from that phone call? I hardly said anything."

"Nothing clever I'm afraid. Having made it obvious in Tunbridge Wells that I had spotted them I was waiting for them to try something different. When that call came through I thought it qualified as 'different' and decided to play it safe and check it out."

"Well, it's left me feeling quite uncomfortable. It's my usual day off tomorrow and I'm going to phone my manager Paul and ask him to come in for the next couple of days as well. He's always keen to show he can handle things without me, so now he can prove it."

They decided to turn in shortly afterwards and as Martin and Anna sat in their room she asked, "What are you planning to do now?"

"I'm going to concoct a report saying that following a run-in with a couple of heavies who we believe are working for Yelenkov, we were able to scare Anne Silverdale into handing over the Egg which she had been hiding all of these years. We have promised her a share of our finder's fee, called off the hunt for Jase as we have run out of ideas, and will be flying directly into Basel the day after tomorrow."

"Won't that put whomever it is on notice, and enable them to prepare a reception of some sort?"

"Even if they manage to establish contact with the two clowns it won't contradict what I am saying. I won't be telling the whole truth, because I thought we should actually fly back tomorrow. Arriving more than twenty-four hours early should catch them off guard. Now, while I do that would you mind catching Anne Silverdale before she goes to sleep and ask if she fancies a trip to Switzerland. If so, we can swing past her place early tomorrow morning and pick up her passport and some clothes."

Rather than phone, Anna decided to walk down one floor to Anne Silverdale's room and when the bemused woman asked how expensive it would be told her that it was an all-expenses paid trip courtesy of CKC Bank. Returning to her own suite she found that Martin had completed and sent off his report as promised. "Right, bed for us and an early start tomorrow. We leave here 7.30 am and I've booked us a flight from Heathrow at around midday. We travel First Class so a car will pick us up here, and then after a short stop in Grove Road, it's on to Heathrow and fast tracked through to Departures. We will get to Basel at around 1.30 local time and I've arranged to pick up a car at the airport."

"What about the RAV4?"

"Hire company will collect it from the downstairs car park."

"Very efficient Martin, I'm impressed."

"I wasn't co-ordinator of that…., uh, never mind."

'Damn!' She thought, 'he almost forgot himself and let something from his time in the military slip out.' Although she knew a great deal more about his army experiences than in those first few months leading up to their marriage, he was always very reluctant to impart anything other than a bare minimum. Even though she knew he would never tell her a blatant lie, she shrank from trying to ask him outright all about what he did in the forces. It would have been disloyal, and one of the major factors forming their relationship was their mutual trust. Each knowing that the other could always be relied upon to do the right thing. She actually blushed with embarrassment at the thought as she recalled just how wrong-footed she had initially been only a few months ago when, during the Welsh 'dig', he had felt obliged to become involved for several days in thwarting a terrorist threat in Lincolnshire.

The previous day had been so eventful that Anna found herself half dozing as, having stopped long enough to allow Anne to collect her things and satisfy herself that her flat was secure, they were expertly ferried by Jaguar to Heathrow Airport. Anne was almost bubbling over with excitement as she had only previously visited Spain. The instantaneous decision to hop on a plane and fly to Switzerland was a novel experience and only served to heighten the almost God-like status which Martin was rapidly achieving in her eyes. She had no regrets about her slightly misspent youth, but now, as she looked at Anna, she did wonder what her own life may have been like if she had met a Martin Price herself all those years ago. But still, she had chosen her own path through life and here she was, swept up in an exciting, if somewhat unnerving, episode originating from her own youth and travelling with two people she had only recently been reading about in the colour supplements and watching on TV - and First Class!

During the trip to the airport, Martin had made a phone call which, to Anne Silverdale's mystification and Anna's frustration was conducted entirely in French. Despite her slow familiarisation with the language Anna could still not follow French speech when it was delivered at what always seemed to her as lightning speed. Anne's complete ignorance of anything other than English also ensured that when Martin ended the call he was immediately cross-questioned by his two travelling companions.

"I heard the name Lascelles didn't I Martin? I know enough about you and Monique to know it wasn't her. What was that all about?"

"I wish I could speak French" sighed Anne. "I remember Jase saying that if I could then I would be able to come on tour as the band's interpreter. That's how Tatti was able to work her passage. Perhaps if I did speak French she wouldn't have had the opportunity to, well, that's all in the past. Was your phone call to do with us?"

"Yes it was to do with us Anne, and no, it wasn't to Monique, Anna. I was making an appointment to see Celeste Palin under the guise of a wealthy individual named Edouard Lascelles who has inherited ten million Euros, having been given her name by Count Emiliano Ruffolo. I apologised for the short notice but I have to fly to Rome this evening so if she could spare an hour this afternoon I would be very grateful."

"And she agreed?"

"I didn't speak to her, but one of her assistants arranged it."

"Suppose they check out this so-called Count whatsisname Martin?" Anna asked.

"They will find he is a well-known elderly resident of Milan and deaf as a post. He's an old friend of mother's and quite wealthy. It's all short notice but CKC isn't going to miss the chance of managing a portfolio worth ten million or more and I said I would only speak to Celeste."

"But if she is the one who has been organising the yobbos you dealt with yesterday, won't she simply deny everything? We don't have a scrap of evidence, and she will be expecting the Egg."

He grinned, "That's right. Now this is how it's going to work."

His explanation was short and despite her doubts, Anna had to agree that the element of surprise should be enough to carry the day. Anne decided she had somehow strayed into an alternative reality seen only on TV and would try to enjoy the experience while it lasted.

Their plane touched down in Basel at 1.35 and Martin insisted on stopping at the Laderach chocolate shop as he threaded the hired Volvo through the city streets. By the time they entered CKC via the old fashioned revolving doors Anne Silverdale was in a state of such excitement that she could barely string two words together and contented herself with staying as close to Anna as possible. She realised that her companions had clearly been to the bank before as without hesitation Martin veered to his left and led the way through a door and into a small comfortably furnished windowless anteroom.

"Grab a seat, these settees are nice and comfy as I recall", he said as he pressed the bell-push at the side of another door on the far side of the room. The time was exactly as arranged with Celeste's assistant and it was Celeste herself who appeared. She stopped dead at the sight of her visitors and for once the cool composure that had marked her demeanour at previous meetings slipped. "Oh, M-Martin, Anna, I wasn't expecting you."

'Not a good start' thought Anna as she gazed at the dark-suited Swiss.

Celeste swiftly regained her composure and as she glanced discreetly at her wristwatch said, "I am so sorry, but I am expecting a possible new client, in fact, I thought this must be him when you rang. Would you mind waiting in another room, I will get one of my people to conduct you, it may take at least an hour, though."

She reached for the bell push but stopped short as Martin said, "I'm afraid Mr Lascelles won't be arriving Celeste."

Her expression registered amazement at the comment, but before she could respond he added, "But never mind, I've brought you a rather unusual Egg." He accompanied the statement by placing a plain cardboard box on the coffee table in the centre of the room.

Anne Silverdale watched as the Swiss took a pace forward, undid the top of the box and looked inside. When she looked up her face was wreathed in a smile of pleasure as she said, "But how nice, and patted her own bottom saying, "It will not help this particular area, but I do so love chocolate."

Martin glanced appreciatively at the woman's rear before catching the warning glance arrowed at him by his wife.

"Please, please do sit down, I will have some coffee sent in." Her fingers deftly extracted the small tablet from her suit and skittered across the keys as she elegantly lowered herself onto a settee. "Now please tell me why you have played such a pleasant trick on me. We are all so serious here and so this is a very enjoyable surprise indeed. How is your work on the Imperial Egg going? You have been very quiet since you started. Is there any progress, and I have yet to be introduced to your companion?" She gestured towards Anne and as the introductions were made, the coffee trolley was wheeled into the room.

It was Anna who returned to the matter at hand once the ritual of coffee and biscuits had been completed by asking "Have you read our reports, Celeste?"

She was rewarded with a blank look and upraised eyebrows as Celeste replied "Reports?"

"We've sent several progress reports over recent days," Martin interjected.

The confusion was obvious on the woman's face and so Martin launched into an explanation of what had occurred since their arrival in England, all of which was clearly of news to the listener. Finally, as Martin finished his story Celeste Palin said "Angelina. My assistant, Angelina Flavio!"

Then, as realisation dawned she added "But you thought it could have been me and that is why you arrived unannounced. You needed to be sure I would be here so you set up the meeting with the fake M. Lascelles and you knew that my reaction would be enough for you to see if I was the guilty one. I am most impressed."

"You may wish to check out the one piece of hard evidence we have, in the form of a BACS transfer made to this English bank account a few days ago Celeste," Martin said as he pushed a piece of paper across to her. "I imagine you will be able to trace how it was initiated, from your internal audit system?"

She laughed "Ah yes. Thank you, Martin. Will you kindly excuse me for just a few moments while I attend to what is now an urgent matter.?" She inclined her head and tapped away at her tablet, paused, tapped again, and then waited until the door through which the public entered the room opened and a tall man in his twenties appeared and conversed rapidly with her. There was no doubt just who was in charge out of the two of them as the woman fired several short sharp comments at him, each of which elicited a nod and single word of agreement before he withdrew. "My apologies" murmured Celeste as she returned her attention to her visitors. I have just arranged for Angelina to be detained by our internal security pending the arrival of the police."

"Has she actually committed any crime in Switzerland?" Anna asked, appalled at the speed and extent of Celeste's reaction to their news.

"I believe conspiracy to defraud, misuse of privileged data, and I suspect, theft of bank funds should cover the situation. We do not take this sort of activity within our banking system lightly."

"I believe a boyfriend may also be involved," said Martin as he recalled Ray Priest's reference to a man with a foreign accent.

"Thank you, Martin." The fingers again went briefly to work before Celeste turned to Anne, saying "Now, Miss Silverdale, your considerable inconvenience, exposure to danger, and co-operation in this entire episode is gratefully acknowledged and I will authorise an ex-gratia payment to you that I hope will make amends for this unhappy incident."

Anne was startled out of the daze she had found herself in since first entering the room and managed to stammer "Oh, thank you. It was alright really. Martin and Anna have looked after me."

Celeste swept her gaze back to the other two occupants of the room and said, "So, am I to take it that the search for the account holder and possible owner of the Faberge Egg has come to nothing?"

"I'm afraid it looks that way, Celeste. We are at a dead end and the only people who could now help are either dead or untraceable. We will send you our final conclusions within the next few days but it very much looks as if the little gold bust of Czar Alexander will remain unclaimed and revert to ownership by the bank."

As they walked back to the car Anna said "Wow. I don't think I would like to make any mistakes when Celeste is around. Talk about decisive or, more accurately, incisive. I bet poor Angelina Flavio has already felt the swish of the executioner's blade whistling past."

Before he could reply Martin was forestalled by Anne Silverdale who said, "Would you mind dropping me off at a decent hotel so that I can sort out my flight tomorrow?"

"I thought you had arranged to take a few days off?" Anna responded.

"Well, yes I did because I didn't expect it to be all wrapped up so quickly, but I may as well go back now."

"Why not spend a couple of days at our place? We are less than four hours' drive away and I can rustle up something to eat at home, especially if I phone ahead. Marcel and 'Etta won't mind tidying up a spare room will they Martin."

"Nothing 'Etta likes better. Ask her to make sure there is wine available and tell her not to worry Marcel about seeing us in. We can pitch up and take Anne round to say hello tomorrow morning."

"Are you sure your neighbours won't mind?" Anne asked.

"Perfectly sure Anne, and we can have the pleasure of showing you around our little corner of France."

"Well, that would just about complete a marvellous couple of days. This time yesterday I was getting ready to have dinner with you in London, and now I'm about to be driven from Switzerland to France in a posh Volvo. I haven't enjoyed myself so much since I was a teenage groupie - well, you know what I mean" she hastily added.

Martin drove in what Anna was wont to describe as his 'positive fashion' with the result that they were approaching Château Sarony via the access road through the fir forest in a little over three hours.

"Oh, my goodness you really do live in a Château," said Anne, as she suddenly recalled what she had read in the English press. Overawed, she then subsided into awkward silence as Martin drove straight towards the gates and paused to let Anna hop out and phone Marcel before they trundled slowly along the gravel driveway.

They had barely drawn to a halt when without a word Anna flung her door wide, ran across the drive, bounded up the steps to the front doors and, after a short fumble with the lock disappeared from view.

"Is something wrong?" Anne asked in a confused tone.

"Don't mind her," laughed Martin as he took hold of her overnight case. "She's in love. Come on, let's get you settled."

"You are a lucky man" answered his guest as they ascended the steps in a more dignified fashion.

"Oh yes, it is beautiful here and Anna's been in love with the place from her very first visit. "Don't be surprised if you find her sitting in a corner somewhere crying her eyes out. She has been suffering untold misery these past days in London, wondering if the old place is still standing without her. Come on, let's find the silly old bat and check the wine supply."

Chapter 19 - Monique

When Anne Silverdale awoke the following morning it took her a few moments to recognise her surroundings. She showered, dressed, and quietly made her way along the passageway, to the galleried landing, and down the long staircase. Music and the sound of movement from the rear of the house drew her left along the hallway into a large kitchen with French doors at the far end which, in better weather, she could see would open onto a flagstoned terrace and rear grounds. Martin was seated at a large refectory table attacking a plate of scrambled eggs and smoked salmon, with a cup of coffee in close attendance. Mouth full, he cheerily waved a fork in her direction as Anna looked around from her work and said, "'morning Anne, eggs and salmon like Martin, or would you prefer something else?"

"Lovely thanks."

"Grab a cup and help yourself to coffee,' added Martin having finished his mouthful.

It felt very odd. Here she was, being waited on in a French château, by a couple whom she hardly knew but had seen on TV and in the newspapers and treated as a favoured guest. By the time breakfast was finished she felt more at ease and Anna took her on a leisurely tour of the East Wing, confessing as they passed the impressive pictures hung alongside the stairs that she no idea who most of the subjects were. She did, however, explain the significance of the family group pictured at the top of the stairs and then linked it rather self-consciously with the large painting down in the library that, on closer inspection, proved to be herself and Martin despite their medieval garb. The East Wing, she explained, was the part most in use. They were gradually smartening up and buying furniture for the

West Wing but had, since the Boudica matter and then the recent Christmas holidays, found spare time hard to come by.

They were soon joined by Martin and for the rest of the morning she was given a general tour of the château grounds including the Sarony family vault and introduced to Marcel and 'Etta Morane who provided coffee and mangled English in their comfortable cottage. It was a wonderfully lazy day with a trip out to Pont De Tresor and Colmierre during the afternoon. The finale was an evening meal at Auberge Fleurie, once again in the small dining room due to the cool winter weather, which Anne looked forward to with some trepidation due to her lack of a smart dress. Anna, however, assured her that she too would be wearing jeans and a blouse so there was nothing to worry about.

Their arrival was the most peculiar that she had ever experienced when attending a restaurant. First of all, as they entered the main salon she was thrilled to recognise the tribute behind the bar to Alois Lascelles and Phillipe Albert that had caught her eye in a colour supplement feature about Sarony some weeks before. There were smiles and murmurs of acknowledgement from the few customers in the bar area but she was caught unawares by the welcome from the woman named Monique. They had told her that Monique was a great friend but the blur of movement as the French girl almost literally jumped into Martin's arms with a shout of "*Marti*" was itself surpassed by the passionate kiss she delivered full on the Englishman's mouth. As Anne looked nervously towards Anna, the French woman, having released Martin, brushed by her and planted an equally effusive greeting on the mouth of the blond before saying, "Cherie, are you well? England is not good for you. I know. You belong to Sarony." She accompanied this small speech by stroking the golden hair that framed Anna's face. The blond herself appeared completely unperturbed by the assault on them both and actually slipped her arm around the woman's shoulders saying as she did so, "Monique, we have only been gone for a few days."

"Oui Cherie, but Marti must take care of you. London of all places! Here in Sarony, you become one of us and we love you for loving that man."

It was only then that Anne understood what the colour supplements had totally failed to convey. Sarony wasn't simply a quaint French village in which a wealthy English couple had chosen to live. It was the place where they *belonged* just as surely as if they had been born there with generations of ancestors reaching far back into the past.

"Monique, I would like to introduce Anne, an English friend of ours." Anna drew attention to the third member of their party.

Monique immediately turned on the charm, "I must apologise for my rudeness Anne. These two keep running off to England and it is my great fear that Sarony will lose them."

"No chance of that Monique." Martin laughed and then consciously adopted the French woman's mode of speech, as he indicated his wife, saying "This one would die if I suggested it."

Anne looked at Anna and thought to herself *'Many a true word spoken in jest.'* Martin barrelled on, unstoppable in his good humour. "This new method of greeting your customers should go down well. Are takings increasing as a result?"

Monique said something in French which missed the two English women by some distance but elicited a grin from Martin and a snort of appreciation from Thierry behind the bar.

"Come, come," she ordered and sweeping up two bottles of red wine led the way to a large table that Anne noticed was set for five. That mystery was solved when she said "The others have not arrived yet as you can see. Dinner is venison and I will come back later for your final orders." She glided away to attend to the other diners who were also clearly local as they had nodded and waved to her companions when they were led to the table. She was totally unfamiliar with France and so when drinks were dispensed said, "We don't have a choice of main course then?"

"If you are brave enough to go against Monique when there is venison you may regret it." Anna laughed "Take my word, Anne, unless you have some sort of allergy it has to be venison."

They amused her with stories of the small incidents and characters encountered since Anna's arrival in 2013, particularly the American girl, referred to as Marilyn because of her looks, but by profession a US Marine Corps Major. It was a world totally unfamiliar yet fascinating, and she slowly slipped into the comfortable warm feeling that she was now experiencing a *real* French evening, despite the nationality of her hosts. The cosy ambience was suddenly shattered by a very English voice calling "Hey you two drunks. How many bottles have you put away? I've a copper with me and he takes a dim view of boozy English tourists. Isn't that right Dixon old bean?"

The expression of irritation that almost reached Anne's lips was stilled when she saw the smiles on the faces of her companions as they rose to greet the newcomers. A slim young English girl embraced Martin and Anna in turn and a very tall older man who, with his good looks and pencil moustache could only have been French, repeated the procedure. It was Anna who performed the introductions as Nikki and her Capitaine de Gendarmerie took their seats. Anne ran an appreciative eye over Jean-Paul as he smiled at her and the thought *'Ooh, I could fancy some of that'* lingered only briefly as she caught the look that he bestowed on Nikki. The English girl promptly shattered the illusion of a typical Brit abroad by hurling a stream of French at the barman who had served one of the other guests. He grinned and uttered something that caused Jean-Paul to bark a short laugh and then address Nikki in English with the words "You are so rude, Ma Petite. He only forgot two glasses, castration is not the appropriate punishment, even in France! Now, what is this Dixon you referred to just now?"

While JP was educated on one of the finer aspects of British nineteen-sixties TV, Thierry rectified the lack of glasses and said something from the corner of his mouth that reduced Nikki to a helplessly giggling mess. Anne sat bemused as she realised that her 'typical French evening' had been exploded by an English firecracker who in contrast to poor Anna had an impressively fluent grasp of the local patois. She looked again at JP who was gazing in undisguised adoration at his sparkling companion who, in deference to Anne's presence, outlined in English the character Dixon of Dock Green for her mildly perplexed man.

Dinner passed slowly and enjoyably with the starter being a soup called Garbure that Monique had unashamedly pinched from an entirely different French region. Amazed at the large metal pot that was brought to their table, Anne watched as the others dipped in and ladled a helping onto their plates. "Go on Anne, it's delicious" encouraged Nikki "But not too much, it's easy to overdo it because you can take as much as you like."

It was good advice, and by the time they had their coffees, at which point Monique, to Anne's surprise, simply joined them without asking, the evening had again slipped into that warm, relaxed mode that she so liked. Despite the irrepressible Nikki's repeated attempts to draw her in, she was happy to say little and let the conversation swirl around her, offering only an occasional comment. She noticed Anna looking at her on a couple of occasions with a thoughtful expression but then turn back to Monique and Nikki who were more than making up for her own reticence. The talk had fragmented, as often occurs, and while the women's exchanges were more animated, full of laughter, and of a naturally higher pitch, JP and Martin spoke in a more desultory fashion, rumbling along, their speech very often punctuated by a single word or a nod of the head. It was, thought Anne, just like those far off Christmases in Halifax when, as a child, she would sit quietly, listening to the grown-ups, hoping that her parents would not notice it was way past her bedtime.

For the second time that evening it was Nikki who broke the spell. Monique had asked Anne whether she worked and as the music shop was mentioned Nikki leapt to her feet with a loud "Bloody hell JP, I only left it in the car. You're a copper as well, I bet Sherlock Holmes wouldn't have let that happen." As she scampered from the dining room JP rolled his eyes at Martin and in response to the upward twitch of an eyebrow said "Do not ask Mon Ami. I am in love with a crazy woman."

"Would you have it any other way?"

A smile and slow sideways movement of the head provided the answer.

Anne could not resist saying "Do you find it odd that Nikki more often addresses you by just your initials Jean-Paul?"

The Frenchman turned to her and said "It is her way, Anne. But there are occasions when she calls me other things."

Although he used English it was Monique who got the joke first and burst out laughing with the comment "Ah yes, that is what you men like Jean-Paul."

Anne felt her face redden but before the discussion could expand, Nikki came hurrying back to the table clutching what could only be an old fashioned vinyl long playing record encased in bright wrapping paper. "For you, with the compliments of a country copper and his missus," she announced as she thrust the item at Anne.

Mystified, she slowly peeled the paper away and there for the first time in several decades saw the words *'Tread Carefully'* and *'Wheelspin'* in the familiar yellow writing, emblazoned across a stylised picture of a Ford Mustang. The conversation had died and, aware that all eyes were suddenly upon her, she turned it over in a pretence of reading the sleeve notes. "Oh goodness" she gasped 'It's autographed! How on earth did you get this? The album itself is almost impossible to get hold of, but I've never heard of an autographed copy coming to light. You can't give this away."

"It's just a memory of an old boyfriend and his brother" shrugged Nikki. "Much to my man's disgust I recorded it earlier today so I can still listen. You actually knew them, so keep it with my blessing."

"May I see?" Martin asked from the far side of the table. She handed it across and he looked briefly at the front cover, then read the sleeve notes and was in the process of handing it back when his hand paused in mid- air. He looked again at the record and then pushed it in front of Anna saying, "Notice anything?"

She scanned the item before her and shook her head. "What am I looking for?"

"The signatures Watson, the signatures!"

"There are four of them Jase, Hal, Griss and Mikey. They look genuine enough." She passed the record back to Anne saying, "They are the real thing aren't they Anne?"

"I think so, although Jase is the only one I was particularly familiar with. That's definitely his with that sort of squirly finish and the way he used to drag the pen back as if he was underlining his name. I used to tease him about it and he would say 'One day I'll be famous'. Why are you looking puzzled Martin?"

"Because it's somewhat different to the signature on the CKC forms opening the account in 1977. I'll show you when we get back home."

"That's a relief" piped Nikki. "I thought for a moment that old Archie had pulled a stroke all those years ago."

"Archie?" Martin and Anna chorused incredulously.

"Alright. I was only fourteen you know" answered Nikki defensively. "A chap can't help his name can he?"

The party finally ended amidst many hugs and kisses, and as Martin headed for the X3 Anna said, "How much have you had Martin?"

"Very little my love. I was heavily watering it as I thought dinner would go on a bit, and JP is a copper as the adorable Nikki keeps reminding him." Then in a statement that left Anne speechless, he said as he fastened the seatbelt "I do love that girl."

Instead of an explosion of seismic proportions, she heard his wife say, "Me too Price. I take it we are agreed on the Timewarp matter then?" A nod of the head left Anne none the wiser and, as they eased along the access road towards the château, she wished she could stay forever in the back of the X3 and that the evening would never end.

Once in the library, Martin began rummaging through the papers littering the desk. "Now where are those bits and pieces Celeste left with us?"

Anne excused herself with the words "Too much wine, back in a moment", as Anna said, "Try that pile of stuff on the end of the desk" and headed in the direction of the kitchen. She was absent longer than he expected and having finally located what he was searching for he brandished them at Anna when she returned.

"Where's Anne?" She asked.

"Thought she had gone to the loo" answered Martin absentmindedly

"Oh come on Martin. I've made some coffee and knocked up a tray of sandwiches with the remainder of the salmon. I know she's a woman, but it shouldn't take that long."

"Perhaps she isn't feeling well. She's only little, and it's not everyone that comes home from a fine venison dinner and starts making sandwiches you know."

"So you don't want any then?"

"I didn't say that."

"Right, I'm going to see if she is OK. In the meantime, keep your grubby paws off the food until I get back."

Anna slipped upstairs, knocked gently on the door of Anne's room and then stood irresolutely when there was no response. Finally, she inched open the door and was surprised to see their guest sitting up on the bed with her legs drawn up in front of her and the LP clasped across her chest. It was when she became aware of Anna's presence that she looked up and the streaks from tears could clearly be seen on her face. So often embarrassed by her own emotional fragility Anna was momentarily nonplussed, but then hurried over to the bed and wrapped her arms around the older woman in the way that Martin so often did to her. They sat side by side for several minutes until a voice echoed up from downstairs saying "If you two don't want the sandwiches I'm going to eat them. What's going on up there?"

It wasn't often nowadays that Anna snarled at her husband but her loud "For Christ's sake shut up and stay down there. I'll be down shortly" had the desired effect.

Rarely had she raised her voice in anger against him in recent months and this sudden throwback to the less congenial Anna drew to mind the proverb concerning Angels and Fools. Ex-military Martin Price may have been, but he wisely refrained from joining battle on this occasion, and it was fully fifteen minutes more before the two women reappeared. Anne had repaired her makeup and said "I'm sorry Martin. It all got a bit too much for me. Such a lovely evening, your wonderful friends, the LP. It all just hit me and……!"

Her lip trembled and before he could answer a forceful Anna cut in with "Don't worry Anne. Believe me, I know we live in Paradise and I never stop offering thanks. It's been a hectic 36 hours and you are just worn out. It's our fault for dragging you off to the Fleurie. Now can you manage a sandwich before Martin faints away with hunger poor thing?"

The reference to the man, whom Anne had begun to hero-worship, as a 'poor thing' brought a smile back and she surprised herself by enjoying the sandwiches and coffee at what was now almost midnight.

"Now look and you will see what I mean," said Martin as he pointed to the signature on the CKC form. "Even allowing for the fact that no two signatures are ever identical in every respect I am sure the one on the form was by a different hand. No doubt It was a passable imitation of the one on the passport. I suspect that it only received a cursory glance and when combined with the photograph, passed muster at the time. If the signature on your LP is genuine Anne, then this one on the form is clearly a fake."

"I'm not sure I quite understand the significance" answered Anne.

"It says to me that Jase didn't open the bank account and, therefore, in all likelihood he never was in possession of the Egg. We have worked all along on the basis that Jase opened the account, but if he didn't then there is only one likely candidate."

"Dave Fairfax the roadie," Anna said. "It makes sense, several people, yourself included Anne, said that there was quite a close resemblance between the two men, and passport photographs are notoriously poor - particularly in those old black and white days. Don't forget, 1977 was, in security terms, like the Wild West compared to today. Swiss banks were very relaxed about their account holders. Having had a passport waved in front of him with a photo bearing a strong resemblance to the living breathing person the bank employee is likely to have thought it unnecessary to specifically check the signatures, particularly if the ID was produced some time before the form was completed and signed off. It was only what you described as the squirly end and the underlining that made Martin take a second look."

"I don't suppose it's possible that the man who fell from Suicide Bridge was actually Jase and not Dave?" Anne dreaded the answer, but Martin shook his head.

"No Anne. I did wonder at one point whether that may have been the case, but in a local paper report it says identification was made easier by the discovery of a driving licence in the man's jacket pocket. It was Dave Fairfax alright."

She mulled over what had been said and then commented "It's ironic, isn't it? That row at the airport back in 1977 blew up because Jase was late and couldn't find his passport. That's what had happened to it. Dave Fairfax had it."

"Wouldn't that have caused a problem coming back from the French tour?" Anna asked.

"No, I don't think so. It was fairly standard in those days for a roadie to take care of the small details and they very often collected the passports from band members who could never be relied upon not to lose things."

"So poor Jase never was involved with this damned Egg?" Anne didn't know whether she wanted a positive or negative answer.

Martin threw a swift glance at Anna before saying "No, I don't think he was. He was a victim of what is nowadays referred to as 'identity theft' but without being aware of it. All of our huffing and puffing trying to track down Jase Wooldridge was completely pointless."

"I'm glad. I told you I was sure he wasn't a thief and knowing that he never even knew about the existence of the wretched thing makes it all much better. All I have got regarding Jase are my memories and now this signed LP. Nothing has been messed up. Everything I knew, both good and bad, about him is unchanged, even the mad thing like hating travel and fuss. He used to tell me that he only ever wanted to write his music and lead a quiet life. I do wonder whether the row at the airport was just an excuse to pull out of the whole thing. I just wish we had still been together when it happened."

Chapter 20 - Kev

"Sterling work my love," said Martin as they crawled into bed.

"Pardon?"

"Little Anne Silverdale. You really took care of her earlier."

"I was watching her over dinner Martin, and she was like a child in a toyshop. We were all carrying on being frightfully happy and jolly and I saw Anne looking from one to the other of us and at one point thought she was going to burst into tears. Thank God for Nikki, that LP made all the difference I'm sure. Although it was all too much for her along with everything else when we got back here."

"Everything else? You mean the business back in London with those two comedians at her flat?"

"Partly, yes. That flat is the one thing that she has after fifty or so years of life. No family, a few friends but nothing very close."

"Don't forget the business, Anna."

"Ah yes, I was also taken in by the air of confidence when we first met her. I've been there myself, as you know, and I still didn't recognise it until I was upstairs earlier. The business is about to go under Martin. She hasn't done badly over the years but her lease rental has shot up along with her overdraft and there is, of course, a recession that has meant lower sales and tougher conditions by her bank. From what she told me earlier, it's not a question of 'if', but 'when' the shop has to close down. These past few years she's been borrowing against the equity of her flat, and so she's worrying about having to pay that off if she's got no business left. All the talk and bravado at our first meeting was just that. She never expected to see us again and she could put on an act. I thought I might offer to make her a loan from the Trust money I've got piling up, but now is probably not the right moment, and I'm not sure she would accept anyway."

"I hadn't realised. I just thought all of this, you know, coming to France with us for a few days, carrying on the way we normally do, would be nothing other than run of the mill and a bit of a nice change for her. Apart from the first class air tickets, I haven't been ostentatiously chucking money around."

"No, but we do live in a French château, the fact that the entire female population of Sarony appears to fall at your feet, and even simply grabbing a hire car and sailing off to Switzerland to a Swiss bank isn't at all familiar territory for Anne. She has only ever been on package holidays to Spain, and the last of those was some years ago. She's led a quiet unassuming life and this is a huge contrast. Plus, of course, we have recently become quite famous and, without wishing to sound big headed, that has probably also reminded her of what she thought was glamorous back in the seventies."

"Did you mean what you said just now?"

"About the loan?"

"No about the *entire* female population of Sarony falling at my feet."

"Bastard. None of that for you tonight, I'm whacked, but if you wake early in the morning who knows what could happen!"

None of them awoke early, and it was almost midday before they completed breakfast and congregated in the library where Martin explained to Anne how he had come into possession of Château Sarony, and the fact that most of the books she could see had been accumulated by his late stepfather. She appeared far more relaxed than the previous evening and listened intently as he described the famous archaeologist Armand Furneaux. "I've just been fantastically lucky," he said. "Old Armand was a typical shambolic academic but, boy did he have a super instinct for making money. Complete contrast to my natural father who was a military man and, from what I can gather, a very organised creature of habit. Even in his private life he never strayed outside his own personal comfort zone. Must have been due to being a professional soldier for more than twenty years. Always read the same newspaper, always dressed in a very conservative style with clothes from the same few shops. Mum said that even when he was on leave he went to the local pub at the same time on a Sunday and only ever drank two pints of bitter. All he wanted was a nice orderly life doing familiar things in familiar places. Mum certainly managed to land a complete contrast when she married Armand."

Anne expected him to trot out a few of his academic stepfather's eccentricities but instead, he stopped speaking and she saw a faraway look appear in his eyes.

"Is everything alright Martin?" She ventured.

"What? Oh yes. Sorry, drifted off for a moment. Now you said you wanted to travel back to the UK tomorrow didn't you, and it's just occurred to me that Anna and I have also got a couple of loose ends to tie up over there, so I hope you won't mind some company?"

"N-no, that will be very nice" stammered Anne, but she could not see that behind her Anna was standing with her mouth open and a look of amazement on her face.

They had dinner at the château that evening and in anticipation of another energetic day of travel, Anne decided to turn in at ten o'clock. This was the first opportunity that Martin and Anna had been given alone together and Anna sailed straight into the attack "OK Martin, just what loose ends do we have in the UK that require tying up? No sooner have I got away from the bloody place than you are proposing to cart me back off there again. What part of 'I want to spend my time in Sarony' don't you get?"

"Sorry Anna, but as I was telling Anne about my father being happiest within his own familiar little world, I was suddenly struck by a very odd thought. All the things that Anne has told us about Jase Wooldridge point to him having similar traits, you know - only wanted a quiet life, kept going back down to the Eastbourne area, pulling out of the band and just walking away. Not to mention managing to do a disappearing act for almost forty years having been on the brink of fame and stardom"

"And?"

"Well, supposing we have been looking *too* hard? We now know that he had probably never even heard of the Faberge Egg. Granted, we did that radio show and got a small response, but we didn't really look too deeply into Jase's character, did we. Other lines of enquiry, particularly Tatti, came up and off we went on the assumption that we would find Jase wherever we could track down the Egg."

"So what? The Egg's gone, God knows where. CKC have satisfied their compliance people, and Jase was a complete red herring. Just why the *fuck* do we have to go back to England?"

He recognised Anna's escalating annoyance by her use of the expletive that often saw daylight as a sign of her exasperation and pointed upwards. "Anne is still in love with Jase Wooldridge. I understand that as a mere man I should leave these finer observations to the fair sex, and I must say that sex with you is pretty fair, but don't you think it's worth one last fling for twenty-four hours, to see if we can find our personal Scarlet Pimpernel?"

"Alright, you've got the moral high ground on that. But don't think I'm going to spend a minute more in the land that also harbours my mother than is absolutely necessary."

"Agreed."

"Oh, and don't think you've got away with that smartass crack about sex with me only being pretty fair. I'll bloody well show you whether it's just pretty fair when we get back from the UK."

She stomped out of the room and so missed seeing the smile of triumph that spread across her husband's face.

The return flight was uneventful as was the drive from Heathrow. Anne was dropped off at her flat and, following a brief examination of all locks and catches, they went on their way, having promised to look in and say goodbye before they flew back to France. They had driven themselves in a hire car and Martin was soon following his favourite route out of London in the direction of Eastbourne. He had mollified his resentful wife with the promise that they would again stay at The Grand, and she had slowly thawed to the point where she was now fully engaged with their mission. Having settled back into the same hotel suite Martin listened as Anna telephoned South Downs Radio.

"Is it possible to have a word with Alan Keene, please? This is Anna Price. Hello Alan, I've a favour to ask. Did you happen to retain the phone number of the man who said he shared a flat with Jase Wooldridge and, if so, are you allowed to pass it on to me? Brilliant, yes I can hold. Oh, that was quick, OK, I've got that. Martin sends his best, and yes we will make sure you hear whether we have any success."

She turned to Martin saying. "Nice chap Alan. He's given me the number of Mark Braithwaite, now living in Sheffield. Shall I call him or would you like to?"

"No, that's fine, you go ahead. I'm happy to listen."

She called the landline number which Alan Keene had passed to her, and again Martin heard one side of a conversation.

"Mr Mark Braithwaite? My name is Anna Price. You kindly telephoned the Alan Keene programme when you were in Sussex last week."

"Yes, *that* Anna Price. Oh, how kind of you. It was a real thrill for us as well. Your mother? Oh, I see, she lives in Eastbourne. Yes, there is a book coming out. We will be happy to sign it, and I will arrange for Alan Keene to include a mention when he gives out an update on the Jase Wooldridge affair. Which brings me to why I have telephoned. First all many thanks for taking the trouble to phone in last week. We are particularly interested in the comment you made about Jase playing in various pubs here in Eastbourne. I appreciate it was nearly forty years ago but......., pardon? Yes, I can't believe how it flies by. Do you recall the names of any of those pubs? Oh good, hold on, let me jot this down. Now Mr Braithwaite, ah yes, Mark. Now Mark, is there anything you can tell me about Jase on a personal level? No, I do understand that you were flatmates rather than close friends, but how can I put it? Impressions. Yes, what impressions did you receive of his character? I see. Hmm. Interesting. Well, thank you er, Mark. No, I won't forget."

She broke the connection and faced a grinning husband who said "He sounded a bit of a handful. Anything of interest?"

Duly lubricated she referred to her notes and read out "The Mockingbird, The Plough, and The Three Crowns. Those are the pubs that Jase used to play at most often. Character-wise, Mark Braithwaite said he was only interested in his music but wasn't particularly ambitious. In fact, it was a bit of a surprise when he actually bothered to go for that audition and completely out of the blue when he announced he was forming *'Wheelspin'* and moving up to London. Their flat sharing was really just a financial arrangement, but he was always conscious that Jase was exceptionally honest. If he found a 2p piece on the floor he would hand it to Mark. That's about it, what do you think?"

"The character traits fit with what we have heard elsewhere, and we can quite easily check out the pubs. It just occurred to me yesterday when I was speaking to Anne, that Jase might still indulge some of his old habits like playing the local pubs occasionally. All of this is now just a long shot and if we strike out then that's it, no harm done. Come on let's find the pubs. Oh, hold on, I've just thought of something else." He tapped his mobile and when the connection was made said "Hello Nik. This is just a quick question, but the *'Wheelspin'* brand of rock - what sort of audience did it appeal to? I see. Did you own one? Yes, guilty secret indeed. Can't imagine it myself. No, I won't tell JP. See you soon."

He rang off and Anna immediately asked "What was all of that about? What won't you tell JP?"

"It turns out that our Nikki was a bit of a wild one when younger, and her boyfriend Archie was a wannabe Hell's Angel following the example set by his older brother. She said that even that late in the day *'Wheelspin'* were pretty popular with the leather-jacketed fraternity - a sort of cult thing. Nikki even had a jacket with studs and whatnot and used to ride pillion with Archie. Fluffy Nikki was an underage rock chick. That's what I won't be telling JP because she's embarrassed. Now let's find those pubs."

Interrogation revealed that all three establishments were still in business although The Plough had become part of a chain of 'family pubs' that had bouncy castles, children's menus, and Sunday carveries so they relegated it to the bottom of their short list. The Three Crowns was located near to the town centre, and The Mockingbird to the East of the town.

"My vote goes to The Mockingbird" as our first port of call" announced Martin.

"Shall I phone them?" Anna asked.

"Not worth it. If he appeared under his own name, we would have found him days ago. Look, the website says The Mockingbird will be holding its usual Rockers Evening on Saturday, that's tomorrow. That's sorted then."

Despite her misgivings, Anna agreed that they should attend the event and if it turned out to be a waste of time they would move on and check out The Three Crowns. She did, however, insist that Martin accompany her on a short trip into town so that she could purchase some black jeans, top, and jacket. She remembered how she had stood out at the pub in Dorking and had no wish to attract any more attention than necessary.

"How do I look?" She asked as they were preparing to set off on Saturday evening.

Unfortunately for Anna, she had been endowed with the sort of physique that would have made a bin-bag look as if it carried a designer label. Martin's response off "Dead sexy" was not what she wanted to hear and her spirits were further depressed as they drew up at The Mockingbird. It was a very large sprawling building, and not terribly well-maintained judging by its shabby appearance. There were a number of cars in the car park, but they were by far outnumbered by the motorbikes and even tricycle-bikes. Inside she saw that the pub resembled a small theatre with a stage occupying the far end opposite the entrance, a long bar manned by several male and female staff stretched along the left-hand side, and the remaining area was filled with small tables and chairs, a number of which had been pushed together by some of the larger groups of patrons. The stage was littered with equipment and the blast of noise emanating from a five-piece band almost took Anna's breath away. She felt her mouth go dry as Martin looked hopefully for a spare table nearest to the front and shouted to her "Look, there's a table for two just past that large crowd on the right, go and bag it while I get the drinks."

She nodded and, with an air of confidence that she certainly did not feel, began to ease her way between the various tables and over uncaringly sprawled legs. The fact that among the sea of leather jackets, long hair, boots and even peaked caps she could discern a significant female representation did nothing to calm her nerves. With the music pounding around her she kept her focus on the small vacant table until when she had almost arrived she found her way blocked by a tall man in his thirties with hair slicked back in old fashioned rocker style, and an unpleasant look on his lantern-jawed face. As the band came to the end of their set, the music died down and she tried to sidestep him. With a grin, he moved in the same direction and when she tried to edge past him he moved forward and she found herself face to face with him, trapped by his pelvis against her and the backs of her legs against one of the tables. The unpleasant confrontation was suddenly ended when with a look of surprise on his face her tormentor was abruptly jerked backwards by his collar and Anna found her herself propelled several feet in a grip of iron and plonked unceremoniously onto a chair among the large crowd of disreputable men and women she had noticed earlier. The people sitting either side shuffled away from her as her rescuer grabbed the two chairs from the vacant table and dropped one either side. The man slumped onto the chair in front of her and when he turned to face her she found herself gazing into the smiling face of Kev, the biker from Dorking.

"Where is he?" He asked.

"G-getting the drinks" she stammered as she looked across and saw Martin in the act of turning away from the bar.

"Maaartiin!" Kev roared above the hubbub as he stood up to wave his arm. The action was rewarded by a nod from her husband who began to make his way towards them. Once Martin was seated and Anna's adventure explained she said, "What about that other man, er Kev?"

"Ah, that's just Terry from the St. Leonard's Chapter. Great lump of nothing, fancies himself as a ladies' man. It'll get him into big trouble one day. Lucky I didn't belt him when he went for you. Now how are you both? Still looking for this Jack person?"

"Jase, Jase Wooldridge. Yes, we are. We know he used to occasionally play here back in the seventies and he went on to become the frontman of a band called *'Wheelspin'.*"

"Yeah, I've heard some of their stuff. Good rock band in their day."

At that point, the lights dimmed rapidly and Anna's ears were assaulted for a further thirty minutes. Despite the noise, she and

Martin were slowly introduced to Kev's wife and another half dozen couples at the table. The drinks flowed and knowing that Martin would be careful Anna gave up after the one revolting glass of warm wine and switched to lager and lime. Alcohol made the music somehow more endurable and she even found her feet tapping to one number.

At the next intermission, she turned to Martin and said, "Should we move on?"

Kev overheard and said "If you go now you'll miss the best bit. It's when guest singers are invited up to sing in front of The Mockingbirds - that's the name of the resident band you've been hearing since you arrived. Guests tend to do old numbers and the place can really rock."

"OK" acquiesced Martin. "It's the guest players we are interested in. The next round of drinks is on us, Kev."

"Oh God," thought Anna.

Having warned his friends not to 'take the piss' Kev took the orders and fresh drinks soon arrived at the table.

"Ladies and gentlemen." To a chorus of catcalls and abuse, the announcement was made from the stage that the part of the evening they had all been waiting for had arrived, and would they put their hands together for their first guest Mickey Strand.

Anna sought refuge in guzzling her drink, although she had to admit that the performances of this and two further guest singers were surprisingly competent - if you happened to like that sort of thing.

They had decided via sheer unspoken inertia to give up on visiting The Three Crowns, and as the evening was drawing to a close the announcement from the stage advised "Now our last guest this evening will close tonight's entertainment. An old rocker familiar to many of you - Johnny Sumner." There was an eruption of noise from the audience and Kev leant over to her and said " You're in for a treat now. He's good."

She looked at Martin and saw that he was frowning as his eyes followed a figure moving rapidly along the far side of the room towards the stage, guitar in hand. Once on stage, he plugged in his instrument spoke briefly to the band, nodded and turned to face the audience. "Here's an oldie that thanks to Jeff Beck is on everybody's list of favourites." Even Anna recognised the strains of *'Hi Ho Silver Lining'* and found herself swept up in the exhilaration that rippled around her as hands thumped tables, feet stamped, and the audience roared along with the lyrics. At the end, the singer stood for a moment with sweat glistening under the spotlights and a broad smile. He was a man in his fifties by the look of him, about five feet eight inches tall and, as he shrugged off his leather jacket and played the opening bars of *'Rockin' all over the World'* Anna could see that the quality of his performance was way above that of his predecessors. She found herself standing and wildly applauding along with everyone else as the number ended. The singer bowed low over his guitar and unbuttoned the waistcoat he wore over a simple white shirt. He looked around at the grinning band members behind him then turned back to the audience and held up a hand. "Any requests for the last number?"

To her complete surprise, Martin's voice roared out from behind her *'Burnin' Rubber'*.

The singer looked in the direction of the voice, turned and said something to the band, turned back to the microphone and said "OK.

Let's go." The first pounding chords crashed out and the pulsating sound swept across them filling the room. Anna swore afterwards that she could feel the floor vibrating long before the audience was again on its feet in a sea of wild movement. The guitar solo screeched to a crescendo amidst ecstatic cheers and as the old rock number finally died away she was standing waving her arms and cheering along with everyone around them.

The lights went up, the singer unplugged his guitar, swept a hand towards the perspiring backing band and retraced his footsteps from the stage along the far side of the room.

"Fuckin' brilliant!" It was Kev's verdict on the performance. "He ought to be a pro - seen him once before down here. Just the same - bloke's got talent."

There was no chance to hurry out to the car park thanks to the press of bodies all moving towards the exit and it was only when they were finally outside in the open air that they were able to properly exchange words with Kevin and his wife.

"I owe you one Kev," said Martin "Thanks for looking after Anna."

Kev wrapped an affectionate arm around the dumpy middle-aged woman in leather by his side and said "Wives are special Martin. Pauline here is the most precious thing that ever came into my life. Good choice of number by the way, really brought the house down. Don't often hear that one nowadays." He held out a hand "Got to make a move so I'll say cheerio."

"Goodbye Kev, Pauline." Martin shook hands with them both. Anna did likewise with Pauline but couldn't resist holding onto Kev's hand and giving him a firm kiss on both cheeks. "If you ever find yourselves in Sarony, down near Dijon, look us up. Just ask in the village and they will direct you."

As Martin drove out of the car park onto the main road he said, "Never had you painted as a rocker, I didn't think you were that keen on loud music."

"I'm not really, but the atmosphere, when that last fellow was playing, was unbelievable. I couldn't stop myself. You knew it was Jase didn't you - that's why you asked for that particular number. Too bad we couldn't get hold of him. I couldn't see him when we came out but spotting anyone would have been difficult at night in that crowd. We can probably trace him via the pub, don't you think?"

"No need" was the surprising response. "I know exactly where to find him. By the way, have I ever told you that you look very sexy dressed all in black?"

"Oh I see Price, take her out, get her all revved up, and then try it on, eh?"

"Got it in one."

Chapter 21 - Jase

It was only when she surfaced the following morning that Anna remembered how Martin had craftily side-tracked her as they drove back from the pub, and she still did not understand the comment he had made concerning the whereabouts of Jase Wooldridge.

"Hey, Price you evil molester of innocent women. Make my coffee strong please and then tell me where we can find Jase."

He handed her the drink and said "I will do much better than that my love. I thought we would look in on him this morning. It's Sunday today and I reckon we have got a good chance of finding him at home."

She decided to indulge him and restrain her inquisitiveness on the basis that she would give him hell if it turned out to be a misguided attempt on his part to have some fun at her expense. With breakfast concluded they finally drove out onto the road along the Eastbourne seafront, then gradually turned inland to follow an easterly direction.

"Two things surprised me last night," he said. "One was the sight of you knocking back gallons of lager, and the second was just how good a guitarist Jase is. I thought Hal was meant to be the great man on that instrument when the band were making their records, but I can't imagine he was better than what we were treated to last night. I thought for a moment you were going to end up dancing on the table."

"For your information, I wasn't knocking back gallons. The wine was horrid and it was really hot in that place so I decided to try lager and lime. You are right about the music, though. Although I've never been into that sort of thing I admit it was exhilarating. I've never been to a place like that in my entire life. The sight of the people frightens me to be honest although Kev and his crowd are a pretty nice bunch. Mind you, I wouldn't want to upset Kev. He reminds me of you in some ways, very sure of himself." She paused and looked more closely either side of the road they had turned into. "Martin, this is where the Trafalgar Court Children's Home is."

"And it's where we should find our elusive former rock star," he answered as they slowed and turned into the beginning of the drive. "I don't usually do this," he said as he banged his hand on the car horn several times. After a short pause, Anna saw the door of the nearby gatehouse open and the figure of the gatekeeper appear. Martin walked over, exchanged a few words with the man and then returned. She watched as the gates juddered, then swung slowly open allowing them to creep through. There was a small parking area to the right and Martin halted alongside a Citroen Berlingo displaying the livery and name of the children's home. "OK let's go," he said and without waiting for her, hopped out of the car, walked across to the gatehouse and through the door that the man had left ajar. Anna hastily strode after him and arrived in a small hallway with an open door to the right. Inside the room Martin was facing the gatekeeper and turning to her said "Anna, may I present Jase Wooldridge, late of *'Wheelspin'* and I would guess for a good many years John Sumner of Trafalgar Court."

She recognised him now. The superb singer and guitarist from last night in The Mockingbird and smiled as she held out her hand saying "Thank you for the performance at the pub last night. It made the evening worthwhile for me."

His hesitant manner changed slightly as he shook hands with her and replied rather stiffly "Glad you enjoyed it." Then he looked at Martin and said "You're the bloke who asked for *'Burnin' Rubber'* aren't you, and you both visited here a few days ago, but in a different car. What's going on?"

Martin held up a hand and replied "Nothing to be unduly concerned about. If we may sit down, we will explain." He related a much-abbreviated story of the Swiss security box and their conclusion that it was the roadie with Tatti's help who had got hold of the Egg.

Jase shook his head and said "So that bugger Dave Fairfax used my name did he? Never cottoned on to him that much although a lot of people said we had similar looks."

"You were happy enough to pinch his girlfriend though" responded Martin.

Anna saw the man's neck redden and he replied "You mean Tatti. Well, nobody pinched Tatti because it wasn't necessary. She was happy to put it about whenever it suited her. She and I had a bit of a fling and then it fizzled out."

"You dumped her you mean" needled Martin "Like you did with everyone back in those days. Provided good old Jase was OK then sod everybody else."

Anna waited for the explosion, but it never came, and instead Jase sat back in his chair and she could see his body relax as he looked silently at her husband before saying "It wasn't like that. You've been nosing around in my past life so you may know I was brought up in a children's home - oh yes, of course you do, that's what brought you here last week wasn't it? Well, I'm not asking for sympathy because I was one of the lucky ones, and the home I grew up in was run by kind caring people. By the time I left it was obvious they were in trouble financially as the place was beginning to go downhill quite quickly. I bummed around, doing a few odd jobs including some gardening which eventually stood me in good stead, but I'd always liked rock and roll. As soon as I could afford it I bought myself a decent guitar and taught myself to read music. Then I started to play at one or two of the local pubs like The Mockingbird and realised that I had a bit of a talent for song writing. Everything was rubbing along quite nicely. I set up and quite enjoyed running a little gardening business and with music as a hobby I was more than happy to stay down here in Eastbourne and see how life panned out. The children's home was boys only and it took me a long time to feel at ease with girls so they didn't feature very much in those years.

Everything changed one day when I went back to the old children's home for a visit. I used to look in from time to time because to me it still represented the only proper home I had ever experienced, and Mr & Mrs Burnett were a bit like substitute parents. Well it had been a few weeks and when I arrived it was obvious something was wrong because instead of Mr Burnett clumping down the stairs to say hello, it was Mrs Burnett who came down and I could see she had been crying. It turned out that her husband had suffered a severe stroke a few weeks before and it looked as if he would be permanently bedridden. It was a very unhappy visit I can tell you and after I had left them I tried to think if there was any way in which I could help. It was very shortly afterwards that I saw the advert in one of the music papers inviting musicians to an audition in London and it suddenly struck me that I might be able to sell some of my songs.

Off I went and didn't have too much trouble getting through the weeding out process but got dumped before I made it to the finals without being given a chance to show anyone the songs I had written. It was basically all a publicity stunt of course and so I ended up in a pub drowning my sorrows along with a few other rejects. That was where I met up with Hal, Mikey and Griss. We were drinking and talking and talking and drinking and realised that we had the basic ingredients to set up our own band. We even had original material written by me. Mikey and Griss came from nice middle-class families and could afford to buy their own instruments and even Hal actually owned a couple of guitars. I'd got my own business, as I said, so I had a bit more money than the others although we were all of a similar age. Because of working for myself I had a bit more experience of life as well and so when I suggested the name *'Wheelspin'* I went straight off to see a local lawyer and got him to take basic legal precautions to make sure the right to use the name belonged to me. Growing up in a home, however good, conditions a person to always want to protect their own property and rights, at least that's how it was with me.

When Hal eventually found out it, was what caused the first falling out I had with him. He objected to what I had done and I told him it was tough luck as I'd been the one who had come up with the name. By that time though we were getting quite a lot of bookings and so it would have been silly to change names. We soon had enough money to buy a decent second-hand van, and so were able to take bookings further afield than Eastbourne because there is a limit to how many instruments and bodies you can cram into a small gardener's van and survive.

Now you may look at all of this and think I wasn't playing entirely fair although, to be honest, I don't really care what you think, because I had it in mind that the thing with the band was only useful until I could get some of my own material recorded by some well-known names. I knew it was the publishing royalties that made the real money and I thought I could assign the rights to Mr & Mrs Burnett so they would have money to keep the home going and maybe even help the old boy out if there were medical bills. I wasn't too far off centre as it happened because a bloke from Tornado Records was at one of the gigs we played at a university in the Midlands, and then he pitched up again a few weeks later and asked if we would come up to London for an audition.

It all took off from there and I immediately moved up to the big city and got myself a crummy little flat in Earls Court. What I hadn't bargained for was the fact that after six months of living on a shoestring financed by Tornado they were very keen on a great many of the songs I had written and used in some of the test recordings we did for them. As soon as I could see the way the wind was blowing on that one I hightailed it back to my lawyer and used the rest of the money I had saved to set up what they called an 'offshore arrangement' involving trusts and limited companies. In those days tax rates were as high as 83% so it made sense to take precautions.

After that first six months, Tornado offered all of us new contracts. We were each individually contracted to their management company but I also signed a separate deal with my own music publishing company, and it was that company that Tornado had to do a deal with so far as the song writing royalties were concerned. My company was in turn owned by an offshore trust. I still don't fully understand it, but it works."

"You mean it's still operating?" Anna asked.

"Of course. I've never given up song writing. Anyway, this was the cause of an ongoing rift with Hal. He didn't like the idea of me earning extra although it was not at all unusual within the industry - look at Lennon and McCartney compared to Ringo and George. We had several hit singles; our first album went gold and then so did the second. We were touring, appearing on TV, and although I was earning a fortune from the song writing I was living a lifestyle I hated. It wasn't without some compensations though and for a time on our last tour I actually got into the whole thing and landed the beautiful Tatti. It didn't last of course and I got rid of her not long after we returned to the UK.

I was rapidly becoming disenchanted with the whole thing. Mikey and Griss were getting bored, Hal was pretending to be a big star but, at least, the royalties were beginning to come in. Then, I received word that Mr Burnett had died and that Mrs B - I always called her that - couldn't continue with the home. We were on the point of going on our big US tour when I managed to lose my passport. When I got to Heathrow, late and still minus the passport, all hell broke loose. Hal went completely off his head and even tried to attack me, the great fool. Suddenly, I knew what I was going to do and I said goodbye there and then. I was able to arrange for a new company to be set up that was fully owned by the offshore trust and that company bought this place from Mrs B using my ever increasing royalties."

"At this point you changed your name, using your middle name Sumner," Martin interjected.

For the first time, Jase smiled "Well done. Via the new company I insisted that Johnny Sumner should be hired as groundsman and gatekeeper etc. For almost forty years I've been quietly writing hit songs using a variety of names but all contracted to Trafalgar Music Ltd. That company puts money into the trust which in turn makes donations to Trafalgar Court which has always been a registered charity. The royalties have continued to flow and I have built the home into a top class environment caring for its boys and equivalent to a great many private schools. Nobody knows who I am and I even give gardening lessons to those kids who are interested. It's all worked like a dream and, over the years, I've also turned into a useful handyman. I even manage to play the odd gig at a local pub, like last night."

He sat and looked from one to the other and added "So you see, all your efforts to trace me were pointless because until this morning I had never heard of this Fabergé Egg. Dave the roadie set things in motion all those years ago when he used my passport. I've simply got on with my life achieving exactly what I wanted. I've no regrets."

He made as if to rise from his chair but Martin sat forward and said, "That's not entirely true is it Jase."

"Are you calling me a liar?" The words came fast from a face that had acquired a very deep shade of red."

"Not unless you equate the sin of omission with telling lies" replied Martin evenly.

"What are you talking about?"

"I mean that you have taken us on a brief tour of your life to date and in particular those very significant years in the nineteen-seventies. You have mentioned the other band members, the record company, and even the half-Russian nymphomaniac that you had a fling with. It may interest you to know that Dave Fairfax died as the result of falling eighty feet from a bridge in North London only hours after you last saw Tatti at the party in her flat. Tatti, by the way, was last heard of decades ago receiving a prison sentence for blackmailing one of her clients. She had been working as a prostitute. As a matter of interest just why did you show up at Tatti's party? You had already split up with her hadn't you?"

Jase looked for a moment as if he would ignore the question but as his temper cooled he said "We had become involved just before that tour but it only became obvious once we arrived in France. She was used to getting what she wanted and she just turned up one day and with a load of her stuff. I was still living with another girl at the time so I got the bloke in the flat downstairs to look after her cases. When we were on tour my other relationship ended and Tatti kept on and on pushing for us to get a posh flat together in central London financed by what she thought was my rock star income. It was one of the things that turned me off her. It was the lifestyle she wanted, not me.

Dumping her wasn't a difficult decision and I started to spend most of my time down here in Eastbourne as the property purchase had gone through and I wanted to be on site. There were still other things continually needing attention regarding song writing contracts and the like so when I found myself seeing an agent in north London I decided on the spur of the moment to drop in and tell her that I would soon be clearing out of the Earls Court entirely, and she had better collect her stuff if she wanted it. It was weird because when she first saw me she was angry but I simply said that if she wanted to let me know when she could collect her stuff I would be happy to buy her dinner. No hard feelings. Then she seemed to change and became very pleasant and friendly. She said she would phone me and come down to collect her stuff early the next week. The days passed and I heard nothing from her so I wrote to her, gave her my address down here and told her to let me know what was to be done. I never did hear from her again. Now I've been very patient and answered your questions even though I didn't need to say anything. So what was that crack about a 'sin of omission' in aid of?"

"You have very carefully omitted any mention of the one person who actually liked you and cared about you back then. A person by the name of Anne Silverdale."

Anna saw the man's face lose its remaining red hue and, if anything, turn pale. "She left me, and then went off with some singer in another band."

"When you were snuggled up with Tatti in France" retorted Martin. "She played you at your own game and you can't blame her for that."

Jase sat quietly and to Anna's eyes seemed to sag and grow smaller in his chair. Finally, he nodded and said "You're right. It was probably the worst decision I ever made, but not long before I finally moved out she visited the flat in Earls Court while I was away. I was slowly shifting things down here piecemeal each time I visited Eastbourne. I didn't have a car so went by train and slept here. There was plenty of room and I was able to use it as a base from which to liaise with the solicitors and architects and all of those people who would be involved with modernising the home. I was letting the rent agreement run down on Earls Court and being able to ferry stuff down here in dribs and drabs while I made this old gatehouse habitable was very useful. While I was down here for a few days Anne turned the place over and left her key behind. I suppose she was just getting back at me and I knew I had asked for it so I took it as her last word and moved on. I did make some discreet enquiries a few years later and found out that she was married and living somewhere up north so she had done the same as me.

It's true. I don't think of her in the same way as all the others. It's ironic because at first, she was just a nice little groupie. She didn't deserve to end up with Hal, it was a bad move and it ended up with her moving in with me. It was only meant to be temporary but nature has a way of taking its own course." He shrugged and looked sideways out of the window.

"I can tell you that it wasn't Anne who turned your flat over. She found it in that state and thought *you* had made the mess. That's when she left the key for you to find. The mess was made by somebody who thought you had the Egg"

Jase shrugged again. "Whatever the reason, it's all ancient history."

"It's never too late to put things straight," Anna said.

"Go searching the north of England for a married woman I haven't seen for nearly forty years you mean?" The acerbic nature of the words was not lost on Anna but she persevered.

"Anne Silverdale is long divorced, lives alone and runs a small failing record business in north London. She spent three days with us last week, two of them as our house guest. I can give you her number here and now if you like. Instead of thinking only about yourself why don't you make an effort for someone else? She could do with a little care and attention at present. Or are you only good at building monuments to the past?"

Martin looked at his wife in admiration at the final comment then back at the groundsman. Her words must have hit home because Jase suddenly jumped to his feet and walking over to where his jacket was hanging on the back of a chair pulled a mobile phone from one of the pockets. Turning back, he hesitated, looked at the phone in his hand, then out through the window across the neatly kept grounds of Trafalgar Court.

"Give me the number" he uttered in a sullen voice and looked surprised when having entered it there was an almost immediate response.

"Hello is that Anne?"

"This is Jase. Jase Wooldridge."

"What? Some friends gave me your number. I thought…."

"Oh yes. Ok please do."

He placed the handset on the table and said "She started to cry. She's going to phone me back."

"We won't take up much more of your time," Martin said. "One last thing I would like to ask is what did you do with Tatti's stuff. The things she never collected?"

Jase looked bemused for a moment then replied "Well, I was expecting her to get in touch as she had promised at the party, and when she didn't show, I stuffed her odds and ends back into her suitcases and brought them down here, she hadn't even fully unpacked. I wrote to her saying that she could always come and pick them up if she gave me a call first."

"And she never did?"

"No. As I said, I haven't heard from her since the party."

Martin briefly looked at his wife and then asked, "So what became of her things?"

There were another few seconds of hesitation as if Jase was having trouble understanding the question. Then he said "Well, I think those cases are still where I put them. There's a decent sized loft here and I slung them up there to start with, then a few years later when I was having the old place rewired I think they were moved down to the far end of the roof space with all the other bits of junk I'm never likely to use. That must be where they still are. I only ever use the loft to dump odds and ends and those are all close to the trap door for easy access."

"If you don't mind me saying so, I think you should open those cases up and have a good look through their contents. If you find something that looks like an egg, then perhaps you would give one of us a call. We will be able to help matters along from there. Now, we have taken up a great deal of your time without having the slightest right to do so other than our friendship with Anne Silverdale. Apart from the clue of your phone call just now she has no idea that we have traced you. As far as she is aware, our interest ended a couple of days ago and we are spending a short time here tying up a few personal loose ends."

They left Jase Wooldridge at the door of his gatehouse from where he could operate the gates to let them out. He didn't smile or wave and the impression Anna came away with was that of a rather sad person despite his stated satisfaction with life.

"I confess Martin that I was bloody irritated when you suddenly announced to Anne that we were coming back with her for a few days to tidy up, but I'm very happy now that you did. Do you really think that the Egg has been sitting in Jase's loft all of this time?"

"It would make sense of some of the genuinely loose ends Anna. Tatti had the Egg and it needed to be kept in a safe place. She thought she was on a good number with a rising star in the shape of Jase and stashed the Egg at his place. Anne said she seemed pretty keen to track him down after the airport fracas and assumed it was for emotional reasons. Jase said she started off angry at the party but then changed her attitude, I think that was because all of a sudden she knew she would be able to get hold of the Egg. That also explains why she and Dave Fairfax went beetling off in a state of drunken euphoria. No doubt he was giving her a hard time about the whole thing and she was thinking she could bounce straight back from Jase into partnership with Dave again. She intended to pick up her things from Earl's Court, but later that same night Dave went over Suicide Bridge and she cracked up completely. What with the drink, drugs and the shock combined with a nervous breakdown she probably never even recalled meeting Jase at the party."

Chapter 22 – Woman in Black

The phone call they hoped to receive arrived late in the afternoon as they sat in one of the public rooms on the ground floor of The Grand. Anna sat patiently as Martin took the call and by the time he was finished she was almost quivering with excitement. He looked at her and nodded.

"There are now only six missing Imperial Eggs. Jase retrieved those old suitcases from the loft and at first thought it was a waste of time although he did say it brought back some memories of Tatti. He then realised that a cuddly toy he had slung to one side was actually a little bit heavier than would be expected and when he shook it and squeezed it he could feel something hard inside. There it was, the Egg that so many people were keen to possess. You heard me tell him that the last Egg to be sold on the open market was quite recently and made something like 20 million dollars. Even though that was solid gold and his one isn't he would still be looking at a likely value of several million once reunited with the present that CKC is holding. He's driving over here with it now."

The three of them sat having the excellent afternoon tea with a cardboard box placed on the vacant fourth chair.

"I've lived almost my whole life down here in Eastbourne and this is the first time I have ever been inside this place." Jase looked around him and then at the cardboard box. "Were you serious about how much that thing is worth?" Martin grinned, "Just think in millions - somewhere between five and fifteen in sterling I would guess, but if the Russian state was willing to buy it you may well be able to ask Mr Putin to cough up a bit more."

"Hold on a minute. I brought it here to hand it over to you I've plenty of money that's piled up from my song writing. Over recent years the home has received substantial donations from successful former Trafalgar boys so the Trust hasn't needed to use so much of the royalty income. I've no use for this thing."

"Well, all of the evidence, such as it is, points to you as the owner. If you've no use for it why not sell it and donate the proceeds to a good cause, or better still use it to fund a scholarship for Trafalgar Court boys at one of the universities."

"Now that's worth thinking about."

"I will be asking Celeste Palin from CKC Bank in Basel to contact you so that they can arrange to return the gold present."

Anna leant forward in her chair and asked, "Is it rude of me to ask if Anne phoned you back?"

For the first time since his performance at The Mockingbird, she saw a smile of pleasure appear on the man's face and his words displayed genuine eagerness. "I'm taking some time off and driving up to north London to see her tomorrow. It should be an interesting meeting. I've never been so scared in all my life."

"I can't believe we have actually escaped at last." They had collected the X3 at Dijon airport and a watery sun was shining as they followed the familiar route towards the turn-off for Colmierre. Anna leant back against the headrest and revelled in the fact that they were once again in France and only a few miles from her beloved home.

"It's been a strange couple of weeks since Celeste visited Sarony" answered Martin "In some ways, it seems a great deal longer than that."

"It's not the sort of thing I want to get involved in on a regular basis. It was a good little earner as Nikki would say but having built a reputation for chasing down historical oddities this feels a long way from what Timewarp should be all about. The seventies may be history in one sense but I prefer something a little further into the past."

They drove across the Pont De Tresor and soon approached the left-hand turn onto the access road that would lead them to Château Sarony. Within an hour Martin was sprawled on one of the library settees whilst Anna had made coffee and then disappeared on an unknown mission. They had first telephoned Celeste and reported the recovery of the Egg and asked her to call Jase Wooldridge who had been in possession of the item for almost forty years and appeared to be the only traceable owner. She sounded delighted but immediately asked if they would be interested in a similar project concerning a diamond necklace. They had politely but firmly declined.

When Anna returned to the library she was dressed in the black outfit acquired for the evening at The Mockingbird and said "I've phoned Nikki and Monique and a table is booked for an hour's time at Auberge Fleurie. I thought I would wear this stuff as you seemed to be so keen on it. I've booked us a cab, so you can relax on the drinking front but don't over indulge. Now take your coffee and buzz off to the shower and make yourself look respectable, otherwise, I will have to find myself a greasy haired rocker to have dinner with."

They arrived early in order to have a glass of wine together. Apart from being admonished by Monique as a 'bad boy' for forcing Anna to return to England, their entrance was more subdued than on their last visit although Monique did run her gaze up and down Anna and murmur "Tres Bon, Cherie" as she winked ostentatiously at Martin.

Nikki and JP arrived fifteen minutes later and true to form Nikki's voice reached them in advance of her body as the words "Every time I see you two you're knocking back the booze. Wow Anna, cool outfit." They seated themselves and as she raised the glass to her lips Nikki added "So, tell us all about it. You went diving off back to England pretty smartly so it can only be to do with the *'Wheelspin'* job."

"Before we do that Nikki, and before we consume too much plonk there is something Anna would like to tell you, and the fact that JP is here makes it better somehow." Martin looked across at his wife and nodded that she should go ahead.

Anna, although dressed to kill, was never greatly enamoured of holding centre stage, but as all eyes turned in her direction she gulped down some more wine and spoke.

"We feel there should be more than just an employer/employee relationship between you and Timewarp, Nik. It goes without saying that you have become very close to us both this past couple of years." She waved down an attempted interruption and finished what was in her glass. "We have had some quite remarkable success particularly with the Considine and Boudica jobs and the financial rewards are beginning to gather pace. Your contribution has been invaluable and you have turned your hand very successfully on our behalf to the whole PR and contractual side of the business. Without your contribution we would have been swamped. Hopefully, your salary is acceptable in a general manner of speaking, but we want you to have a bigger stake in the business. So, we would like to offer you twenty percent of the company shares. Now it's not as if we are offering you a slice of the action in Microsoft I appreciate, but Martin and I will soon commence taking dividends from the company and we would like to think that your share of the additional income will be partly as a reward for all of your hard work and partly an ongoing thank you for being so important to us on a personal level. The only condition is that if you leave the company then you will have to sell us your shares at whatever the value is at the time. Are you happy with the idea?" She waggled her empty glass at Martin who attended to his wife's needs with some alacrity.

Nikki said nothing for a moment although JP did stretch out a long arm and stroke the back of the younger girl's neck. She found her voice finally and said "I love it here, working with you guys, living with JP. It all changed for me back in Grantfield when you invited me to your wedding. I would love to be a proper part of Timewarp so yes, of course, I am very, very happy indeed. Thank you both. Now excuse me while I nip off to the ladies for a minute. " She jumped to her feet and almost ran out to the bar area."

JP then said "Thank you, Mes Amis. Seeing that crazy girl happy is the thing I live for."

When she returned they told Nikki about the evening at The Mockingbird and how they had been able to track down Jase and as a result the long lost Egg. "So you're a *'Wheelspin'* fan now, are you Anna?" She asked.

"I wouldn't go so far as to say that I am a fan, but that live performance at The Mockingbird was memorable. Something about that rhythm and the noise made me very…"

"Horny!" Nikki shouted with a peel of laughter. "It's great, isn't it. Yeah, *'Burnin Rubber'* ba-boom-bang-bang."

JP looked at Martin and shrugged.

They paid the taxi driver and walked slowly up the steps to the front doors. Martin slipped his arm around his wife's waist as they entered and said. "It went well with Nikki. Well done, it was your idea and you were dead right. Now, have you had an awful lot to drink Spindles, old girl?"

"I suppose I could manage to do my wifely duty, only I haven't forgotten about your comment that it's only fair so I'm warning you that you had better not have drunk too much yourself."

When they reached the landing at the top of the stairs Anna said, "This whole *'Wheelspin'* thing is now pretty much a closed book, but I can't help wondering what became of Tatti."

Epilogue

In early March the weather in the south-east of England turned very cold and London received several inches of snow.

They found the body huddled under some bushes in Waterlow Park. Nobody knew her name as she had always been referred to as 'the bag lady'. Her life had consisted of a fixed routine that took her on a circular walk each day down Dartmouth Park Hill, back along Junction Road, up Archway Road and then along Hornsey Lane, across Suicide Bridge to Waterlow Park. For years they had tried to stop her staying in the park at night, but somehow she always found a way in.

Somebody mentioned that she had always seemed to be permanently looking for something. She would rummage through the pavement waste bins and those attached to lamp posts then walk off empty handed, muttering to herself.

Always searching for something that she would never find.

Printed in Great Britain
by Amazon